PRAISE FOR *BEAST*

'In *Beast*, Matt Wesolowski brilliantly depicts a desperate and disturbed corner of north-east England in which paranoia reigns and goodness is thwarted. It's a big ask to come up with a new vampire tale, but Wesolowski achieves it magnificently. He is an exceptional storyteller.' Andrew Michael Hurley

'Endlessly inventive and with literary thrills aplenty, Matt Wesolowski is boldly carving his own uniquely dark niche. I'm always excited to see what he does next' Benjamin Myers

'Matt Wesolowski writes some of the darkest, most inventive crime fiction available today, and *Beast* is his best yet. Disturbing, compelling and atmospheric, it will terrify and enthral you in equal measures. Simply superb' M.W. Craven

'Beautifully written, smart, compassionate – and scary as hell. Matt Wesolowski is one of the most exciting and original voices in crime fiction' Alex North

'Such a fantastic, creepy read! I love the sense of place – and the combination of ancient horror and modern technology is very compelling' Elodie Harper

'A fantastic book that ticks all of my favourite boxes; it is creepy, exciting and very well written to boot' Yrsa Sigurðardóttir

'I get so excited when a Wesolowski comes out, and he always goes RIGHT TO THE TOP of my book pile. And this was worth putting everything aside for. He is a genius. He always takes a traditional legend or tale and tells it with a shocking or surprising modern-day slant. This time we have vampires. And boy, do they live among us' Louise Beech

'*Beast* is a flawless thriller, but once again Matt Wesolowski does not hesitate to turn the spotlight on human flaw— ~he need for attention, t~ ~ ~ ~—~ ~for other people's fe~ ~er must read' Fron~

'Each book Matt Wesolowski writes is imaginative, captivating, and cleverly constructed … as good if not better than the last. Once again he's written the epitome of a page-turner' The Book Review Café

'Matt's incredible talent to create a novel is awing, his ability to steer the reader in the exact directions he wishes is brilliant … The concept is absolutely haunting … a contemporary take on classic horror' The Reading Closet

'Gothically inspired and deliciously dark. I had all the feels, the chills, the horrors mixed with excitement and trepidation. Visually stunning and chillingly complex. Five stars are not enough' The Book Trail

'If you love a good thriller and haven't read Matt's books before then I definitely recommend them … love the style' Independent Book Reviews

'Full of creepy atmosphere, completely gripping and with ingenious plotting, *Beast* is another spectacular read from Matt Wesolowski' Emma's Bookish Corner

'By blending contemporary issues with a rich pagan folklore, steeping it in darkness and presenting it in the setting of an episodic crime podcast, Matt Wesolowski has created something truly special with his Six Stories series' Book Worm Hole

'*Beast* doesn't disappoint, once again finding Wesolowski on addictive, chilling and macabre form … a compelling journey down dark paths and through stormy waters with a palpable sense of creeping unease that courses through the pages' The Tattooed Book Geek

PRAISE FOR THE SIX STORIES SERIES

'Bold, clever and genuinely chilling with a terrific twist that provides an explosive final punch' *Sunday Mirror*

'This is the very epitome of a must-read' *Heat*

'Haunting, horrifying, and heartrending. Fans of Arthur Machen will want to check this one out' *Publishers Weekly*

'A genuine genre-bending debut' *Daily Mail*

'Impeccably crafted and gripping from start to finish' *Big Issue*

'Thanks to Wesolowski's mixture of supernatural elements and first-class plotting, this is one of the most addictive of new crime novels' *Sunday Express*

'Fans of Ruth Ware will enjoy this slim but compelling novel' *Booklist*

'A dazzling fictional mystery' *Foreword Reviews*

'A genuine chiller with a whammy of an ending' C.J. Tudor

'Original, inventive and brilliantly clever' Fiona Cummins

'Wonderfully horrifying … the suspense crackles' James Oswald

'Wonderfully creepy … Inventive, unnerving, bold. Loved the story structure and the use of forest folklore. EXCELLENT' Will Dean

'This is a creepy, chilling read that is ridiculously difficult to put down. The ending is just incredible' Luca Veste

'Frighteningly wonderful and one of the best books I have read in years' Khurrum Rahman

'Wonderfully atmospheric. Matt Wesolowski is a skilled storyteller with a unique voice. Definitely one to watch' Mari Hannah

'Wonderfully clever and chilling … a series which just keeps on getting better and better, it surprises, thrills and enthrals in equal measure' LoveReading

'They're all brilliant, very different despite following the same format and prove that Matt Wesolowski is one of the best emerging horror/crime writers' Off-the-Shelf Books

'This is bold and clever story-telling at its best and it fulfils that much used phrase "a must-read novel"' Books are my Cwtches

'Dark, incredibly intense, full of supressed rage and emotionally gut wrenching. It blew me out the water. I rather think Matt Wesolowski is destined for stardom' Live & Deadly

'An intense, dark and utterly absorbing book. The pages crackle with tension, the characters have real depth and the writing is truly stunning' Bibliophile Book Club

'A dark, emotional and honest book and to my mind, the best Six Stories yet' Hair Past a Freckle

'Another outstanding addition to this series. The writing will pull you in from the first page, and you won't be able to stop reading until you find out the truth about what has happened' Hooked from Page One

'Intensely dark, deeply chilling and searingly thought-provoking … an up-to-the-minute, startling thriller, taking you to places you will never, ever forget' Segnalibro

'Matt has once again created a chilling plot that blurs psychological thriller with a touch of the paranormal; suffice to say you will never look at a wood in the way same again' Random Things through My Letterbox

'Completely unique, with a tight narrative, dominated by unnervingly atmospheric tension and with a magical blend of crime, thriller and a trace of horror' Jen Med's Book Reviews

The Six Stories Series
Six Stories
Hydra
Changeling
Beast

ABOUT THE AUTHOR

Matt Wesolowski is an author from Newcastle-upon-Tyne in the UK. He is an English tutor for young people in care. Matt started his writing career in horror, and his short horror fiction has been published in numerous UK- and US-based anthologies, such as *Midnight Movie Creature, Selfies from the End of the World, Cold Iron* and many more. His novella, *The Black Land*, a horror set on the Northumberland coast, was published in 2013.

Matt was a winner of the Pitch Perfect competition at Bloody Scotland Crime Writing Festival in 2015. His debut thriller, *Six Stories*, was an Amazon bestseller in the USA, Canada, the UK and Australia, and a WHSmith Fresh Talent pick, and film rights were sold to a major Hollywood studio. A prequel, *Hydra*, was published in 2018 and became an international bestseller. *Changeling*, book three in the series, was published in 2019 and was longlisted for the Theakston's Old Peculier Crime Novel of the Year and shortlisted for Capital Crime's Amazon Publishing Reader Awards in two categories: Best Thriller and Best Independent Voice.

Follow Matt on Twitter @ConcreteKraken and on his website: mjwesolowskiauthor.wordpress.com.

Beast

MATT WESOLOWSKI

**ORENDA
BOOKS**

Orenda Books
16 Carson Road
West Dulwich
London SE21 8HU
www.orendabooks.co.uk

First published in the United Kingdom by Orenda Books, 2020
Copyright © Matt Wesolowski, 2020

A catalogue record for this book is available from the British Library.

ISBN 978-1-913193-13-3
eISBN 978-1-913193-14-0

Typeset in Garamond by www.typesetter.org.uk

Printed and bound by CPI Group (UK) Ltd, Croydon CR0 4YY

For sales and distribution, please contact info@orendabooks.co.uk

'He believed that a vague, singular aura of desolation hovered over the place, so that even the pigeons and swallows shunned its smoky eaves. Around other towers and belfries his glass would reveal great flocks of birds, but here they never rested.'

HP Lovecraft, *The Haunter of the Dark*

So in six days, I'm going to meet a vampire.
That vampire is going to kill me.
I'm going to die in six days' time.

Well then, I bet that took you by surprise didn't it? I think you've pro-
bably guessed: today's video is going to be something very different and
I'm just so excited to do this one, it's such a departure for me, but I'm
totally up for this and you're going to love it.

No one else is doing this. Everyone round here is too scared. Parents
and teachers are all freaking out, but I'm not. I'm the first person who's
daring to do it and you're coming with me. I'll be with you all the way!

Oh my God, have you seen the snow? It's like Christmas has come
all over again, but it's February! I mean, what the hell is going on,
weather? Honestly, winter. I'd thought we'd put the cold behind us now
and here you are, again. I'm freezing!

There we go. Heating's on. I've got one of those, like, mini radiator
things, which I'm frickin' cuddling more or less. My mum reckons they're
a waste of energy but, um, have you seen it out there? They're calling it
the Beast from the East: a 'polar vortex'. Whoa there with the drama,
guys, it's just a bit of snow! I'd make a snowman, buuuut I can't be arsed!

Let's get right into it, shall we? Last week's shopping haul video is
still available and thank you so much. I think that's the biggest number
of views I've had yet – it's 'effing brilliant, if you'll excuse my French.

You can still see all my shopping hauls and unboxing archive by clicking the links below and don't you forget to hit 'like' and 'subscribe'.

Thanks guys! Let's go do some vampire-bothering shall we?

Admin done, let's get dark and spooky, because today, guys, I'm going to be doing the – drum roll please – DISD Challenge. Yeah, that's right, I'm going to be…

DEAD. IN. SIX. DAYS!

So for those of you who haven't *heard of it, this challenge is all over my hometown. No one knows exactly* where *it started but that's how these things go, right?*

If you've been locked in a box or whatever, the Dead in Six Days challenge is pretty simple. Six days, six challenges, and if you don't pass it on, you're going to meet a vampire who 'vonts to drink your blood!' Simple as a pimple, right?

Let's do this.

OK, as you can see here, I've got WhatsApp up on my phone. Sorry, it's not my actual phone; so don't be trying to get in touch. No, I got my mum to get me this old one just for the challenge.

So what you do is … look here … you send a message to this number. Which I'm totally gonna blank out – sorry guys! And you'll get a message back. So I'm doing it now – live, right now. You have to use the magic words, apparently, so let's type it out:

Creature of the night,

Listen to my plight,

Your challenge is my goal,

Let us battle for my soul…

And here it is … sent!

Now let's wait a few minutes. I'll put my phone here so we can all see and hear if it replies. It doesn't take long, apparently.

So guys, what's going to happen is the vampire's going to send me a challenge; something I have to do. It'll be a prank of some kind, that's what everyone's doing round here. You have to do the prank, upload it onto YouTube and pass on the vampire's number to the next person.

What if you don't pass it on? Well then you get another prank. A harder one. And so on ... for six days. At the end of the six days, you have to go and meet the vampire.

And it kills you.

But the thing is, it's not going to kill me.

Why? Well, you'll have to subscribe to find out, won't you?

So ... guess what? The vampire's replied. It has a name too! 'Vladlena' – is that, like, the female form of Vlad? Who knows? If only there was some sort of information superhighway, accessible at the click of a button to find out...

Yeah, it's female. It means 'to rule'. Ooh, feisty.

Let's have a read of what Vladlena has to say, shall we?

'Hi Elizabeth' it says – how did it know my name? That's spooky as hell. I told you, didn't I? It's probably a subscriber, to be honest; most people round here are!

Yeah I'll be doing an unboxing of fresh virgins' blood next week, hun. Chill your little undead beans!

'Your challenge is: "Play Lurky in the Dene".'

Wow. OK. So Vladlena wants me to hang round Ergarth Dene in the frickin' snow? Fine. No problem, mate. Oh look, she's sent another message. Hang on.

'This is your first challenge, it will also be your last, pass my number on or your days are numbered and your soul will be claimed in six days.'

Oh, it's like that, is it, Mrs Vampire? Well don't you worry your undead little head, because this will be one game of lurky you'll not be expecting.

Bring. It. On.

If you want to join me in a game of lurky that no one's ever going to forget, just hit 'like' and leave me a lovely comment and I'll hand pick a few of you lovelies to help me out.

OK, guys, so that's it for now. Don't forget to raise your thumbs, give me a big thumbs-up if you liked it. Hit that subscribe button – then you'll be able to see as soon as I upload the next video. Also, hit the bell icon; that way, wherever you are, you'll be able to see if I survived day one!

Keep leaving some love in the comments section, guys. Let me know if any of you out there have met the vampire. Is she hot? Can she handle a girl like me? What do you reckon?

Ha! Thanks guys and I'll see you soon!

Episode 1: What Have We Done?

—We'd like to warn viewers that there are details in the following report that some may find disturbing.

—This is Matthew Manning for BBC News in Ergarth. A grieving family awoke this morning to find a terrible, taunting and sick message scrawled on their garden wall.

The Barton family are shocked and appalled to discover someone has spray-painted the words '*Who locked Lizzie in the tower?*' on their property overnight. This simple message has reopened a still-raw wound, both for the Barton family and the small town of Ergarth on the North-East coast. As viewers will know, Elizabeth Barton was the young woman found murdered in Tankerville Tower two years ago, in 2018. Tankerville Tower a thirteenth-century ruin on the clifftop just outside the town, has been described by locals as an 'eyesore' and a 'death trap' with countless petitions put to Ergarth Council begging for its demolition.

Elizabeth, just twenty-four years old when she was callously murdered, was a popular and high-achieving young woman, with a burgeoning career in video blogging or 'vlogging'. Elizabeth's 'shopping-haul' and 'unboxing' videos attracted thousands of subscribers.

It was her participation in a deadly Internet challenge known as 'Dead in Six Days' that ultimately led her to her death. A death that prompted warnings to parents, countrywide, to be extra vigilant around their children's Internet use. Many schools in Ergarth and the surrounding area have since banned students taking part in any such challenges.

This new graffiti has, yet again, drawn attention to Elizabeth Barton's killers; most notably, Solomon Meer, Barton's former schoolmate. Meer, twenty-four, was sentenced to a minimum of thirty-three years behind bars. His two accomplices, Martin Flynn and George Meldby, twenty-three and twenty-four and also former school-mates of Elizabeth Barton, were sentenced to a minimum of twelve years each for conspiracy to murder.

The three killers used the Dead in Six Days challenge to lure the young vlogger into the local ruin before imprisoning her inside. As temperatures plummeted during one of this country's worst cold snaps in two hundred years, she passed out and died of hypothermia.

A deleted video was recovered from Solomon Meer's phone showing the three men standing around Elizabeth's body as Meer's voice repeats 'What have we done?' This, combined with the perpetrators' DNA, which was found on the council-erected barricades that surrounded Tankerville Tower, provided the crucial evidence that condemned the three.

The most disturbing aspect of the case was the decapitation of Elizabeth Barton's lifeless body. This was said to have been performed at some point after the video was taken. The implement used was never found, and is presumed to have been thrown into the sea. None of the suspects would admit which of them committed this depraved act. The jury on the case took exactly two hours of deliberation to find all three guilty.

Solomon Meer and his accomplices did not defend or explain their actions during their trial at Newcastle Crown Court, save to describe the killing as a 'prank gone wrong'. Since the trial, however, there are those who have suggested that the decapitation of the corpse could have been an 'apotropaic practice' – something performed on dead bodies in post-medieval Poland to prevent 'vampires' rising from the grave. This has, of course, brought Ergarth's own vampire legend to light, a story relatively unknown in the national consciousness. Until now.

It is considered unlikely by those who were close to the case that the graffiti found on the Barton family's wall will raise new questions about the guilt of the three convicted men. Instead it serves as a stark reminder of what the Bartons have lost.

This is Matthew Manning, BBC News, Ergarth. Back to you in the studio.

—Thanks Matthew. Earlier, we spoke to a number of Ergarth residents, to get their thoughts and feelings about the scrutiny this terrible event placed on their town.

'That poor lass, she had her whole life ahead of her. Pretty little thing, wasn't she? Them lads: monsters, all three of them. They weren't happy to just let her die. Doing that to her afterward. What's wrong with people? I tell you what it is; there's no moral guidance anymore. All that rap music and the nonsense on the Internet. They all thought they were vampires or something, didn't they? If that's not the result of a damaged mind, I don't know what is. Bring back national service. That'll soon get it out of them. What are they teaching them at those schools?'

'Aye, she was proper lovely, was Lizzie: dead pretty. She wasn't ever nasty to no one, just dead ... nice. I don't know no one that had a bad word to say about her. She was smart as well. Always top of the class; A's in everything at school. She was on the teams as well: debating, netball, football. She was just good at everything. She had thousands of followers, you know. On Instagram. Even more on YouTube. She was doing charity work wasn't she? Giving something back? That's why those lads picked on her, I reckon. It's cos she had a good heart, lads like them don't like that.'

'It's that blooming vampire story. Folk were saying they'd seen it all over. That's what got that poor lass killed; just gossip on Facebook about the Ergarth Vampire. Them lads? Proper bunch of freaks. I swear down, something should have been done about them. They all thought they were vampires and that – devil-worshippers, drinking blood. Cutting off her head: I ask you. I heard that the leader one, that Solomon Meer, was caught killing pigeons and cats and using them for sacrifices to the devil. What got done about that? Nothing. Then they go and do that to some poor lass who never did no one any harm. It's a disgrace. And where were the parents? That's what I want to know.'

'I just think there's more to it than everyone says. I just think it's not so straightforward. Do I think they did it? It got proved they did in a court of law, so what does my opinion matter? I just believe there's two sides to every story is all.'

'I don't know if they're innocent. Maybe it *was* a prank gone wrong? I don't know. Maybe that's what the graffiti is about?'

'I just think there's more to it than everyone thinks.'

—So, as you can see, this is a sad and tragic time for the people of Ergarth.

Welcome to Six Stories.

I'm Scott King.

Over the next six weeks we are going to look back at the brutal murder of Elizabeth Barton in 2018. We're going to examine the events that led up to her death from six different perspectives, through six pairs of eyes. What I want to know in this series is what turns someone from a town like Ergarth into a killer; what brought three young men together to commit such a terrible crime? This is something that has never, in my opinion, been satisfactorily explained. Was this just a prank that got out of hand, or was there more to it?

For my newer listeners, welcome. For those of you who've been following Six Stories, *welcome back.*

Before we go on, I suppose I should take a moment to address the elephant in the room. Me.

I've only ever wanted to be a vessel for this podcast – a mouthpiece for six perspectives on a crime. I was never supposed to become the story. I used to try my hardest to be anonymous. I used to hide myself away behind a computer, wear a mask when conducting interviews, do everything I could to be nobody.

Yet it seemed the more I hid – crawled beneath my rock – the more the spotlight searched me out.

It's been a while since the last season of Six Stories, *a year since my own story was told; since what happened to me played out in the public eye. I wondered for a while, in the aftermath of all that, whether I should hide away, vanish. But I didn't. I made myself more obvious; more accessible. I shed a lot of the myth that I had hidden behind. I've* had my fair share of criticism for doing that. But I'm back. And I refuse to hide anymore.

So now I'm facing everything head-on. I'm placing myself in the spotlight, conducting every interview face to face. Without Six Stories I wouldn't be where I am now. We owe it to each other to go on.

For all the messages and the support you've offered me after last season, I want to say thank you. There are too many people to name, but rest assured, I read every single message and every one of you made a difference to me. Those of you who are still fighting monsters, keep going.

In this series we look back at crimes: cold cases, missing people, the motivations for murder. We rake up old graves. Some of them don't want to be unearthed, though. Sometimes I hit a rock, find an impasse. Sometimes cold cases are called that for a reason. The following is one of those.

I actually began the research for this one a while back, but I'd only delved just below the surface when I realised there was no real mystery here. This case was simple. For, as you'll see, on the surface, the case of Elizabeth Barton appears not to be about who, or even why. It is open and shut. Maybe that's what attracted me to it. Maybe this time I just wanted to report what had happened. I didn't want to be drawn in. I asked myself what I could possibly say about this that hasn't already been said? Why open a raw wound?

Then, two years after Elizabeth was killed, the graffiti on the Barton's house appeared, as you've just heard at the top of the episode. Someone wants this case reopened.

Dead in Six Days. The challenge that lurks around every bend in this case. Six days … six stories. I don't know; it felt like it fitted. But there was something else, something that's important to me now: this is not a case that I would become part of. I needed one that isn't personal.

I packed a suitcase and I travelled to Ergarth.

Because I'm not hiding from monsters anymore.

*Ergarth is an oddly named and oddly placed town on the North-East coast. Unlike the quaint tourist hubs of Whitby or Scarborough further south, Ergarth is not your typical seaside town. Its coastline boasts no fossil banks, wildlife watching or boat trips out to the headlands …
In fact, there's very little of anything, just a grey, rain-flecked cluster of buildings that ends abruptly in a cliff edge where the ruined Tankerville Tower stands; an austere and crumbling monolith square-edged, five storeys high, made from thick, dark-coloured basalt and limestone. Unlike other pele towers – the fortified keeps and defensive structures built on the borders between England and Scotland – Tankerville has no arrow slits in its walls nor a proud weathercock on its roof, pointing above the crenellations. It is instead, a Brutalist, black rectangle.*

Talk to anyone in Ergarth and they'll tell you they want it torn down. Even in the summer, it looks no better; a benighted blight that everyone can see from their window and wishes they couldn't.

And now, two years after Elizabeth Barton's death, the tower stands as an unpleasant reminder of what happened here in 2018.

Despite its grim outlook, the town has a charm that does bring in a few tourists. There's a caravan park up on the cliffs, a couple of miles from Tankerville Tower. It's small but neat. The town itself has a couple of bed and breakfasts and guest houses, which would probably be considered 'retro'. The town itself isn't terrible; there's even a small parade of amusement arcades before a short pier where the cliff drops to sea level. It's hardly Brighton Palace, but it's well kept and affable; the flash of the lights, the jangly music and the smell of fried doughnuts during the summer. There's also an array of coastal walks along the cliffs, where kittiwakes nest and seals can occasionally be spotted, bobbing up out of the water with their blunt, oily-looking heads. On an unpleasant winter's day, though, with few visitors, the steel shutters closed over the amusements and wind warnings keeping people off the pier, Ergarth is slightly forlorn.

Perhaps, then, the one feature that makes Ergarth stand out from the other small towns that huddle along England's northern coasts is the great, black ruin that is Tankerville Tower.

Occasionally there'll be a ripple of interest in the place: a scheme, a crowdfunder, a local entrepreneur who has big ideas for Tankerville Tower. But then it'll all fall through. People say that's because it's cursed.

The people of Ergarth don't refer to the tower by its real name. They call it 'The Vampire Tower'.

We'll get to that in due course.

It's autumn, and the sky is blue and clear. It's cold, though, and our breath steams. We're inland, my first interviewee and me, on the edge of Ergarth Dene – a wooded public park that dates back to the Victorian era, and sits close to the remains of the Fellman's pasty factory, which burned down a number of years ago. Originally created for genteel perambulation; the park sits in a small valley and has a multitude of trees, paths and ornamental pools. Almost directly opposite, on the other side of the town, Tankerville Tower looms. It's easy to believe you have been sucked into a time warp down here and that around the corner you'll see women wearing crinolines and men carrying canes. The air is thick with the earthy scent of the season: damp leaves and a faint tang of stagnant water. The trees that rise up all around us are turning, preparing for the coming frost. It's a stark contrast to the site of the tower or the centre of Ergarth itself. The wind bites through your clothes along a desolate high street where betting shops have lit up like luminescent fungi. In nearly every doorway there are people huddled together to keep warm.

The cold is more intense here than I've ever felt before, and despite my gloves, the tips of my fingers and toes are like blocks of ice. I imagine how it was for Ergarth two years ago, during the cold snap of 2018. The roads were blocked both in and out, the cold permeating through walls and roofs that were totally unprepared for this onslaught.

—We were proper busy during that cold snap. What did they call it – the Beast from the East? It was proper harsh; there wasn't enough grit to go round, ice all over the roads; people falling over, old people freezing. Half the roads round here were closed; no one could drive into or out of the town. It was like we were suddenly in Siberia.

Pipes froze, leaving some wrapped in bedclothes on their sofas at night, praying that headlights would round the corners of the coiling roads, black with ice, bringing supplies. But the old and infirm of Ergarth were more isolated than ever. My interviewee wants to tell me that people pulled together, helped each other out, checked on neighbours, but that wasn't the case. Ergarth is not affluent; there was little money and little hope. This bred a deadly apathy.

—It was a dog-walker what found her. Isn't it always? She didn't *find* her though, that's not strictly true. We was proper busy and I was on the night shift; I'd just arrived at work, and there was already lads getting ready to go out. They said someone was stuck in the tower. I remember thinking, what on earth someone was doing there in this? It's bad enough in the peak of summer. I knew that this wasn't going to end well. Not at all.

Tankerville Tower dates back to the thirteenth century. A five-storey structure that stands on the edge of the cliff and stares over the green rage of the North Sea. Nothing else, just the wind and the cliffs and the ghostly cries of the kittiwakes. Unless you're walking a dog, or specifically visiting the place, there's absolutely no reason to go there. It's windy there all year round: swirling, freezing Siberian winds and sea fret most of the year. The inside provides little shelter either; the tower is crumbling into the sea.

The tower's origins are somewhat murky; some say it was the beginning of a castle or the leftovers of an attempt at a pele tower, should the 'Border Reivers' move their raids further south. Some say it was a purpose-built prison. With its windowless walls and cell-like interior, this seems the most plausible idea. What we know for sure is that the tower was purchased and given its name by the earls of Tankerville in the early 1700s. They had grand plans to turn it into a residence with an adjoining mansion house, but these never came to fruition. The tower remained unmodernised and was eventually forgotten.

During the twentieth century, the Tankervilles sold the tower to the local authority but not a single use could be found for the place.

The inside of Tankerville Tower is worse than its outside – black,

*sea-scarred stone; a winding staircase that's crumbling and treacherous,
impossible to climb, leading to a bare, windowless room at the very
top. Birds roost in the places where the topmost rocks have crumbled,
and in the 1990s a colony of bats was discovered roosting in that cell
at the very top, prompting a small ripple of interest in the place. The
Bat Conservation Trust, along with Ergarth Council, worked together
to board up the lower doors and windows and to add a perimeter fence
– thus preventing entrance or exit from the tower.*

*Now the tower is a stark monolith, standing almost as a symbol of
the town over which it looms.*

The fence around it still stands. More or less.

—It's a bloody disgrace how they've just let it go like that. So
much history, and what a sorry state it's in. Just sat on the edge of
the cliff covered in birds' and bats' doings.

*The voice you've been listening to is that of Rob Karl. He's a local
volunteer fireman and was one of the first on the scene when Elizabeth
Barton's body was found in Tankerville Tower.*

—No wonder no one wants to do owt with it. It's a death trap,
that place. The council just let it rot. It'll be good riddance when
it does fall down; the sea can have it. You get all sorts of people
hanging about in there. They say there's bats in the roof, don't they?
That's the reason they can't do nowt with the place. You can't
disturb the bats.

—*You said you get people in the tower. Why?*

—Aye, druggies mainly; smack-heads and the crazies. We often
used to get calls from folk saying that kids were going in and out
of the Vampire Tower and that they're worried for them – scared
that one of them's going to hurt themselves, fall into the sea. And
you only need to get close to it to see they've been in there: graffiti,
them tags all over the walls.

You'd get calls saying people had heard stuff, too. Screaming and
that coming from inside. It used to be easy to get in there; the
boards across the doors were all rotted away with the damp and
the rain and the sea. We used to have to go there regular.

Don't get me wrong, now. I'm not saying that any of those other sightings were real. It was all rubbish, all of it.

—*Sightings? Of what?*

—Let's just not talk nonsense, eh? Let's talk reality. I think sometimes people round here get carried away.

Rob becomes cagey and defensive at the mere hint of anything other-worldly associated with Tankerville Tower. You see, there's a story that surrounds the 'Vampire Tower' and its strange nickname. While the ruin is now synonymous with the grisly murder of a young woman, before Elizabeth Barton, there was another female associated with it. I know Rob doesn't want to tell me the story but he knows as well as I do that it's going to have to come out.

—Folk think we're all stupid round here because of that silly old tale. It's like the folk from Hartlepool getting called 'monkey-hangers' cos of some daft old story. You know it, don't you? Back in some war or other, olden times, them up there hanged a monkey cos they thought it was a French soldier.

But our bloody vampire story, it's a hell of a lot worse. It's all a load of rubbish, though, just like the monkey.

—*Can you tell it to me?*

—I'll tell it once. I'll tell you the official version.

—*Fair enough.*

—So it goes like this; see back in the Victorian times, 1860s, I believe, there was a problem in Ergarth. There was a freak cold snap like the one in 2018. It was serious. Folk up here were dying. They were finding bodies frozen in their beds, washed up on the coast, see; all mangled, white, drained of blood. It was the weather; it cut the whole town off. No one could get in or out, and people were ill, starving, throwing themselves into the sea. Horrible times. Back then of course, they knew nowt about polar vortexes and diseases, so they blamed a vampire instead.

—*It seems like an odd conclusion to come to, even in that era.*

—Aye but there was a reason. You see, back then, some soldiers had this prisoner from the Crimean war – a hostage. They say the British and French captured her at the Battle of the Alma when the Russian scarpered. They said she was found in a prince's carriage with a load of money. They brought her here cos no one would ever find her.

—*Who was she?*

—They reckon she was a Russian sorceress or some rubbish like that. Brought down from the Tundra in Siberia; her witchcraft to be used as a weapon. At least that's what the soldiers thought. They brought her back to England as a hostage, kept her prisoner in Tankerville Tower, hoping for a ransom, but no one ever paid up. It's said they didn't want her back. So she was a Trojan Horse type of thing, you see? Then the cold snap came; the place was all snow and freezing temperatures. They say it was the sorceress what done it, like. So they killed her.

Thing is, after that, people round here believed she came back from the dead. As a vampire, like.

Rob's story matches up with some old ideas about vampires. The British and French troops that sailed to fight in the Crimean War landed at the Bulgarian port of Varna, the very same Varna from which Bram Stoker's Dracula launches his ship, the Demeter. *North of Varna are Wallachia, Moldavia and of course, Transylvania. You don't need me to tell you what that particular region is famous for.*

Another piece of lore that's significant here comes from the north of Russia, where vampires were often believed to be powerful sorcerers. If they were killed, it was thought they could return as the undead, and were able to command the winds and tides, the birds and beasts. These creatures could only be finally killed by staking them through the heart, by burning or by decapitation.

Could it be that these folk stories, which were so entrenched in those far-off lands, were brought back to Ergarth by the troops, along with their prisoner?

—*That was when the vampire rumours began?*

—Aye. They say the ship they sailed her back on ran aground on the coast near here; when the locals boarded it, they found the crew dead or dying – but she was alive. They said she'd survived on rats; drank the blood of the crew. Bram Stoker wrote a similar story – and set it down the road at Whitby, fifty or so years later. Seems a bit of a coincidence, doesn't it?

—*What happened to her?*

—Well, the story goes that two Coldstream Guards that came with her went missing the night they locked her in the tower. That's when the snow came; they say she brought it all the way from Siberia.

They found the guards' bodies all mangled at the bottom of the cliff; as if they'd been thrown out of the tower. After that, folk got too scared to go anywhere near the place. They said that she terrorised Ergarth night after night – killing cattle, people; throwing the bodies off the top of the tower. The Russians didn't come to get her back, and the Ergarth folk were so terrified, eventually, they decided they had to get rid of her.

—*How did they do it?*

—The story goes that they tried a few ways. First, they sent a soldier in with a rifle. His body was found on the beach a few days later. Then they sent a hunting party up to the tower with dogs and all sorts. They never came back. They were all found frozen to death, dogs and men, all drained of blood. No one would come to Ergarth anymore after that. And with the weather the way it was, no one could get out either. Diseases were rampant, there was no food, there was no hope. So the people of Ergarth decided to sort it out once and for all. These three farm lads went up there, in desperation really. They supposedly battled with that vampire for three whole days and nights.

At last they managed to lock her in the tower; barricaded the doors and waited for her to die of cold. And when she did, they cut off her head so she couldn't come back.

The next day, the snow thawed and Ergarth was saved.

There is a long silence, disturbed only by Rob's ragged breathing. I don't want to mention what's obvious here.

—*Did she have a name? Who was she?*

—The story goes that her name was Vladlena, but she was known as 'The Beast from the East'. I'll warn you now, you don't want to talk to folk round here these days about the Ergarth

Vampire. Not after what happened to that lass. It doesn't go down too well.

So there you have it. That's how the Vampire Tower got its name. There's certainly no evidence that could even remotely confirm the vampire story. It's almost like the bats that have made residence there have done so to maintain the myth.

I've visited the tower myself. It is certainly a foreboding and rather unpleasant place, even if you don't know the rather farfetched legend about it. The clifftop on which it stands is exposed to the elements; there's an almost constant spray of sea fret, and the wind is even stronger and colder than on the high street, where it screams around the boarded-up shops with a sharpened blade.

The fencing around Tankerville Tower has been reinforced since Elizabeth Barton was murdered. Ergarth Council have assured me they now impose a penalty on anyone who trespasses onto the site. But, according to Rob, before her death it was a beacon for drug addicts and the homeless, and held a fascination for the young and the wayward of Ergarth.

It's no wonder, as it seems there's little else to do here. The nearest cinema is an hour's bus ride away, and I see no places where people, let alone the young, can congregate, save for a few pubs and a low wall outside Ergarth Frozen Meats on the high street. I've been warned by the staff in my hotel not to wander around Ergarth at night. At first I dismissed their concerns, but as the day darkens, there's a distinctly ominous edge to the place. Shutters are pulled over Ergarth Bus Station at sunset and the public benches around the dried-up fountain in Ergarth Market Square have been removed to deter rough sleepers. Rob tells me that plans for a skate park close by were successfully appealed by the Ergarth Residents' Association, and the idea was abandoned. Gangs of youths congregate under the concrete stairs that lead up into the shopping centre or wander aimlessly through Ergarth's streets. There are so many homeless, aimless and addicted people here, it's staggering. No wonder towns like Ergarth feel forgotten. The smell from the abattoir wafts in one afternoon, thick and pungent, like some terrible fog. Some residents pull scarves over their mouths but most go about their business as if it's nothing.

There is no money here; certainly not enough to demolish Tankerville Tower. But it's the lack of hope that has more impact on me.

But when I stood in the shadow of the tower one afternoon, I had the distinct feeling I was being observed. It was unnerving. The wind is savage on those lonely cliffs, and as the day began to die; the cold once again began to burrow into the ends of my fingers.

I turned away, heading back towards town, when something caught my eye; some movement in my peripheral vision. I turned and looked at the tower, that sense of unease increasing. I saw a black shape. A gull or some other sea bird, most probably, roosting in the tower. But the size of it – its wingspan a blot against the sinking sun – for some reason unnerved me. I understood at that moment why the people of Ergarth want rid of this terrible place.

And as I started to make my way back into town, I was approached by a man asking me for change; I wondered if he'd been watching me from the ruin. I almost wanted to tell him to get as far away from the place as he could. The whole thing felt like it was getting to me, gnawing at me like the cold.

I want to know what Rob Karl saw people actually doing in Tankerville Tower. As those of you who are new to the case of Elizabeth Barton will come to find out; this plays rather an important role in what happened.

—Oh aye, all sorts were going up there and getting up to mischief. It's out of the way, see. When people saw kids in there they would usually call the police, not us. We were only summoned when there was a potentially dangerous situation. Like if they were lighting fires or trying to climb to the top.

—*And were those situations common? You said before that it was mainly the homeless and drug addicts who went to the tower.*

—That's right. Look, it sounds harsh but … well … that lot can look after themselves, can't they? I mean it's no skin off anyone's nose if … The kids though, you can't ignore that. But as soon as we arrived, they'd scarper. We only ever caught kids in there once. I'm going back a few years now, mind. Group of ne'er-do-wells had got in and were causing trouble, lighting fires, messing on, the usual.

—*What happened?*

—We heard this shouting, and we shone a light up onto the side of the tower. This one lad, he'd tried climbing up the stairs to that top room and caught his trousers on something; he had those shiny tracksuit bottoms on, see? They'd ripped and he was hanging on to the stones, shouting at us to eff off, with his arse hanging out! Sorry, I shouldn't laugh about it, not when you know what happened to that poor lass, but this was a long time ago.

—*What drew people to Tankerville Tower, do you think, of all places?*

—What do you mean?

—*I've been up there to have a look, and I just can't imagine why anyone would want to be there, even if there was nowhere else to go.*

—Grim, isn't it? My advice would be to stay well away, especially on your own.

—*Were these intruders just vandals and drug dealers, or was there a more … nefarious reason for them going in there?*

—I know what you're getting at, I think. Was any of them into dark stuff – witchcraft and that? Like that Meer lad.

—*Right. I'll just ask you straight. You've been inside that tower on several occasions, correct?*

—Correct.

—*And the last time you went in there was the fourth of March 2018, right? The day Elizabeth Barton's body was found.*

—Also correct.

—*Have you ever, in all your years, seen anything in that tower to suggest occult activity? Strange symbols painted on the walls? Evidence of sacrificial altars, that sort of thing?*

—I've never seen nowt in that tower that I couldn't explain. Until I saw Elizabeth Barton. But that was cos I couldn't fathom *why* someone would do that to such a lovely young thing. To me, that place is the Vampire Tower in name only. There are some round here that'd like to see that place demolished and I'm one of them. I'll tell you that for nowt.

The case against Solomon Meer suggested that he was obsessed with the occult and the idea that there was a vampire in Ergarth. It has not gone unnoticed that the removal and subsequent placement of Elizabeth's head coincides with medieval European practices concerning the killing of vampires. There are many in Ergarth who say that Solomon Meer was an unpredictable and ghoulish presence around the town, as well as being a petty vandal and a thief. George Meldby and Martin Flynn fare no better. Searches on Solomon Meer's computer show that he was a member of several vampire discussion forums. All of this Meer admitted in court, but he would not be drawn on whether Elizabeth Barton's death had something to do with his belief in vampires.

With a case as complex as this one, a case that has been debated and dissected throughout the media, it is hard to know where to start. So let's start here, in Ergarth, and work backwards. We'll hear again from Rob Karl about the discovery of the body, and I want to do this in parallel with more recent developments, namely the graffiti on the Bartons' garden wall:

'Who locked Lizzie in the tower?'

Mr and Mrs Barton live in an affluent new-build estate just outside Ergarth, where graffiti of any kind is rare. There is, perhaps, more to the thoughtless question in white paint. It appears crassly rhetorical, but is it? I feel like this question has a specific purpose, but what?

Solomon Meer, Martin Flynn and George Meldby are all serving time for what, by their own admission, they did to Elizabeth Barton in March 2018. Is the message on the Bartons' wall really questioning their guilt?

—It must have been minus ten out there on the cliff, with the wind, and the snow still coming down. I've never felt cold like it in this country. My son went over to Sweden one New Year and said it was so cold that your tears froze on your cheeks. This wasn't far off. When we got the call about someone being trapped in the Vampire Tower, we were over there like a shot.

—*What time of day was this?*

—Morning, around nine, ten-ish? We park the van as close as we can to the tower. There's this woman stood there, all bundled up in her scarf and hat; her dog going crazy on the end of the lead. She says that there's something in the tower. A body.

—*How did this woman know? Had she gone inside the tower?*

—It was the dog. This great excitable beagle – great daft thing it was. So she's taking it – what was its name? Henry. That was it. So she's taken Henry for a walk along the cliff; not so much snow there, see? Not so icy. She lets him off the lead and he's gone bounding off into the tower and come back with something in his mouth.

—*Oh...*

—Nah, it wasn't nothing horrible, not fingers or nowt like that. Henry comes back with a scarf.

—*And this woman, she called you because of that?*

—Oh no; apparently Henry's not finished there; he's off again, back and forth into the tower until he's stood with a hat, a scarf and some gloves in front of his owner, wagging his tail for a treat like he's Jack the biscuit!

—*I'm assuming these were Elizabeth Barton's things?*

—That's right. We wondered why it was so easy for this dog to get them all off the body. We hadn't seen it yet.

—*That must have been difficult – not knowing what you were about to face in there.*

—Aye. We thought something else had happened to her – there's plenty of maniacs and weirdos around here who would do … something … to a pretty young lass like that. But we had no idea what we were about to see in there…

There were a few nasty coincidences too.

—*Really?*

—Yeah. Not nice ones either. First one is that the woman who's walking her dog has been listening to a podcast. Not yours, but one about the Crimean War.

—*Really?*

—Yes. And the episode she was listening to was about the Battle of the Alma. Same battle they captured the Beast from the East in.

—*With respect, it's just a coincidence – quite a big one, I'll grant you. A coincidence all the same.*

—The woman who found her was listening to this podcast about the Battle of the Alma *when* Henry began bringing her the clothes. It's not right is it? It's horrible.

There's another unpleasant coincidence at play too: the cold snap in the UK that began on the 24th of February 2018 actually came from Russia as well. An arctic air mass that, combined with Storm Emma, covered most of Europe, bringing sub-zero temperatures and winds direct from Siberia. The UK Met Office issued red weather warnings.

Elizabeth Barton's death was one of eighteen attributed to this new 'Beast from the East'.

The autopsy on Elizabeth Barton's body was unable to ascertain exactly who or what removed Elizabeth's head, save that it was done post-mortem. It is likely, according to the coroner, that at some point in the night the young woman lost consciousness in the extreme cold.

As it was back in 1854, when the Ergarth Vampire legend began, this weather was utilised by Solomon Meer, Martin Flynn and George Meldby. We'll get to them presently. Let's stay with Rob, Elizabeth and the tower.

—So you had to break in to Tankerville Tower to find her?

—Yes, more or less. By then the police had arrived too and we were instructed to go inside. The security around the place was pretty shoddy – not like it is now. Then it was just a flimsy, chicken-wire fence with some half-hearted barbed wire on top. Someone had lopped through it long ago, so it just opened, like a door. It took us all of a few minutes to find the opening. We pulled back the fence and went in first. We had our helmets on and all our protective gear, thank God, cos the cold out there … The boards over the door to the tower had rotted away long before, so the council had just recently put new grates over the doorway … *again*. But the grate was all dented and battered, half hanging off with this gap at the bottom where the dog must have got in.

It's dark in there, even in broad daylight; it stinks as well: bat shit, bird shit, salt. The stone's all wet and slippery. No snow had got inside. There was a load of rubbish in there – sleeping bags and that from the homeless. She was all crumpled up in the far corner. No clothes on; head on her legs, staring at us. I'll never forget that sight, long as I live.

Elizabeth Barton had been dead for hours; she was naked, her fingers and toes were blue, and the hair on her decapitated head, placed on her prone legs, just above her knees, shone with ice. An ambulance was called and the body was taken away by paramedics. Rob and the other fire-fighters and first responders left the tower and a perimeter was set up and forensics attended the scene. The poor weather conditions made the investigation difficult but the following theory was eventually constructed:

At some point during the evening of the third of March 2018, the grate that covered the doorway into Tankerville Tower was partly removed. Elizabeth Barton entered the tower alone and the grate was bent back into place by the three young men – their DNA was found all over it. Elizabeth Barton was too weak to move the grate herself, and died of hypothermia after, it's assumed, undressing herself at some point during the night. Paradoxical undressing can occur when hypothermia sets in. When the body's core temperature has dropped too low, the blood vessels contract to prevent loss of heat – resulting in a hot flash that makes the already weak and disoriented hypothermic person think they are too hot. Elizabeth's body, save for the decapitation of her head, had not been interfered with … eliminating a sexual motive for her murder.

Solomon Meer, Martin Flynn and George Meldby were accused of bending back the grate and then coercing Elizabeth into the tower and leaving her there until her death. Phone records show that it was Solomon Meer who told Elizabeth she should come to Tankerville Tower, presumably to complete her online video Dead in Six Days challenge. As Elizabeth Barton reportedly had little to do with Solomon Meer, it is still not known why she answered his summons. Maybe we'll never know. I put this to Rob.

—It's always those what are trying to do good, isn't it?

—*I'm not sure what you mean.*

—I don't know the ins and outs of it, but a lot of people round here say that Elizabeth Barton was setting up a good cause, a foundation to help people.

—*Help who?*

The druggies in the town, and the … well … them what hung round in the tower, I suppose. Like I say, it's always the good ones…

There's an unpleasant piece of irony here. The Elizabeth Barton Tower Foundation unfortunately never came to fruition. Instead, this well-intentioned young woman ended up dead in the very place she was trying to do some good.

Perhaps most shocking was what happened to Elizabeth after she passed out and died from cold. Her head was severed with something very sharp; it is assumed a blade from the abattoir owned by the family of Martin Flynn. It is not known for sure which of the three committed this particular act as the weapon was never found. DNA from all three perpetrators was found on Elizabeth's body but, in view of Solomon Meer's penchant for vampires, it is assumed that he committed this diabolical act.

—*Rob, did you know Solomon Meer, Martin Flynn or George Meldby? Were any of them known to the police or the fire service?*

—Oh aye. Georgie bloody Meldby – the little firebug; we all knew him. Even before the Fellman's factory burned down.

Martin Flynn … well, everyone knew the Flynns.

Martin Flynn's family were the owners of Flynn's Meats – an abattoir on the edge of Ergarth – and while not exactly criminal, the Flynn family had a reputation for being tough. I'm told that no one wanted to get on the wrong side of the Flynns of Ergarth. There was controversy surrounding Flynn's Meats as the result of an undercover investigation in 2017. That's something we may explore in a later episode.

George Meldby is a very different character. He was best known in Ergarth for burning down a factory when he was fifteen. George Meldby's issues with fire are well known throughout the town. Like Tankerville Tower, the ruins of the old factory stand like another black tooth on Ergarth's already sorry gumline.

—*George Meldby was a 'firebug'.*

—Oh yes. Big time. He had a problem, that lad. A real problem. George wasn't a thug like the Flynn lad, but he liked to burn things. He was obsessed with fire. His poor mother – at her wits' end she was. An odd lot, the Meldbys. Old Ergarth family. Lived up at the Primrose Villas Estate. That place makes Helmand Province look like Benidorm.

You know Fellman's, the bakers? They used to have the factory here; just outside town. Most people in Ergarth worked or was related to someone who worked at Fellman's factory. George Meldby and his mam lost a lot of friends after that place burned down. That was back a good few year now, the whole place going up in smoke. George Meldby, he was only fifteen, for Christ's sake!

—*It wasn't official though, was it? It was never proved that George Meldby did it.*

—Not officially, no. Lack of evidence. But everyone in Ergarth knew it was him. George was a sly little thing, see? Managed to wriggle out of that one. But, like I say, everyone knew.

—*Was there a particular reason George burned down Fellman's factory? Like you said, it was an important part of the town.*

—Hmm, there's a lot of rumour that goes round in a place like this. Thing with Georgie was he wasn't slow like Martin Flynn, but he was … *malleable*. If someone told him to do something, he would more than likely do it. Specially if it was a lass.

—*There was no mention of fire in connection with Elizabeth Barton's death, though, was there?*

—No. None whatsoever. I was surprised when they said Georgie was involved if I'm perfectly honest. But maybe it was escalation. First a factory – he got away with that. Then this. I reckon just the fires wasn't doing it for him anymore. He needed a bigger kick. Don't get me wrong; he wasn't like a lot of them round here; he didn't go round smashing things up and robbing people. It was just about the fire, for Georgie. Nowt else.

—*Is it true that George tried to burn down his primary school when he was nine?*

—Georgie provided Ergarth Fire Service with plenty of work, I'll say that. What most people don't know is *that* fire never actually started. He was stopped at the last minute. I was one of the fire officers who went to his house afterwards. To 'have a chat'. It was us, the police, and social services were there too. It seemed a bit excessive, like. I thought the lad must be shitting himself!

—*Wasn't he?*

—Not *really*. It was strange. *He* was strange. You know when a little one seems older than their years; an old man in a kid's body? That was our Georgie alright. He just sat there on that massive sofa next to his mam, looking up at us. That house was full of dogs; and there were tanks full of lizards and snakes. It felt like there were thousands of them, and there was all of us squeezed into that living room. We were gentle – tried to explain to him about the consequences of his actions, gave Mam a load of leaflets, all that.

—*What was George's response?*

—Just … nothing. He just nodded. Like he'd heard it all before. Six or so years later and Fellman's burns down. Fat lot of good we did, eh?

—*What about George when he was older? Was he still the same?*

—He was quiet, a little odd bod. Everyone knew who he was round town, but apart from the fire-setting, he was harmless enough. I didn't think he had it in him to … No one did.

—*So, from your experience of George, his part in what happened to Elizabeth Barton came as a surprise?*

—Yes. It was a surprise. It's a small town; everyone knows everyone round here, and I can tell you that all the coppers I know felt the same way about him. We all sort of *liked* him. OK, 'liked' might not be the right word, and now, we certainly don't like him. But we did. He wasn't like some of the kids you hear about; torturing puppies and birds and that, robbing old ladies. That wasn't Georgie. He just liked fire. He didn't try and kill people with it, he just liked it. He just liked watching things burn.

—*What about the others? Solomon and Martin?*

—I'll come to them. All in good time.

George Meldby was never charged with setting fire to Fellman's factory when he was fifteen, causing hundreds of thousands of pounds worth of damage and the loss of a great many jobs. The company, despite being from Ergarth, decided to relocate their production premises to Redcar in Cleveland, much to the disgust of the Ergarth community.

Rob Karl's interview raised several questions – sprouting up like weeds around this case: why was Elizabeth Barton murdered? Why has the guilt of the three who murdered her now been questioned, and why would a boy like George Meldby be involved?

It's easy to assume that, because George had a problem with fire, he had the potential to do worse. Yet, if what Rob is saying is correct, George wasn't that type of a kid. Maybe he was just easily influenced.

I'm going to dig deeper into the back stories of Elizabeth's killers in later episodes. For now, though, I want to explore something that's been troubling me. According to Rob there was no evidence of 'occult' activity inside the tower, so I don't understand quite yet how the idea of a vampire fits into the story. Let's hear an allusion to the Ergarth Vampire in the case of Elizabeth Barton in a local news report.

Audio excerpt from *Look North* (North East and Cumbria) March 5th 2018

…It has become clear that the three convicted of the killing were part of an online 'challenge'. Their friendship began at Leighburn Adult Education Unit where the three killers formed a close bond, and Solomon Meer emerged as the trio's leader. It is thought they were behind a spate of vandalism and cult activity in Ergarth Dene. During the trial at Newcastle Crown Court, none of the accused denied participating in the 'Dead in Six Days' challenge, but none of them would explain their part in Barton's death, save to say it was a 'prank gone wrong'. However, many people in Ergarth suggest Meer's fascination with the local legend of the Ergarth Vampire may have had a part to play in the gruesome, ritualistic killing.

'Cult activity' and 'ritualistic killing' are interesting terms. As far as I'm aware, there was no actual evidence that the three convicted men were involved in occult activity. The removal and placement of Elizabeth's head, however, has to be significant. Was it a grisly coincidence? I'm not so sure.

…Video evidence from Solomon Meer's phone shows the three stood near the body of Elizabeth Barton, with Solomon Meer repeating 'What have we done?'

Solomon Meer, who was sentenced to a minimum of thirty-three years, was suggested to have instigated Barton's death; it was his text message to Elizabeth Barton that brought her to Tankerville Tower that night. It was Meer, according to the judge's summing up, who coerced the others into carrying out his plan to barricade Elizabeth Barton in the ruin and leave her to die of hypothermia. No clear motive has yet been established for why the three committed this act.

It is believed Elizabeth knew her killers, as all three were her former school-mates. There is also some speculation that Elizabeth Barton's burgeoning YouTube fame played a part in her murder.

All three defendants underwent psychological examination and all three were deemed fit to stand trial. The Barton family are calling the sentencing 'a degree of justice'…

There's a lot to think about here, not least the still-unanswered questions about why the three perpetrators did what they did. The story from some quarters is that some sort of esoteric activity played a part. Solomon Meer's obsession with vampires haunts this case, but the actual role it played in the killing remains only rumour. Depending on who you talk to, he either believed he was a vampire or was attempting to start some sort of vampire 'cult'. I'm still searching for clarity here.

All I can find so far is that the murder of Elizabeth Barton mirrors the story of the Ergarth Vampire – the original 'Beast from the East'. But is this mere coincidence or the result of delusion? What is it that links Elizabeth Barton to the story of the Ergarth Vampire?

Rob Karl admits he finds it hard to understand this aspect of the case. He tells me that these days everything happens online, and that he and his generation don't see what the young people of Ergarth are doing until it blows up like this.

We know that Elizabeth Barton was participating in an online challenge known as 'Dead in Six Days' before she met her fate in Tankerville Tower, and that the challenge would apparently culminate in meeting a vampire. And Solomon Meer admitted without question that he'd messaged Elizabeth Barton to meet him at Tankerville Tower on the night she was killed.

Rob shakes his head when I mention the Dead in Six Days challenge to him.

—All that's playground gossip and nonsense. It was just one of those daft crazes the young 'uns dream up.

—Was the vampire story discussed much around the time Elizabeth Barton was killed?

—Well, I think it's one of those that's been passed down and it got twisted up in her death, it took place in Tankerville Tower, after all.

—It's interesting that such an elaborate and frankly unbelievable story is still perpetuated here.

—Oh aye, talk to anyone round here. Everyone's got a story. Everyone reckons they've seen her.

That's where this vampire business moves from a folk tale to actual sightings. And to be fair, a vampire story is a lot more exciting than most local legends.

—So people in Ergarth have seen the vampire 'in the flesh'?

—Well, no one's had a first-hand sighting. It's one of them: someone's mate's girlfriend's hairdresser seen her. You know what I mean?

—Do you know any of these stories?

—I've heard them all, more than once. Since I was a kid in the seventies. Everyone here has a vampire story.

—The Ergarth vampire was that prevalent? I had no idea.

—It's difficult for anyone who's an outsider to understand … no offence, like.

—None taken.

—But up here, you know, there's not a lot for us to focus on. Westminster doesn't know we exist; we've never been a ship-building place like Sunderland or Newcastle; not a fishing port like down Whitby; we've not even got a power station, like Middlesbrough has. There's no jobs – there never has been, there's no industry really, save for the abattoir and, well … there *was* the Fellman's factory. It's hard living here. That's the unfortunate reality.

A lot of kids grow up and never escape; the lucky ones work in the supermarkets or down the arcades. The ones what leave school with nowt usually go work at the abattoir, the unlucky ones end up on drugs or dead. That vampire story, it's *ours*. When you've not got a lot, you hold on to what you have, however weird it is.

—*So what was it about the story of the Ergarth Vampire that motivated Solomon Meer?*

—Come with me.

We walk further into Ergarth Dene. The path squelches beneath our feet and the trees rise up, tangled and heavy with sodden leaves. It's another world down here, the slim, winding paths and the stone bridges. Away from the screaming wind and the crash of the sea, nature is allowed to bloom here, pushing away the harsh reality of the town, where chicken bones line the gutters and empty shop windows stare sadly at the deserted high street. I can see why coming down here, for some, might feel like an escape. However, I still don't feel entirely safe.

—Back when I was a kid, people used to say they saw her here. See these old iron lampposts? They were the old gas lamps. When I was little, they put electric lights in them. Costs too much now, to light it down here. I tell you what: I wouldn't come down here at night, and that's not cos I'm afraid of a vampire. You understand me? Plenty of bad 'uns knock about down here, and I'm not just talking about kids. There's all sorts come here: the homeless, the druggies, the mental, the mental *and* homeless druggies, now they can't get in the Vampire Tower. Sorry, not very PC of me is it, to say that? The mental-health ones anyway. It's dangerous down here, let's leave it at that.

Anyway, the vampire. When I was a kid I had this babysitter, Maureen. I was about eight or nine. Maureen was a young lass, only in her twenties. Anyway, she used to tell me this story. I used to beg her for it, and she would always say no, reckoned she'd get in trouble. But she'd tell me if I nagged her enough.

She'd been walking through the Dene, late at night, see. God knows why, cos even back then it can't have been a very safe place to be at night. Anyway. Maureen said she was just walking along, minding her own business, when she hears a noise. At first she thought it was the wind, a sort of high-pitched, screeching noise. She didn't like it, she said, it got in her head this wailing, screaming wind noise, confused her; she started wandering, staggering about.

Look, come here, I'll show you where she says she went.

Rob leads me along the path, passing a stream that gurgles beside us, its voice carrying above the skeletal shopping trolleys sitting in the water. Then we go uphill slightly where a slim stone bridge passes over our heads and casts a rough shadow on the path.

—Pretty nice, huh? Picturesque? The bridge was built when things were made to last. It doesn't really go anywhere in particular, just connects up the paths, but the Victorians liked stuff like this; dinky bridges and stepping stones. When I was a kid, we called this the echo bridge. Nowadays the kids just cover it with graffiti.

Rob steps into the arched black shadow and shouts out; his voice reflects back at us. Ivy interlaced with old graffiti creeps up the sides of the bridge. There is a strong smell of urine, which, for a second, makes me share Rob's disappointment with 'the way things are these days'.

—So Maureen was right about where we are, not quite under the bridge. That light was on back then, so she could see a figure standing on the top of the bridge. But in silhouette, from the lamp, see? The figure's a woman, she said, in a dress; but the dress is all ragged and ripped, soaked in mud.

It's her what's making all the noise, but it's all wrong, it's high-pitched – like a kid. In fact, she said, it didn't even sound like screaming at all, it didn't even sound *human*.

Anyways, it's dark and it's cold, and this figure is up there, and Maureen swears she can feel that it's looking down at her. So she decides to get out of there, she's not having any more, she's done. So she's just about to turn round, pretend she's forgotten something, go back the way she came when that figure starts coming after her.

—*Down the path?*

—Down the bridge. She said it just climbed over the side, hands and knees, climbing down the side of the bridge like a *spider*. Maureen stood there, frozen; watching as this thing in a dress creeps down the wall. It opens its mouth, she said, and it's got these *teeth*. Like knives, she said, a mouthful of daggers. I swear down, that gave me nightmares.

Poor old Maureen screams, she said, and she turns round and she's out of there. She doesn't stop. But she can hear it coming after her, this pattering of feet, this rustling of a dress, but worse than all of that is the screaming noise it's making. At first, she said, she thought it was all the breath coming from that mouth, the mouth full of daggers, whistling through those fangs. But when you ask other folk what they've seen, they say that the Ergarth Vampire – the Beast from the East – can't speak.

—*What do you mean?*

—They say that those three farm-lads what killed her, in the story, they cut off her head, right? But they didn't do it properly, so she can only make a whistling, screaming noise through her throat. It's why she's still here, is what some people say.

She'd never ran so fast in her life, Maureen said, and she never went down to Ergarth Dene since, not even in the daytime. When she's not in the Dene, Maureen told me, she's up in the tower, in that top room; sleeping … In the form of a giant bat.

I swear that story kept me up for about a week. I wouldn't open the curtains, because my bedroom faced east and I could see the tower. I had nightmares every single night. Great, black wings in the sky. No wonder my mam and dad gave poor Maureen the boot. Poor lass.

I think suddenly of the ragged shape that thrashed at the edge of my vision that afternoon I visited the tower.

—*Did you believe her?*

—Aye, at the time I did. But then, everyone's got a vampire story round here.

—*Do you know any more of them?*

—I've heard them all, man. Everyone has.

—*Can you give me an idea of them; do they cover similar ground?*

—Well all the ones people told when I was a kid had something to do with the Dene. Maybe it was someone dressed up or something, but a lot of people said they saw her down here. People still say they've seen that mouth full of daggers, this great cut in her throat; they say that if she catches you, she'll bleed you dry. All that nonsense. Come with me, I'll show you something.

I'm surprised, if I'm honest, that this grim tale of the Ergarth Vampire reoccurs so frequently; but it seems it's almost become a touchstone for the town and its people. I certainly don't believe Rob's babysitter, so, as we turn from the bridge and take a narrow path downhill, past a wall of ferns and stinging nettles, the mud squelching under my feet and the soily air thickening with every step, I wonder why I'm feeling a sense of foreboding, why I don't want to look back because I'm worried I'll see something watching us, some blurry figure with a mouthful of daggers.

The path ends abruptly in a small clearing carpeted with yellow leaves, above it a canopy of poplars, leaning together conspiratorially. It's damp and shady down here and the only thing that shares our space is a dilapidated folly, cloaked in moss and black with age. It looks like a half-formed cenotaph made of the same dark basalt as Tankerville Tower, a waist-high tri-pillared thing that ivy is slowly demolishing.

—This is it.

—*I'm rather underwhelmed if I'm honest.*

—Yep. What a mess, eh? Believe it or not, this is actually a grave. Of sorts.

—*Really?*

—That's what the story is round here. Look.

Rob walks past the folly and pushes aside some bushes; they soak his sleeves.

—Look here: three paths. This place is a crossroads. Or at least it was. Now look.

Rob walks back over to the folly and lifts a great pile of thick, bottle-green ivy. Beneath it, brown roots coil, silvery insects scurry. There is a small stone plinth, its recesses filled with mould and moss. There are four words carved into this plinth, surrounded by faded carved skulls:
  'Never shall thee wake.'

—This is where they buried the vampire. At a crossroads. After they cut off her head. This is Ergarth's best-kept secret. Only one or two know it's here. Well, at least that used to be the case. I'm guessing when your podcast comes out, we'll be getting a load more visitors to Ergarth Dene. We can charge them a fiver to come splodge round the mud down here. Nice little earner.
  —*Is it really the vampire's grave?*
  —Course not! It's some daft thing the Victorians built. Who knows? Who cares?

I feel like in a short space of time, we've veered off topic. Hugely. It's more like careering off the road with no brakes. We began talking about the discovery of a dead body in Tankerville Tower and now here we are, somewhere in the depths of Ergarth Dene, facing another ruin, talking vampires. But if I've learned anything doing these series, then it's to roll with the punches and see where we end up.

  —*And what does this have to do with Elizabeth Barton, if you don't mind me asking?*
  —Of course. That's why you're here. That's why we're here. As I say, not a lot of people know about this place. They all think everything happened at the Vampire Tower. You want to know a bit more about those lads that killed her? Well you'll need to look down here, in the Dene. This was where Solomon Meer first came to our attention. Right here.

I can see why Ergarth Dene is more of a lure to the young and the bored than the tower. Tankerville Tower is damp and ruined, exposed to the elements. Even with a fire lit, I can't imagine any sort of comfort being found there. Down here though, in this little valley, there's trees, hidden paths, bridges and the cover of darkness. Unlike Ergarth High street, or out on the pier, where faded signs inform you you're being watched, there are no CCTV cameras down here.

—It's all drugs and drink down here these days. Fights, graffiti, damage. Worse. The council did spend a lot of money having the paths maintained. But nowadays there's nothing left, so if anything's done, it's volunteers who do it. The loony lefties are always on about doling out money to teenagers – give them more youth centres, give them playgrounds. But why, if this is how they're going to treat things? Why should they get money? When I was a lad, you didn't shit on your own doorstep.

—*What about those three young men: Meer, Flynn and Meldby? Was this their stomping ground?*

—I could tell you the story about something that happened down here. I dunno if the police would tell you it. But I was here. I made it my business to be.

I just want to say at this point that Ergarth Police have told me that they have no one willing to talk to me about Elizabeth Barton or her killers.

—We got a call-out a day or two before Elizabeth Barton died. Fire in Ergarth Dene. Kids. Fights, drink and drugs. All that.

—*Really? During the cold snap?*

—Aye, well, we were dubious too, at first. It was Baltic out there: the roads were blocked, everything covered in ice and snow. But some old dear's called the coppers and says she's seen a fire in the Dene. We guessed it was kids. So we head down. It's the middle of the night. Freezing cold. Luckily the snow had let up but it was brutal out there. Now a car can only get so far down to the Dene anyway, but the road is so steep and slippery, we'd have spent the whole night pulling it out. So a few uniformed coppers and me just go walking down with torches; softly, softly, so as not to spook them, you know? Kids are smart these days, they know their rights. You've got to know how to play them.

It's pitch-black. Our hands and feet are like ice blocks, and we're even wearing those crampons over our boots. The Dene is like something off a Christmas card: thick snow; all the trees hung heavy with it. We see the fire before we get there, flickering through the trees. It's nowt really, just a few sticks burning. There's music on, but it's not that head-banger stuff they like, it's dead slow and miserable, I don't know. It would have been *The Smiths* or something in my day. We get closer and see that there's two of them. They're stood over a fire, heads together like they're in a meeting or something. A bloody coven if you ask me! One of them's got a phone in one hand with the music going. Head down. I thought they were teenagers at first, but when we got closer we saw they were older. Twenties. And one's got a sleeping bag under his arm.

Right here. This is where they were stood.

—Rob points to the vampire's grave.

—So I get down here, sharpish, thinking they're spice-heads or junkies, they must be half dead with the cold. But not a bit of it, and I can see that something's not right. They're still just stood there. No drinking, no fighting. Just these two and a fire. And you know what I thought? I thought they looked … *uncanny*. Like something off a horror film. It just didn't look right.

When they see us coming, they break apart, stand to attention. We tell them to turn that music off, and they do it. And then we notice something else that's odd.

—Like what?

—There was lots of smoke – I thought they were burning a tyre or something, but there wasn't that smell you get; just lots of smoke. Like they were burning green stuff.

—What were they doing?

—Burning flowers! They've got this massive pile of roses and they're burning them on top of the vampire's grave!

—Why?

—Search me. None of them would say owt; they just shrugged – you know how young 'uns do. Shrug and grunt. Thing was, the coppers had another old dear who called the station, a couple of days before, saying she'd seen a couple of hoodies stealing flowers from the churchyard, right off the graves. Sick little bastards.

—Did either of them give you an explanation? What were they burning the flowers for?

—It didn't look right. When have you ever seen teenagers do something like that, let alone adults? I can tell you what it looked like to me – and the other lads agreed with me. We all thought it looked dodgy. Some kind of Satanic ritual. Witchcraft.

The location and the act of burning flowers doesn't seem like run of the mill vandalism. I cannot, however, find much about burning flowers being anything to do with witchcraft. But I can see now, where this idea of cult activity began.

—Rob, I'm assuming one of these two was Solomon Meer.

—Correct. I'll never forget what he said, the impudent little prick, and I don't excuse the language. He said he could do what he liked in his own house.

—What did he mean?

—He was trying to be clever. The coppers asked him for his name and address – and he gave his address as 'Tankerville Tower, Ergarth', all with this smirk on his face. He was showing off now in front of the other lad – thought he was the big man I swear I could have swung for him. I tell you now, if I could go back in time...

—Who was the other one: George Meldby? Martin Flynn?

—No, it wasn't them, it was some other reprobate; a younger lad. Gave us a fake name and scarpered. Little shit.

—So what happened to Solomon Meer? Was he charged with anything?

—I wish. We chucked snow on his fire and walked him out of there, sent him home with a warning, told him to stay out of Ergarth Dene and Tankerville Tower. Biggest mistake the coppers ever made, if you ask me. They should have took him down Ergarth nick for the night, scared some sense into the impudent little shite.

—You couldn't prove they'd stolen the graveyard flowers?

—Nope. It was his word against the woman's who seen the flowers stolen. The flowers were all burned, so we couldn't tell where they'd come from. People's loved ones' flowers on a fire, I ask you … there's something not right there.

—*That's an awful thing to do.*

—You know, I wish we'd persevered that night. Asked more questions. I knew we had to keep an eye on that one from then on. And we did, but I wish we'd done more. Because there's not a day goes by that I don't wish I could have done something to stop him.

—*Who was he?*

—With his bloody Satanic rituals and 'I'll do what I like in my own house', as if he was entitled.

Solomon Meer. I had his card marked, I'll tell you that now.

This story certainly makes you wonder about Solomon Meer's more esoteric interests. Surely he wasn't burning flowers just for the sake of it. And was the place he was doing it significant? Did this have something to do with the Ergarth Vampire? Rob says he's one of few who knows about the vampire's grave. Did Solomon Meer know what it was too? I wish we knew who the other one was. Rob says he looked younger than Meer and appeared more scared by the presence of the police. It's something we might never know. It might not even be important.

—*What do you think he meant by 'my own house'? Was he just being smart?*

—Well, turns out he'd been kicked out of home. Afterwards, folk said he'd been creeping about town, living down in the Dene or up in the Vampire Tower.

—*Really? Is that true?*

—Search me. Like I say, there's not enough money for coppers to be traipsing round Ergarth looking for folk like Solomon Meer. The lad was a bloody show-off, an attention-seeker. I imagine he made up a story about being homeless.

I feel like we've been down here long enough. The temperature is starting to drop as the sun begins to wane. We start moving, Rob in the lead, up the slim track back to the main path that winds up

*through Ergarth Dene. I can't imagine how dark and miserable it
would have been during that cold snap in 2018. Surely it's not possible
that Solomon Meer was living outside at this time. We'll have a look
into that in due course.*

*—There's one more person we don't know a lot about, Rob; I'm
wondering if you knew Martin Flynn at all?*

—Martin Flynn? I only know what everyone knows about him:
thick as two short planks and built like a brick shithouse. Honestly,
that lad was like a grown man at twelve, and as strong as two of
them. He was like the rest of his family; nowt between the ears and
plenty behind them. You know they own the abattoir up Skelton
Way? A few years back there was a problem there with undercover
activists, something like that. But no one dared say anything to
them. You don't mess with the Flynns round here. It was the same
after the Barton lass. And as far as I'm aware he was the muscle
behind the whole thing. Some folk reckon that it was Flynn who
cut off her head, using one of those knives from his bloody abattoir.

—What do you think?

—I wouldn't put it past him, quite honestly. He was always in
trouble, that one, always doing stupid things.

—What sort of things?

—Just mindless really. Vandalism. Breaking things. Your
common-or-garden brainless thug. I might not be very PC saying
all this, but I don't care. People say that Martin Flynn had 'special
needs', but if he didn't know what he was doing then why was he
allowed to wander around Ergarth unsupervised, eh? There was a
rumour went round he busted an animal out of the abattoir too.
His family beat him black and blue. That's the only sort of message
that gets through to someone like that.

*Martin Flynn attended Leighburn Education Unit with Solomon
Meer and George Meldby in 2017. Martin was diagnosed with mild
learning difficulties – or MLD, as it's known. Easily the most troubled
member of the group, Flynn's home live was unstable and chaotic. His
father was not in the picture and his mother, the owner of the abattoir,
worked all hours, leaving Martin on his own from a very young age.*

The incident that Rob mentions happened in 2017, a few years after George Meldby burned down Fellman's factory. According to the spattering of newspaper articles I've found in online archives, Flynn's Meats was subject to an undercover investigation by an animal rights group. Allegations of animal cruelty were investigated when activists posted hidden camera footage showing nightmarish scenes, including inadequate stunning and botched slaughter. This cruelty represented 'breaches of legislation', according to the Food Standards Agency. A number of slaughterhouse workers received sixteen- and eighteen-week prison sentences, suspended for twelve months, along with 250 hours of unpaid community orders. Today, the Flynn's Meats website assures its customers that its livestock are 'reared in an ethical and traditional manner'. There is no evidence that Martin Flynn was in any way involved in this scandal.

I'll explore more deeply the lives of the three young men who committed this terrible crime in later episodes. For now, my impressions are that they seemed like an odd trio. By all accounts, Solomon Meer was the brains of the operation, Martin Flynn and George Meldby either followers or co-conspirators, it's hard to tell.

So what do we know so far? The three young men, who had all known each other since their stint in an educational unit when they were in their early twenties, came together to lure Elizabeth Barton to Tankerville Tower, where they barricaded the entrance and left her to die. One of them, it is not clear who, re-entered Tankerville Tower and removed Elizabeth Barton's head before placing it on her legs.

But why? To me, this question still hangs over everything. There has been much speculation, but as yet I have no satisfactory answer. One more pragmatic theory put forward by many commentators in the aftermath of what happened is that Elizabeth Barton represented everything that these three were not. She was healthy, happy and popular, with a stable home life and budding fame as a vlogger. It is suggested that that was all it took for three angry young men to want to teach her a lesson. In court it was decided that the killing was premeditated: the three intended to murder Elizabeth Barton. Not one of the killers has ever given a reason why they did it, and so the speculation continues.

Rob and I reach our respective vehicles, and as the sun begins to set over Ergarth, hunkering down behind Tankerville Tower, which disrupts what otherwise would have been a picturesque view of the cliffs, we begin our farewells.

—I want to know, before I go, Rob, why you, personally, think that Elizabeth Barton died. Did it have something to do with the Ergarth Vampire? Or were they just angry young men with nothing going for them?

—They still are angry young men with nothing going for them. I imagine Flynn and Meldby might get out early. Meldby won't last five minutes in jail and Flynn is too stupid to do anything but behave. Once they get out they'll need new identities, everything. But they'll get found. They'll spend the rest of their lives looking over their shoulders, and that serves them right. The Bartons have to live with what those three did, all day, every day. As for that vampire stuff? I don't know. Solomon Meer probably believed it at the time – he was into all that, wasn't he? Stands to reason with that cult ritual in the Dene, or whatever it was. But I really think it's more simple than that. I think he just wanted to kill Elizabeth Barton cos she was everything he wasn't. And she was unattainable. I don't think there's much more to it than that. All this vampire stuff – it cheapens what happened. There's a young lass dead and folk are talking about vampires. Give over.

—So why, in your opinion, has this graffiti appeared? Why is someone now calling the whole affair into question?

—There are sick people out there. That's all it is. Some sicko trying to get their fifteen minutes. And it's brought you here hasn't it?

That's a poignant place to end our interview. I don't think there's much more Rob will be able to tell me.

What this episode has given us is an overview; we have seen the backdrop against which this terrible crime was committed, and we have an impression of those that committed it. As we move on through our six stories, I want to explore the three killers, their backgrounds and their lives. We don't solve cases here, we present evidence, we talk and we discuss. Opinions are then formed when the facts are before us.

In the following episode we'll seek to gain the perspective of someone close to the ground in Ergarth, someone who was privy to the unfolding events that surrounded Elizabeth Barton and Solomon Meer. We will also hear, in our second episode, why the notion of a vampire prowling the town of Ergarth, was, for some, very real in 2018.

This has been our first.

Until next time…

Lizzie B

In five days, I'm going to meet a vampire.
That vampire's going to kill me.
I'll be dead in five days.

Hey guys! Lizzie B here. As you can see, I'm still here — so far anyway!
This is, of course, day two of the Dead in Six Days challenge.

Guys, I've been sent my first challenge from a vampire called Vladlena.

And I smashed it. Of course!

If this is all a bit too spooky for you, please head on over to have a look at my shopping-haul videos, which are all available down there in link-land. I'm also going to be un-boxing some wonderful products that the lovely people at Vainglorious have sent. As you know, Vainglorious are my absolute fave make-up brand. They could even make our friend Vladlena look half-human, they're that good.

So it's still snowing here — still snowing everywhere — still freezing. Like, it's not even fun snow, that you can make snowmen in and stuff. It's so hard to do anything. It's like someone's pressed pause. Everything's just ground to a halt. The gritters can't grit cos it's too icy. I mean, how is that even a thing? You see all the little kids on their way to school, slipping about, cars getting stuck, roads being closed. I swear, when I was a kid, snow was much more fun. Half the schools round here are shut so there'll be kids everywhere.

I'm staying in. God, when did I become so old? I'm twenty-four and literally five days from death.

If you want to see my day-one challenge, 'Play Lurky in the Dene', you can click the little linkaroo down there. If a load of screaming girls in the dark is your thang then go for it. Let's just say, maximum lurky was achieved. But not like any game of lurky you've ever seen before.

Off you pop. Go on, have a click, I'll wait here.

Righty-ho then! Onward with the challenge. So, as I said yesterday, I won't be passing the next challenge on; I'll be doing it myself. You better believe, Vladlena.

Soooo, I've been reading the comments from yesterday – thanks guys for the love and all the support. Here's some answers:

Thank you so much, but I'm really not that brave at all – but you know I could easily just duck out of the DISD challenge at any point. You know me, though: when I say I'm gonna do something, I'm gonna do it, right?

Yes, those medals in the background – all mine. Yep. Hang on…

Here you go – this one's for, like gymnastics, in, like, year nine! This one's from a brief flirtation with dressage when I was sixteen. I know, right? It was fun and everything, but, you know, you change, you grow up and realise life isn't Malory Towers. Look, here's my commemorative boxed set of all the Malory Towers books – beautiful, aren't they?

The rest of these medals and stuff are for sports mainly – football, hockey, that sort of thing. I was really sad I had to give it all up and concentrate on the channel. I guess that's why I keep them around. Thanks for the question, though! Ten points for originality.

What else is there? Yeah, believe me, I'll be in need of a humongous shopping haul after this one! Primark won't know what hit it! I'll be sure to upload that as soon as the challenge is done, unless, of course, I'm DEAD!

Soooo, the brand, spanking-new challenge, day two! Yes, it's already here. OK, OK, I'll get to it.

It got delivered as soon as I posted my 'Lurky in the Dene' video. I'm only going to show you a bit of it, though, because our undead friend has been pretty specific about who she wants to involve in today's challenge.

So here you go – as you'll see, it's not really much of a challenge, but better than the last one I suppose.

'Snowball Fight in…' and she's told me exactly where this needs to be done. I can't say any more now, you'll just have to wait and see.

OK … wow. So Vladlena clearly knows who I am and wants me deep in the brown stuff with this challenge. That shows that I was right then, doesn't it? Vladlena's a subscriber! Hi babe!

This is where stuff gets real, I suppose. So if you've been, like, living under your duvet for the past few months, the challenge goes like this:

Vladlena sends me a challenge. I have to do it, and do it good!

I upload the video to YouTube. Then she sends me one more.

If I don't wanna die in six days, I pass that task on to someone else.

But you'd better believe *I'm not doing that. In six days I'm gonna meet me a vampire!*

I hope.

So I'm gonna dig out my warmest gloves and hat and thermal leggings, cos you're about to see a snowball fight like no other!

This is a shout-out for anyone who wants to join the craziest snowball fight ever! Just hit 'like' and 'subscribe' and I'll pick a handful of lucky subscribers to join me!

That's it. Ciao for now, lovelies! Please don't forget to give that thumbs-up a little tap if you liked the video, and hit 'subscribe', and if you know what's good for you, tap the bell icon so you'll hear as soon as the next video goes up – the snowball fight of epic proportions! Just think, you could be a part of it!

Keep chattering in the comments, guys. You know I love answering your questions.

Let's see if I survive day two!

See you laters, alligators!

Episode 2: The Flying Monkeys

—My first one was something stupid. Everyone got a stupid one at first, that's how it would start. Like, everyone was doing them. Then, once you'd uploaded it, you got a harder one, and you passed it on. Remember that ice-bucket challenge thing in 2014? It was like that. *Everyone* was doing the Dead in Six Days challenge. No one actually believed it, though. No one believed you'd actually die. It was, for most people, just a laugh. Just something to do.

My first one was 'Drop a bag of flour in Sainsbury's'. That's all it said. But, like, you knew you couldn't just do it dead boring, like it was an accident. Well, I suppose you could, but you wouldn't get many likes. In order for it to be good, you had to make it funny or original.

That was the whole point of it. No one was even bothered about the vampire thing. There were some people who became internet-famous, like, overnight, from doing the Dead in Six Days challenge. Did you see the lad who got 'demon possession in an exam'? I think he got excluded permanently. Didn't matter though, did it? Look where he is now! There was an interview with him on someone's channel the other week. He showed everyone how he made that green stuff that came out of his mouth in his history exam. Chewed up peas and stuff. Gross. But he's a legend now.

Mine was pretty lame really; I just wandered round Sainsbury's with some friends. We were giggling like we were school kids. That's how it made you feel – like a kid again! We got the flour and went to the self-service checkout, and that's when I did it. I just started messing with the scanner until the little red light came on and an attendant came over. It was this dead fat one with a tache – oh God, that makes me sound like such a bitch, but it was so funny! She came over, and I dropped the flour, and it just *exploded!* It went all over both of us and this man next to us, and everyone just started shouting. I just ran out the shop. It felt really naughty, you know? It did OK. I mean it wasn't up there with the best, but it was decent.

But the one Elizabeth did – the snowball fight one – that was one of the best. Even at the time, people were saying it was one of the best, not just after … what happened. It was so funny. My dad was going to report it as a hate crime, you know? He said that it was racially motivated, but how could it have been? It was a snowball fight. Yeah, so some stock got a bit wet. But it's hardly a burning cross, is it?

I can't believe I'm laughing about it if I'm totally honest, like, because my dad was so upset at the time. I can't believe I'm laughing. Not after what happened to her.

But the thing is – and I feel well guilty for saying it – that video banged. Everyone had the snowball fight in dad's shop on their phone. I was getting loads of lads telling me I was fit, and I got a lot of people asking me out. I guess I got to feel what it was like to be her – to be Elizabeth Barton for a while, you know?

I remember the first challenge she got. Day one. It was brutal. What with the snow and everything.

'Play Lurky in the Dene'.

It doesn't sound right now does it? Not without, like, proper context. It sounds creepy. But you see, the whole point of it was that you had to make the whole thing, like, fun. The challenge itself never sounded interesting. Vladlena the Vampire always just sent a boring message – no emojis, just text. It was up to *you* to make it cool, see? That's how people got famous from it.

I have to say, I couldn't quite believe it when Elizabeth picked *me* to help out with that first challenge. There was a good ten of us, and we all knew that being in one of her videos was big. We all upped our game.

We went down the Dene when it was dark, because that would be scarier. It would look better on the video, everyone screaming and running about. Like something off one of those old ghost shows my mam liked, like *Most Haunted*. It wasn't fun, though, not at first, cos it was freezing and snowy, even worse down there Like, all the trees had these icicles hanging off them and the stream was frozen. It was just so still and quiet and weird. It was like everything was just dead. Everyone had their hats and gloves and scarves on. You couldn't tell who was who. We also had masks on – you know those rubber horse heads, yeah? That was Lizzie's idea. That's why it did so well, I think: playing lurky in the dark with everyone wearing horse heads. It was an amazing idea.

I was 'on' so I had to go under the echo bridge while everyone hid. So I closed my eyes, just playing along. I was shivering, my teeth were chattering. It was dark, and the cold was going straight through my gloves. After, like, five minutes standing still, I couldn't feel my toes. I could hear everyone running off, slipping on the ice and giggling. It was dead weird cos it was so quiet, there was no wind down there, just the cold. I counted to ten, dead loud. When I opened my eyes there was just absolute *silence*. It was well weird down there, everything was frozen still. It looked like it must have back in the Victorian times, or whenever. It was like time had stopped. Proper spooky.

I got out my phone and started filming myself doing loads of heavy breathing like I was terrified. It was spooky down there but I wasn't really scared; I was wandering about, up and down the path, like, waving my phone about, pointing it at the bushes, cos I knew someone would jump out at any minute. I kept thinking I was going to slip over. They don't grit the paths down there.

Then I heard a noise.

I looked up and saw someone on the bridge. They had their back to me. I thought none of them would have gone up on the bridge. We never planned that.

We never said we'd do that.

I was a bit scared for a second because, well ... because of all those old stories you hear when you're little. The Ergarth Vampire. The 'Beast from the East'.

The figure wasn't looking at me, they were facing the other way, just staring out. I was just about to say something when I saw they had the horse's head on.

I filmed it on my phone cos I thought it was a good shot, like, maybe Elizabeth could have used it, you know? Just this person stood on the echo bridge in the dark with the moon behind them.

Then they turned around, and that's when I realised who it was and I dropped my phone.

That's when it all went wrong.

Welcome to Six Stories.

I'm Scott King.

Over these six episodes, we're looking back at the murder of Elizabeth Barton, who during the vicious cold of March 2018, was barricaded inside a ruined tower, left to freeze to death, and then brutally decapitated. We want to know why three young men took it upon themselves to do such a terrible thing to an innocent young woman.

I'm here in Ergarth, Elizabeth's home town, where the crime happened, speaking to six people, each of whom have a link to the case.

We're not here to solve a mystery; we're here to discuss what happened.

We rake up old graves.

This small town, which clings to the north-east coastline of England, has a strange legend associated with it; a story of a vampire. This vampire was supposedly brought back from the Battle of the Alma, during the Crimean War in 1854. Around the same time, what was then a small farming community went through a spell of extreme cold – similar to that seen 160 years later. Disease and misfortune plagued the area, culminating in the vampire's death: three young farm hands locked her in Tankerville Tower, before removing her head and burying her body in Ergarth Dene.

This story has been perpetuated through the generations, tumbled and tossed until no one can be quite sure what its true origins are. What is certain, is that the murder of Elizabeth Barton in 2018 shares chilling similarities to the tale of the vampire Vladlena, known locally as 'The Beast from the East'.

Last week we gave voice to someone from Ergarth's older generation, and his perception about what was going so wrong for three young people that they did such a terrible thing to an innocent young woman – someone who was attempting to do good in a deprived town.

This week we're going to speak to someone who knew Elizabeth personally.

Amirah Choudhury is twenty-four years old. She attended the same secondary school as Elizabeth Barton, and both young women worked part-time at a pet shop when they were in their early twenties. I meet her at a chain coffee shop just off Ergarth High Street. It's good to get inside, away from the smell of Flynn's Meats that is particularly pungent today. It's Amirah's lunch break and the place is half full. We wait in the queue together: the clientele is mainly older people and a few young men in suits, scrolling through their phones. A few people looked up when Amirah entered, and one of them smiled. We have to wait awkwardly for a few moments as the baristas try to prevent a man entering the shop. He's muttering incoherently but it's his eyes that stay with me: empty, lost, as if he has given up.

Amirah shakes her head.

—Spice zombies. They're everywhere now. Remember when that stuff was legal? It wasn't even that long ago. There was a shop where you could buy it, just up by the pizza place. You see them all over now; dribbling on themselves and passed out. Elizabeth was trying to help people like him, and look what happened to her…

The man bangs half-heartedly on the window before careering away down the street. Everyone shifts in their seats. Amirah directs me to a booth at the very back.

She lowers her voice.

—You've got to be, like, careful. Everyone's so nosey here; everyone knows everyone else's business. Like, everyone in here now knows I'm talking to *you*. And everyone else will know in seconds.

Amirah's right. Ergarth, being a small town with a few unwelcome skeletons in its closet, has come together since the murder of Elizabeth Barton. I know that since our first episode, there have been a few photographs of me, taken candidly, I may add, circulating on social media. Amirah tells me not to worry.

—Oh yeah. People do that all the time. You have to be careful what you wear, make sure you don't look a state, cos someone'll take your picture, and before you know it, you'll become a meme. No one wants that sort of fame. Like, I'm sure you with … like, what happened last series … I'm just saying people will want photos and that. Plus you're with *me*.

—*Is that a problem?*

—For some people, yes.

Amirah mimes zipping her mouth closed, and she writes something on a napkin, which she then passes to me:

There's still people here who think I had something to do with it.

We communicate in this analogue format for a few more moments. A little later, I'll come to why Amirah's been looking over her shoulder since Elizabeth Barton's death. Amirah tells me she's not really present on social media anymore as a consequence of it. That's hard, she says, because everyone else is.

—*We know Elizabeth was a big social-media user. Do you know if she shared the same fears as you in that sense?*

—Yeah. I mean, I don't know if there was 'fear' – she had haters, of course; everyone who's anyone does. But she just didn't care. There was far more love for her out there. Look here, her Instagram is still up. Take a look.

Amirah hands me her phone and for a few moments we scroll through Elizabeth Barton's photographs. She has more than fifty thousand followers on Instagram; Amirah tells me that before she died she had at least twenty thousand. There were significantly more subscribers to Elizabeth's YouTube Channel, where she went under the name Lizzie B. According to everyone I've spoken to, Elizabeth's channel was on its way to the upper echelons of YouTube fame.

—She was gorgeous. She was funny. She was talented. Everyone loved her. She was, like, Ergarth's very own Zoella! Like, you would see that bright-red car of hers buzzing round Ergarth. She always had it super-clean; those big eyelashes on the lights. I miss that. She could have been as big as Zoella as well; if those three hadn't done what they done. What they did to her is just … I mean, it's just *beyond* horrific. It's beyond normal. There's hating someone and then there's that. It's inhuman.

Elizabeth's Instagram page is mainly selfies: Elizabeth in pyjamas, staring at a dog; Elizabeth grinning with a cocktail in one hand; Elizabeth wearing a swimsuit, licking an ice-cream, laughing. The pictures are captioned simply with long lists of hashtags: '#dayoff #selfie #sunshine #lovemylove #happiness'. Each photo has hundreds of likes and comments beneath them. 'Gorgeous', 'Miss you hunni', 'RIP beautiful lady'.

There are thousands of photos; we don't have time to scroll down through them all.

—*Elizabeth posted a lot of photos of herself.*
—Yeah?
—*Was that normal?*
—Yeah, of course! She was so inspiring – so body-positive and so encouraging. She was, like, someone everyone looked up to. Everyone wanted to be around her. She brought such, *joy* to people.
—*How did she do that?*
—She was so kind, so *giving*. Everyone felt like they knew her.
—*So, she built her following with videos and photographs?*
—That was all part of it. You want to get likes don't you? I mean, like, that's what it's for. Elizabeth deserved it all, though: she was beautiful. She always got thousands and thousands of likes for each photo. That's why she started the vlog – and she was making a living out of it just before she died.
—*Really? How?*

I feel like Amirah's slightly amused at my ignorance. She's patient with me and explains that people can make an actual living from uploading videos onto YouTube. Advertisers send them free products and pay them to feature their products in the videos. Elizabeth had make-up companies and clothing brands constantly sending her stuff. She never wanted for anything.

On each of the six days before Elizabeth was killed, she had uploaded a record of her participation in the Dead in Six Days challenge to her YouTube channel. They still reappear occasionally on YouTube, despite the protestations and appeals from Elizabeth Barton's friends and family. Elizabeth's channel is dormant of course. Her old unboxing and shopping-haul videos are still available to view, though.

The Dead in Six Days videos document each of her challenges, and between each one are additional vlogs where Elizabeth discusses each challenge and answers questions from the comments sections.

—Her usual stuff was shopping hauls, unboxing some stuff she got sent, things like that.

—*I'm wondering if Elizabeth's videos were popular for the content, or for Elizabeth herself. Was it Elizabeth people were into or was it her content? Or a bit of both?*

—Not gonna lie, she got a *lot* of attention for her. So it's fifty-fifty. Like, why are lads watching what some girl bought from the River Island in Ergarth, right? Anyway, she'd built up a huge following, so when she started doing the Dead in Six Days challenge, she just *blew up*, you know? In Ergarth, everyone and their nana watched it. Like, everyone was just *obsessed* with it. That's why no one wants to talk. Like, we all watched the build-up to … to what happened.

—*But it was slightly different for you, wasn't it?*

Amirah nods. She looks around again, slumps into her seat. I feel for her and I wish we could be somewhere less public.

The reason for Amirah's caginess is complex. She tells me that like everyone in Ergarth, she was in awe of Elizabeth Barton, so her participation in Elizabeth's first challenge, 'Play Lurky in the Dene', felt like a privilege. We're going to address later what Amirah saw down in the Dene, but right now I want to skip forwards in time to Elizabeth's second task.

—It was called 'Snowball Fight in Choudhury's'.

Amirah says this in barely a whisper. She can't meet my eye.

Choudhury's is still run by Amirah's father; it's a newsagent on a street corner in an Ergarth housing estate called Primrose Villas. People in Ergarth know it as 'the Prim'. Rob Karl from last episode told me it wasn't a place I wanted to visit – at any time of day. Seeing as more than one person has told me to avoid going anywhere in Ergarth after dark, I think I'll take that advice. George Meldby's family home was right in the middle of the estate.

—Like, it wasn't a racial thing. My dad thought it was though. He thought we were being terrorised by all the bad 'uns off the Prim. At the time it didn't seem so bad but after…

—*What happened?*

—Elizabeth asked for volunteers online to do it – the snowball fight. Hundreds of people volunteered. That's what made me really sad afterwards, seeing how many people wanted to do it.

—*It must have felt like a bit of a pile-on?*

—The thing was, Elizabeth never said exactly where the snowball fight was going to be, not online. That was good of her, I suppose. She only told people when they were all assembled ready to go.

—*How did you find out about it?*

Amirah drops her head again. Her eyes are wet with tears and she begins vigorously stirring at the dregs of her coffee. Eventually, in a choked little voice, she answers.

—Because I signed up. I was a part of it.

—*Really?*

—Yeah. She told us to meet on the edge of the Prim. There was a great big crowd, loads more than she'd actually picked. The snow was coming down really heavy – heavy but silent, you know? It got in your eyes, in your mouth; it just wouldn't stop. You could hardly see who was who or where anyone was, just these lights from people's phones. Everyone was filming; everyone had their phones out. Some people had their torch apps on. Then Elizabeth pulled up in that little red car. I don't know *how* she got it through the snow. Most of the roads were closed. But that was just Elizabeth, I guess. She never gave up! Anyway, she leaned out the window and read out the challenge. Elizabeth didn't let on where the snowball fight was going to be until right at the end. I just remember suddenly understanding what she'd just said … and it was like the bottom of my belly just *dropped*. But this big cheer went up and everyone just swarmed towards the shop…

There's a long and terrible pause. I think of the 'spice zombies' I've seen in the town, and the warnings to stay out of Ergarth after dark.

—…me included.

Amirah and the rest of Elizabeth's followers made great piles of snowballs and surged into Amirah's father's shop. The video of it has long since gone from YouTube, but Amirah says it was chaos: screaming, shouting, kids with their faces covered by scarves and balaclavas. She said it only lasted for five minutes or so, but it felt, to her, like hours. What puzzles me most is why Amirah joined in, why she didn't try and stop it.

—Like, you just *don't* do that. It would have ruined everything. I felt so *bad*. But I couldn't have done a thing. Afterwards, though, that night, it was weird: I was in the bath and I just couldn't get warm. I couldn't feel my fingers, they were so cold. And the wind was making this horrible whistling sound, like it was crying along with me. And I could hear my mum and dad arguing downstairs; it was awful.

The coffee shop door opens and a blast of autumn chill swirls into our booth, Amirah stops talking until she has seen who has walked in. I can feel the air tauten: two lads in tracksuits – they bring with them the thick reek of something that smells burned, almost fish-like. Their eyes are red and swollen, and one of their phones belts out tinny music; the staccato heartbeat of a terrified animal. They stand around for a while, rubbing their hands, before leaving. Eventually Amirah carries on.

—I was now in two Lizzie B videos, and I wasn't going to jeopardise that. Not even for my family. Like, the Dead in Six Days Challenge was really serious at the time. If I'd have ruined it…

—What would have happened, Amirah, if you'd questioned what was happening, if you'd tried to stop it? It was a rather childish prank, don't you think?

Amirah is quiet again, she scrolls absently through her phone before answering with a shrug.

—Like, I couldn't risk it. I couldn't risk what would have happened to me.

—This 'vampire' who set the challenges would have got you?

Amirah laughs, but there's no humour in it – she shakes her head and I feel like I'm missing something, like there's something about all this that I'm just not getting.

—It was the Dead in Six Days challenge. It was more than some school kids' thing, You had to be careful.

What immediately comes to my mind when Amirah talks about this challenge is a couple of other nefarious Internet memes that gained notoriety in the past: Blue Whale and Momo.

Blue Whale was an internet 'game' from 2016 that apparently originated in Russia. Similar in essence to Dead in Six Days, players were assigned fifty tasks via social media channels. These began innocently enough – the tasks were innocuous but challenging: staying up all night or watching a certain horror film. However, the tasks became more and more extreme and culminated in participants self-harming and even committing suicide. Apparently more than a hundred deaths worldwide have been attributed to this game. There is no current official corroboration of these figures – it's simply what you can read online.

But why would anyone want to play such a game? I'm not sure exactly what the lure was to play Blue Whale. Unlike Dead in Six Days, which has a prank-like aspect to it, Blue Whale participants were coerced into continuing to participate by administrators who threatened to post something personal if the player did not do as they were told. The players – teenage girls mainly, reportedly with low self-esteem – would then be targeted on social media and other forums by the game's 'admins'. Exactly how these girls were convinced to continue playing Blue Whale is currently open to speculation.

In fact, a lot of claims about Blue Whale are just speculation. The counter claim is that Blue Whale does not and has not ever actually existed. It has become one of those Chinese-whisper style Internet rumours. According to some, the whole story came from the misinterpretation of a piece on Russian political and social-affairs website Novaya Gazeta. And in an example of how rumour and the idea of a 'good story' get in the way of fact, there were claims that a teenage suicide group known as the 'Sea of Whales' was spreading across Russian social media. There were two significant deaths attributed to online suicide groups, yet there was no evidence of any challenge.

November 2016 saw an arrest: twenty-one-year-old Philip Budeikin, a psychology student who admitted to inciting teenage girls to commit suicide online – describing them as 'biological waste'. According to the BBC, Budeikin admitted creating the game in 2013 under a different name. He pleaded guilty to 'inciting teenagers to suicide' and was sentenced to three years in prison.

More recently, a similar game, called Momo, has emerged from South America, where several teenage deaths are attributed to the 'Momo challenge'.

Momo also has similarities to Dead in Six Days; it involves sending a message on WhatsApp to an unknown number, which will reply with challenges and threats, culminating in suicide. Momo is probably best known for the unnerving image connected with it: a bulging-eyed, black-haired woman with bird-like legs. This image was in fact created by a Japanese artist and has no relation to the game itself. Like Blue Whale, young and impressionable teenagers have said to have been threatened and coerced into harming themselves while playing this game.

Yet there is no evidence, anywhere, that Momo has been responsible for anything of the sort.

We could do a whole series about the psychological intricacies of how and why people obey these tasks, if of course they actually do. I feel, however, that I've had my fill of diving deep into internet games while making this podcast. But it seems what happened to Elizabeth Barton is closely linked to the Dead in Six Days challenge.

—Who was behind the Dead in Six Days Challenge, Amirah? Who was this vampire giving out the tasks?

Amirah sighs and stirs, a look of pained confusion comes over her face.

—I don't think, you know, that there ever really *was* a person behind it. People used to say it was someone called Vladlena – and there were fake Vladlena accounts all over the place. But it wasn't really about meeting the vampire at the end, it was just about, like, the *content.*

—*The challenges.*

—Yeah, it was all everyone trying to outdo each other, getting more likes and shares. That was what it was about really. It was a competition.

—*It was Solomon Meer who messaged Elizabeth and told her to come to Tankerville Tower, wasn't it? Could he have been behind the Dead in Six Days thing?*

—He could have been. I doubt it, though. He probably just made another fake Vladlena account to send Elizabeth that message. I don't know who it was who started it or anything. It just, like, started…

—*You and Elizabeth had nothing to do with Solomon, is that right?*

—I certainly didn't. I'd forgotten about him pretty much, after school. It was only when everyone started doing the Dead in Six Days challenge that he popped up again.

—*Really?*

—Yeah, Solomon Meer did one of the first *big* Dead in Six Days videos. It was, like, amazing. It sounds horrible to say that after what he did to Elizabeth – it's like I'm giving him a compliment.

It's true though. I can't deny it. That's what got everyone going with the challenge.

—*What was his challenge?*

—He got a really good one to be fair: 'Shopping Trolley Sledge'. Everyone in Ergarth probably has that video on their phone still. They'll not show you though.

—*Do you have it?*

—No comment. 'Shopping Trolley Sledge' was the first one that went viral. He had all these dogs; I dunno if they were his or what, but he had them on leads fastened to this ASDA trolley. It was night, in a car park and he was setting off bangers, like, fireworks. All the dogs were going mental, trying to run away and they were pulling his shopping trolley around after them. He'd edited the video and put, like, this silly music behind it. Like a Russian polka or something? And he messed with the speed, so it looked almost professional. It was properly funny.

All the videos that pertain to this case have slowly but surely disappeared from the Internet. They occasionally sprout up again like weeds through the bricks of a driveway. Amirah tells me that it's impossible for these things to ever really go away. Occasionally someone will post Solomon's challenge video; there'll be a flurry of attention, and then it'll be taken down. So far, Amirah says, no one's matched it for likes, not even Elizabeth Barton herself.

—You see, that was the video that got everyone doing the Dead in Six Days thing. Solomon Meer passed on the task to someone else, and it went from there.

—*So he essentially started it?*

—I guess. Maybe. I mean, not really.

—*Would you agree, though, that what you've told me does suggest it was Solomon Meer who came up with the whole thing?*

—Yeah, like maybe. I dunno. There were other people doing it before him. He just did the first big one. Even he was too much of a coward to keep it going for six days, though. It was Elizabeth who did that. She won in the end. She became so much more popular than him.

As unpleasant as it is to say, could it be thanks to Solomon Meer that Elizabeth Barton moved on to another level of popularity? I suggest this to Amirah, but she disagrees, tells me that Elizabeth was way more popular than Solomon Meer. I don't think I'm going to convince her otherwise.

—Like he was just this local oddity. He looked like he was homeless and worked in that weird little bookshop, and loads of people reckoned he slept in the Vampire Tower or in the Dene. I think he was trying to get sympathy a lot of the time, to be perfectly honest. That was the sort of person he was.

While it was definitely Solomon Meer who asked Elizabeth to come to Tankerville Tower on the third of March 2018, it has never been officially suggested that it was him who orchestrated any of the other Dead in Six Days challenges.

I decide to change tack, and take Amirah back to what it was that compelled her to join in with Elizabeth's second challenge, 'Snowball Fight in Choudhury's'. Fear of a vampire … or something else?

—There never was a vampire – it wasn't that I was worried about. It was … it was Elizabeth's followers. Her flying monkeys. They could take people down *instantly*. They could *destroy* her haters. It was amazing really. Imagine having people who loved you like that? The challenges were her most popular videos. If I'd have tried to stop that, I would have been annihilated. Not by her – she wouldn't have done it…

—*What do you mean?*

—It would have been her fans, her followers, her orbiters. I saw it happen, we all did, so many times. If you crossed her, if you did something against her, honestly, they could tear you to pieces, kill your reputation online. I couldn't have that. You wonder why there were barely any negative comments on her YouTube channel? That's why. So I couldn't. It was just a bit of snow, a bit of water. I paid my dad back for it all, you know? I worked there for a whole summer for free to pay back the damaged stock. I said nothing. I said absolutely nothing about the whole thing because at the end of the day, it *was* funny, I suppose.

I just want to clarify some of the terminology here. 'Orbiters' are loosely similar to online followers. The majority of orbiters are male and 'follow' a female either online or in person, commenting and interacting in a needy way, showering them with compliments and defending them from attacks in the vain hope that the female may one day sleep with them. 'Flying monkeys' is a recent term, used in popular psychology to describe those who abuse others on behalf of someone else.

Back to the challenge. I wonder if the frivolity of it – its ridiculousness – was what appealed to the young people of Ergarth. These were not school children embroiled in a craze, but adults in their twenties. Amirah said it was almost self-perpetuating. If there really was no figure behind it, was it in fact symptomatic of a place with little hope? I wonder if such a thing would have been such a big deal in a more affluent location.

—What about your father? Did he know who had orchestrated the challenge?

—No and I begged him, I *pleaded* with him not to report it. I was literally on my knees, I swear. Somehow I convinced him it was all just a joke, a laugh. It wasn't as if Elizabeth did it to be horrible. She did it because that was the challenge: she'd been set it, so she had to do it. And I'd have been destroyed if I'd spoken up.

I understand why Amirah's been quiet about everything. Elizabeth died not long after 'Snowball Fight at Choudhury's' was released on Elizabeth's channel. Amirah tells me she's still scared people think she or her family had something to do with the murder, that they were retaliating. Elizabeth may be dead and her killers in prison, but according to Amirah, the 'flying monkeys' are still a force to be reckoned with online. Elizabeth Barton's death has turned her into something of a touchstone and anything bad said against her is met with a huge amount of online resistance. That was how popular she was. That was how much everyone loved her.

—Did you ever see someone getting destroyed like that?

—It happened all the time. Like, mainly online. Someone literally had to move away from Ergarth. But that was a long time ago. A couple of years before Lizzïe died.

Gemma Hines she was called. She *is* called. Everyone talks about her like she's dead, but she's not, she just went away – her family moved down south. Bristol? Brighton? I don't blame her. Not after what happened to her here. She would never be able to show her face in Ergarth again.

Gemma Hines. There's very little about her in the archived press articles, and what there is makes for rather unsavoury reading. I won't repeat what I've read yet, I'll let Amirah tell the story in her own words first.

—Gemma was in year eight or nine when she joined our school. She was year eleven when it all happened. My year – Elizabeth's year – were gone by then. Gemma was … I don't know how to put it without sounding nasty, without sounding proper shan on her. She didn't have a very stable home, let's say.

—*She lacked guidance?*

—You could say that, yeah. She did daft things. Look, I'll just say it: Gemma slept around. Older lads and that. That's what everyone said. That doesn't make what happened to her OK though.

It is these assertions that the newspapers made; one particularly unpleasant article in the Daily Mail *online shows a blurry still of a crowd of youngsters on the porch of a dilapidated house, bathed in the light of two police cars beside a looming selfie of Gemma, resplendent in a layer of fake tan, mascara and lip gloss. 'What Have Today's Children Become?' bellows the headline. Gemma Hines was around sixteen at the time.*

—She was one of them who had a party cos her mam wasn't there and she put it on Facebook and, like, a thousand people turned up. You know what I mean?

I do know what she means. There have been several high-profile news stories with the same theme: naïve young person advertises a house party on Facebook, thousands turn up, house is trashed. Strangely, for me anyway, these stories are reported with a jaunty, almost comedic tone. I express this to Amirah.

—Can you imagine how scary it would be, having all those people show up to your house: it's just you on your own, and there's lads from all over in their twenties? It was like what happened at the shop. All those bad 'uns from the Prim.

—*What did this have to do with Elizabeth Barton?*

—I don't know for sure, but apparently Elizabeth was, like, the only girl who *didn't* get invited to Gemma's party. So her flying monkeys made Gemma Hines pay.

—*Wow.*

—Half the school showed up to the house plus everyone else and their mates, and Gemma ended up locked in the bathroom – three lads did it. The thing is though, and I have to say this: it wasn't Elizabeth; *she* didn't do this. It was … it was the lads that killed her who did it.

—*What? Solomon Meer, George Meldby and Marin Flynn? They were fans of Elizabeth?*

—I doubt it. They were there though. They were at the party. Everyone was, even Elizabeth's weird little brother. It was them who started smashing the place up, getting everyone to steal stuff. I think they just turned up because they always did when there was trouble. They locked Gemma Hines in her own bathroom while everyone went feral. Me included. It was like Gemma didn't matter.

Poignant words. The few news reports on the incident roundly condemn Gemma Hines for throwing the party and putting it online. There's no mention of the three killers, nor Elizabeth Barton.

—*It seems to me that there was a side of Elizabeth that was … dangerous perhaps? Like she had a lot of power in Ergarth?*

—That's the thing. It wasn't her; she didn't lock Gemma Hines in the bathroom, she didn't trash her house. Elizabeth wasn't even there.

—*Do you think she orchestrated it though? Behind the scenes?*

—No way. Elizabeth was lovely. She wouldn't have done

something like that. And anyway, she was like, a grown-up – she was in her twenties. Why would she care about some little girl's party? It was her followers. They'd do anything for her.

It could be coincidence, but does this show us that Meer, Meldby and Flynn had previous? Does this incident foreshadow what they did to Elizabeth Barton – imprisoning a young female? It's unclear whether Amirah was present at the party herself – despite my attempts, she won't confirm whether she was there or not.

We come now to Meer, Meldby and Flynn. I want to know how they were regarded in Ergarth, which brings me back to what you heard at the start of the episode: Amirah's account of Elizabeth's first task – 'Play Lurky in the Dene'. I ask Amirah to recount what happened from when Elizabeth was given the challenge.

—'Play Lurky in the Dene'. That's all it said. Her channel was getting, like, so much attention. Like I said, people were doing anything to be a part of it.

Similar to the snowball fight, Elizabeth's followers had to like and comment on her video and she would pick some people to join in. Amirah was one of those people.

Amirah then tells the story you heard at the beginning of the episode. She went into Ergarth Dene at night with some friends, all wearing horse masks, and encountered the figure on the echo bridge.

—I thought it was one of my mates. That's why no one said anything. It wasn't what we'd agreed to do, go up on there.

—*Was Elizabeth with you when you saw it?*

—No. She was … I don't know. I was on my own. Everyone was hiding. Elizabeth told us all where to go, what to do, how to film it, all the shots and different camera angles. Everything. We trusted her. We knew that if we did what she said, the video would do well. I thought that it might get me, well … famous.

—*So there you were, looking up at the figure on the bridge. Did you have any idea who it was?*

—It was really dark. The bridge is quite high up and I didn't want to spoil anything by shouting, so I just went with it. I filmed them for a bit, just standing there with the horse's head on. It looked pretty cool. Then they turned around. It was *her*. I swear to God. I swear on my mam and dad's life. On my little cousin's life. I swear down it was *her*.

—*Elizabeth?*

—No! The vampire! The Ergarth Vampire. Under that mask she had pale skin, like she was dead; black eyes and she opened her mouth. This sounds so stupid – it's all going to sound so childish, but I swear to you, she looked dead, her skin was like a corpse. I was scrabbling on the ground for my phone and I could hear her coming. I could hear her running along the bridge and down the stairs on the other side; she was making this horrible whistling noise, and I managed to pick up my phone and run. I swear I've never been so scared. I knew she was behind me, I could sense her. But you know when you're so panicked, you forget how to run? That's what happened, my feet just sort of got tangled up in themselves and I fell. The path was like an ice rink, and I could feel sticks and gravel poking me through my clothes. I remember curling up into a ball with my hands over my head, and I was crying like a baby. I lay there for a few moments but there was just nothing. I swear I thought I was going to die.

Then somehow, I, like, just opened my eyes and that sense of her was gone. Like, I just knew she had gone, so I got up.

—*Was there anyone there?*

—Just me. Just me lying there on the path. In the dark. In the Dene. On my own.

—*What about the others in the horse masks?*

—That's what I thought, right? I had all this stuff going through my head: what if it was a set-up, what if this was the prank? I thought that, despite everything, maybe *this* was the prank.

—*That Elizabeth had created?*

—Precisely. As soon as I thought that, I was angry, but only, like, for a second because it suddenly made sense. This was genius. She'd obviously got one of them to dress up as the vampire and … well, then I got angry again, cos, like, I'd be all over the Internet, screaming and falling in the mud. I didn't know if that would be a good thing or not. All this stuff was going through my head, and I just wanted out of there. I just wanted to go home and sit with my mam on the sofa and watch TV, you know? I just wanted it to be over with. But I didn't want to ruin the video. I thought the rest of them were hiding in the bushes, filming me. So I just started walking down the path, head down, just hoping that it would all finish soon.

—*And what happened then?*

—I was cold, really cold and jumpy, just full of nerves, so maybe that was why I was so scared, But something just came *shooting* out of the sky and flew right at my head. I swear, I've never screamed like that since I was a kid.

—*What was it?*

—I dunno; it must've been a bird or something. But the thing is, I sort of *felt* it, I *smelled* it, it came that close; it was all musty. Then it was gone; back up into the sky, silent. It was horrible. That's when the figures came out of the bushes up ahead. That's when I really thought I was going to die of fright. It was too much.

—*Figures?*

—Those three: Solomon, Martin and George. They all just stepped out of the bushes up ahead of me. I thought they were going to rape me, I swear. I thought they were going to rape me, or kill me and leave me for dead.

—*I'm sorry if I sound insensitive, but what was it about them? What made you so scared of those three that you thought they would do that?*

—They were horrible people, all three of them. George Meldby was an arsonist – he burned down that factory when he was in school. Everyone knew Martin Flynn was a thug, and Solomon Meer was a Satanist or whatever, wasn't he? We all knew what they were. We all know now. We're all still in shock. Sometimes I can't get it out of my head, what they did to her. Sometimes it keeps me up at night.

—*What did they do that night in Ergarth Dene?*

—They stood there, just staring at me. I could see my friends all up ahead in a little group. They were scared too, but, of course, they had their phones out, and I knew they would be filming – in case those three did anything. Cowards. Solomon Meer was all filthy as usual and the other two were stood round him like his guards or something. He leaned right down into my face, so close I could smell him, and he opened his mouth. I remember it being scary at the time but he was wearing these stupid 'fangs' – just trying to be a vampire edge-lord or whatever. What a sad twat!

—*Edge-lord?*

—Like, he was trying to look dangerous, edgy, when he was really just pathetic.

It was only when Elizabeth died that I realised what they were doing. It sort of made sense of why we were down in the Dene.

—*How do you mean?*

—It was them that had tried to get Elizabeth out there; they'd been trying to get her to come out to the Dene by herself. I dunno, maybe they were going to film it; do a prank on her, try and scare her? Something worse…

—*What about immediately after the event? I'm not quite sure I'm following what happened. You were in the Dene, it was dark, you thought you saw the vampire. If it wasn't the vampire, what … I mean who was it? Did you ever find out?*

—Maybe it was a dream or a hallucination or something? I dunno. I thought it was real at the time. I was shitting myself.

—*Did you tell anyone else? Your friends?*

—No. Not about the vampire. They would have been so judgey about it. It deffo wasn't one of them though. I'm sure.

—*Do you think it had anything to do with the three lads?*

—Well yeah, that's the other option. George and Martin were too stupid to have thought up something as elaborate as that, so I imagine it was one of Solomon Meer's friends. Maybe it was some druggie, one of the spice zombies … one of the homeless or the … the people who hung round the Dene? The mentally … you know …

—*I guess I'm interested in why Solomon and the other two actually wanted to kill Elizabeth. They said it was a prank gone wrong. Certainly, Solomon Meer's video – the 'What have we done?' clip – suggests that could be true. It also contradicts the idea that Solomon believed Elizabeth truly was a vampire.*

—I know, right? They were obviously trying to lure her into the Dene to do something to her. Maybe they were going to say that was a prank. It's what they did at the tower, wasn't it? I don't know why they wanted to hurt her. Probably because she was popular and they weren't; because she was beautiful and they weren't … because she was everything they weren't? I don't know.

What does this vampire sighting have to do with our case? Is it unconnected, or was the target of this 'prank' actually Elizabeth Barton? I want to keep Amirah chatting for a little longer, so I offer her another drink. I think she welcomes the break as I stand in the queue to be served – the hiss of the coffee machines, the clank of metal on metal, the spatter of chatter from the gradually filling shop. I have to admit I look over my shoulder a couple of times to make sure Amirah hasn't done a runner. Thankfully, she hasn't and she seems a bit less fraught when I sit back down.

—*I want to ask you about the three lads and your experiences of them, if that's OK? So far I don't know much about them.*
—That's fine. It's just, like I say, you have to be careful around here. You don't know who's listening in, who's filming or recording.
—*Judging by the graffiti on the wall of Elizabeth's parents' house that summoned me here, it seems there are some in Ergarth who think this case needs to be looked at further.*
—Yeah. Maybe. I dunno. Maybe someone knew it would bring you here? People are funny when it comes to fame.

I've been avoiding this but I just want to make a brief note, as it's relevant. Since the last series of Six Stories, *people see me differently. I work differently. Where I used to hide and preferred using Skype or making phone calls, I am now much more comfortable with meeting my interviewees face-to-face. Using my real face. I don't want to say I am a 'celebrity', because I don't think I am. Some people, however, do. Maybe this is what Amirah is getting at.*

—*Can we start with George Meldby? He was responsible for a few arson attacks in Ergarth, wasn't he? Was that well known among people your age?*

—We all knew it and all sort of just accepted it. It was just ... normal I guess, to us. Here's the thing, right: I went all through nursery and school with two of them – George and Martin. Solomon Meer didn't come to Ergarth till halfway through year nine of high school. Everyone knows everyone round here, unless you're rich and you can go to the boys' or girls' grammars. So, yeah, they were all in my year. So was Elizabeth. We all knew each other.

—*There are other people in Ergarth who say that George didn't seem the type of person who could commit such a horrible crime – what he did to Elizabeth, I mean.*

—I'd agree with that. In school, even in primary school, George was just a little weirdo – harmless though. A quiet little weirdo. Not in that sort of broody serial-killer way – that was Solomon. George was actually quite popular.

—*George was kicked out of Ergarth High, though, wasn't he?*

—Yeah, the back end of year ten. He set a fire in a sink in the art room. But he'd been in and out of trouble pretty much all his time in school. I was amazed they'd kept him in normal school for as long as they did.

—*Why do you think that was?*

—Like I say, George wasn't *nasty*; and he had something about him. It's hard to say what – some people are just naturally sort of charismatic, I suppose. And he was friends with the girls, even in primary school. He was actually quite feminine.

—*Were you his friend at any point?*

—No. Not me. OK, so here's something that no one really made a deal of at the time – no one really knew, in fact. But it's the whole reason why George doing what he did was so weird. George and Elizabeth were actually kind of friends. Like, she let him hang around her quite a lot. She even let him help out with some of her videos. Filming her and stuff.

—*Really? It does sound like they were quite close.*

—Yeah but she was, like, helping him out, if you know what I mean? She was just being nice; letting someone like George feel like he was involved. It was her kindness that killed her, I suppose. She let George Meldby get *too* close. You know how he burned down the Fellman's factory? People said it was cos of Tommy Fellman.

—*Tommy Fellman?*

—The 'heir to the pasty throne'. Horace Fellman's kid. He was at the grammar school. A couple of years above us.

—*What did George have against him?*

—There'd been something going on between Tommy and Elizabeth – on some school trip for the high-achiever kids. It wasn't anything really. They'd dated for a bit and broken up, and he'd posted all over Facebook about it, called her a liar and a cheat, which was so not true. George didn't like that. So he did something about it.

—*Was George Meldby one of Elizabeth's 'flying monkeys', as you put it?*

—I suppose he was. In a way. Like I said, she was too nice, and people like George took advantage. To be fair she had known George for years, we all had.

—*Can you elaborate?*

—So in school, like I say, George used to hang about with the girls. The lads all used to call him gay. You'd see him at dinner time, just walking aimlessly around by himself. The teachers must have been keeping their eyes on him in case he set anything alight! So I guess we sort of adopted him; like, he just used to follow us about – Lizzie's gang.

—*Lizzie's gang?*

—In high school, we were, I guess, like, the popular girls. Elizabeth was the queen, obviously. She had all the best clothes, the most expensive stuff, the big house. We all wanted to be seen with her. George just hung on. He used to carry Lizzie's bag for her, sometimes. He was like a little house elf. God that sounds horrible, doesn't it? It was true though. He used to steal bottles of pop and make-up for us from the ASDA near school. Then he got permanently excluded in his last year and sent to a special school for bad kids. After that he just became … I dunno, like, a feature of Ergarth. This little weird bloke who hung about.

—*Did George have a crush on Elizabeth?*

—You mean like every other lad in Ergarth? Yeah, probs.

—*It makes sense though – maybe he burned the factory because he was jealous?*

—Yeah sure. If you want. It's what everyone said.

—*What about the years after you'd all left school? Did George hang about with Elizabeth then?*

—Yes and no. But I wasn't there with her all the time. She had so many people around her all the time by then. She was a local celebrity. Sometimes George was there too, filming, sometimes he wasn't. He came in the pet shop a few times too.

This was the pet shop that Amirah and Elizabeth both worked in – Four Legs Good on Ergarth High Street. It is now closed.

—He kept reptiles I think: lizards. He used to come in and buy crickets for them sometimes, but mostly just came in and hung about. I think he only came in to see Elizabeth, to be honest – like the vast majority of the male customers.

—*Did she ever find this worrying?*

—No. She wasn't fazed by anything like that. We'd both known George for years. He wasn't being stalker-y, he would come in once, maybe twice a month. He was shabby, grubby, smelled a bit, you know? He just hadn't moved on since school, still looked the same. We both felt a bit sorry for him; he was just a lonely little oddball really.

—*Was George's crush on Elizabeth a bit too much, perhaps?*

—It's hard to say cos, like, most people had an obsession with her. She had so many orbiters online, so many fans; she also used to get sent loads of dick pics and that. I don't know how she just seemed so cool with it, you know? Just totally unfazed.

—*So in your opinion, why did he do it? Why did George help kill her, if he was such a fan?*

—Ugh, it was all Solomon Meer, that piece of shit. George was a lost little soul. Solomon got into his head, changed him. If any of them should have been, like, shown mercy or whatever, it was George. But on the other hand, he didn't stop them, did he? He joined in with what they did to Lizzie. The lad was a harmless little weirdo. They, like … weaponised him.

Indeed, there was irrefutable evidence at the scene that confirmed George Meldby's involvement. In fact, the evidence against George was

the most damning. He cut his arm on the edge of the gap in the wire
fence; fibres from his clothes as well as his DNA were found not only
at the scene but on Elizabeth Barton's body. George pleaded guilty along
with the other two, in court. I'm intrigued by Amirah's description of
George as a loner, a hanger-on and an admirer of Elizabeth Barton.
It certainly feels like Elizabeth's kindness towards him – allowing him
into her world to help with the videos and to associate with her – might
have been too much for him.

I ask Amirah about her experiences of the other two, beginning with
Martin Flynn. At the mention of his name, her face contorts into a
look of disgust. She takes another meerkat-like look above the booth
and drops her voice.

—Here's a tip for you: don't go mouthing off about the Flynns
round here. They're one of *those* families. You know? Every place
has them. The Flynns are ours. You don't mess with them. Just ...
be careful who you ask about them, OK?

—*I will. You went to primary and secondary school with Martin,*
correct?

—He was a thick, ugly, nasty piece of shit in primary, a thick,
ugly, nasty piece of shit in secondary, and only got worse as an
adult. No one was surprised when his name came up when Lizzie
was murdered.

—*No love lost there, then.*

—No and if you speak to anyone else about him they'll say the
same. His family owns that horrible abattoir up on Skelton. The
smell of that place, it's like some sort of horrible fog, makes the
whole town stink. They all look the same, the Flynns: orcs, we used
to call them, behind their backs, of course. They are all thick as
shit, hard as nails and stink of meat. Martin would get away with
so much in school because of that, and because he was ... he was
like, slow. Can you say that? He had some disability, some
problem, and he took it out on everyone else.

—*In what way?*

—Like, he would just attack people if he thought they'd said
something about him, or if someone looked at him funny. He was
pulling the wings off flies in primary school, watching them scuttle

round then stamping on them. He used to pull frogs out of the ponds near Ergarth High – pull them to pieces or slice off their skins. Just cruel for no reason. Horrible piece of work.

Amirah drops her eyes and writes on the napkin again:
Everyone round here knows it was *him* who cut off her head.

—*Did Martin have a particular problem with Elizabeth that you can remember?*
—Like, one of the things about Martin is that Lizzie kept him around, no one mentions that because it's not … fitting, I suppose. She kept him near but, like, at arm's length.
—*They were what, associates?*
—That's a good word for it. Martin Flynn would always be around. Like some of the other nastier kids – Lizzie didn't get on the bad side of people like that.
—*You're saying Elizabeth associated with Martin Flynn for what, protection?*
—Ha! Yeah, sort of. Like, she would speak to him but never in front of people, you know? She sort of kept him on a leash. He did have his uses, mind. When Elizabeth was making videos for her foundation, she would go out to the Vampire Tower or onto the streets, filming the homeless people and that. She kept Martin Flynn around, just in case something went wrong, you know?
—*Security detail.*
—You know the worst thing about Martin Flynn? Nothing was ever his fault. Everything he did wrong, he blamed on someone else. They're all like that, the Flynns. We all hoped the abattoir would get shut down when they got investigated, but, of course, his mother blamed cheap, immigrant workers. That's what they were like, if you see what I mean.

It's a harsh assessment but its base is in reality. Martin Flynn, at the time of his arrest for his part in the murder of Elizabeth Barton, had a long list of petty criminality: vandalism, GBH, ABH, drunk and disorderly, the list goes on. In court, it was shown that the DNA evidence from Martin Flynn was found mostly on the barricades

*around the entrance to Tankerville Tower. It was presumed by the judge
that it was Martin Flynn's brute strength that gained the three men
access to the inside of the tower, and that meant they could bend the
grate back, barricading Elizabeth inside. The rumour that it was
Martin who removed Elizabeth's head with a butcher knife from the
abattoir is a common one in Ergarth. Flynn caused controversy during
the trial with his persistent shrugging when asked questions by the
judge. When asked why he had done what he had done to Elizabeth,
Flynn simply stated that he 'didn't know'.*

—I swear down, Martin was helping out in the abattoir since
he was old enough to walk. What he did to Lizzie would have felt
like nothing to him. He didn't even care – you could tell.

—*Was Martin, despite his reputation, easily influenced, like
George?*

—I guess he was. I mean, if you told him to do something
stupid, he would do it. No wonder Solomon Meer got into those
two's heads.

—*Let's move on to Solomon. You said he joined the school in year
nine?*

—Yeah. He'd come from Nottingham; everyone used to take
the piss out of him when he first arrived. They used to call him
Robin Hood. He used to read all these stupid vampire books and
think he was, like, God's gift to English literature.

*Relatively little is known about Solomon Meer before he moved to
Ergarth. By all accounts he grew up in the affluent Nottingham suburb
of Mapperley. The Meer family were relatively well off; Meer's father
a heating engineer, and his mother a dentist. What we do know is that
Mr and Mrs Meer separated and Mrs Meer took custody of Solomon,
moving them both to Ergarth.*

—*What can you tell me about the Solomon Meer you attended
Ergarth High with?*

—He was a bit of an outsider – round here if you're even
remotely different, you're automatically an outsider. I know what
that's like. But cos I've always been from round here, I'm 'alright'

– nice that, isn't it? Solomon liked to make a bit of a show of himself, though. All the charvers used to call him a Satanist and chase him, beat him up. Sometimes it was really harsh. Then, when we got into year ten, he changed; he was different, sort of wild. It was like he didn't care anymore. He always smelled bad, like sweat; his hair was always dirty and his clothes too. It was like … like he didn't care anymore. He certainly didn't care what anyone called him. He didn't hide. Everyone used to pick on him still, and call him a Satanist, but he would, like, play on that. He would act up with teachers as well, get sent out of lessons, that sort of thing.

—*Hang on … 'charvers'?*

—They call them 'chavs' everywhere else. Thugs – nasty people, basically. Some people reckon that when you call someone a chav or a charver, you're taking the piss out of them – looking down on the working class.

—*I've read about that, yes.*

—But it's not. Being a charver isn't about class. It never has been. It's about being a *type* of person. Like, if you call someone 'gay' and throw shit at them because they look different to you, you're a charver. If you bully people, vandalise the town, rob old ladies, you could be from the richest family and you'd still be a charver. In fact a lot of charvers come from well-off backgrounds. That's the reality. It has nothing to do with 'demonising the working class'.

Sorry. Bit of a rant, there. I just wanted to, like, make context.

—*Solomon Meer was targeted, but you say he began to fight back?*

—Yeah, sort of. He invited a lot of it on himself. They used to ask him if he worshipped Satan and he'd say yes. He used to write all this Satanic stuff in pen all over his hands. One time he made this huge cut in his arm with a broken bit of ruler, just for no reason. Said a demon told him to do it. Mr Threlfall, the head, suspended him for a week for that!

—*It sounds like he needed some help, maybe.*

—Solomon Meer wasn't a victim. Sorry, but he wasn't. It was all for attention. He wasn't stupid either, like the other two. He was in my English group. Top set. And he was insufferable. He thought he was smarter than everyone else; 'Oh miss, that's actually a metaphor…' – all that sort of smart-Alec behaviour. He would bring in all these old books about demons, written in Latin, to show off. No one could stand him. He kept telling everyone his mum hated him, that she couldn't handle him, that she wished he was dead, this was every other week until no one listened anymore. No one cared. And you know what? Even if it was true, no one could blame her; it was all his fault.

There is another theory, written by a columnist in a broadsheet weekend supplement, suggesting that Solomon Meer, Martin Flynn and George Meldby were outcasts who had found solace in each other and the idea of a vampire. I haven't seen any evidence yet that Meldby or Flynn had any interest in the Ergarth Vampire. Amirah tells me that this story was a media creation, and not shared by those who knew the pair.

—You see, for all Solomon was clever, he was also a troublemaker. He wasn't this little incel or nerd that got bullied and finally snapped. He only knew Elizabeth because he'd been sent to sit on our table for messing about. In fact, I'll tell you what he'd been doing: he was sat at the back window, making faces and doing impressions of the special-needs kids that came to our school gym on Thursdays. That's a detail I didn't notice anyone pick up on. That, like, sums up Solomon Meer really well.

—*So you and Elizabeth and Solomon sat together in English in school? Did you notice any antagonism between the two then?*

—Actually no. In fact, what was pretty shitty was that, like, when he wasn't acting like a dick, Solomon could be OK, if he wanted. We didn't, like, talk to him much, but he was OK. He could string a sentence together at least. More than most of the lads in Ergarth.

—*What did Elizabeth think of him?*

—Nothing really. Like, she didn't need to associate with someone like that. She didn't have a lot of time or patience with him. To be fair, Solomon wasn't in school long before he was excluded.

—*This was for trying to assault the head teacher, wasn't it?*

—That's right, there was that video of it. Didn't they even show it in court?

Amirah's right. There was video footage online of Solomon Meer attempting to assault the then head teacher of Ergarth High, Dave Threlfall. It was used as evidence in court, despite having taken place a number of years before Elizabeth Barton's death, to try and prove that Meer was prone to violence. For those who haven't seen it, I'll let Amirah explain what happened.

—It was the last day before autumn half term. They always used to do an assembly – attendance rewards, certificates, that sort of thing. It was pretty lame; the head would send us off with some inspirational quote for us to 'think about'. I mean, we were only going to be away from school for a week. Anyway, it was right near the start of the assembly; we were sat in our form classes watching some year-seven dance troupe do their thing. Suddenly there's this commotion up at the back, and everyone gasps. We hear this huge yell, look round and see Mr Threlfall legging it out the hall with Solomon coming after him. He wasn't running, Solomon, he was like, striding with his hands balled up into fists. Everyone went quiet and you could hear shouting and banging all up along the corridor.

—*What happened?*

—What everyone said was that Mr Threlfall had come over to tell Solomon to stop messing about and be quiet, and that Solomon just snapped; he shouted something at Threlfall and then chased him all the way to his office. Everyone says Threlfall locked himself in the office until Solomon went away.

This is more or less what happened. The film – recorded on a pupil's phone – begins with a whispered altercation between the head and Solomon. The sniggering of the pupils and the music from the PA drowns out the sound, but Solomon's roar is audible and the figure of Dave Threlfall can be seen hot-footing it out of the hall with Solomon in pursuit. Solomon Meer never returned to the school.

—*Maybe this was the last time you and Elizabeth had contact with Solomon – until the Dead in Six Days videos?*

—I mean, we'd see him round. He worked at the bookshop for a bit. But yeah, we didn't have anything to do with him.

After Solomon Meer was kicked out of school, he worked full-time at a rather peculiar second-hand bookshop called 'Ergarth Books'. It's a quirky little shop up a short alleyway beside a tattooist. There's no proper sign; just 'ERGARTH BOOKS' written in black paint on the wall. Behind the door steep stairs lead down to a large cellar-like expanse beneath the empty shops facing the high street.

I want to play you an excerpt from a brief chat I had with Bobby Chambers, the proprietor of the bookshop. Mr Chambers is a rather eccentric and, in his own words, curmudgeonly old man. He keeps a baseball bat with a nail through it behind the counter, and when I ask him how on earth a place like Ergarth Books has survived in the town, he taps his nose and assures me he sold his soul back in the sixties. A framed photograph of Aleister Crowley in his famous Eye of Horus hat is nailed to the exposed brick wall. Unfortunately, due to the subterranean location, I presume, most of the recording of our interview came back blank. I'll play you all I have left.

Mr Chambers told me he only employed Solomon as it seemed the young man had a genuine passion for local history.

—*What was he like as an employee?*
—Hmf. Good. He was what I wanted.
—*Which was…?*
—Which was someone who left me alone. Someone who didn't constantly ask silly questions. Just got on with it. Yes. He just got on with it. Did his job. He did all the house clearances; came out in the van, did all the lifting.
—*House clearances?*
—Yes. When the old folk pass on, we get all their books. Solomon would go and do that. He'd spend the afternoon in some old dear's attic, loading all the dusty old books into the van and then he'd bring them here. Sort them.
—*Did you ever notice anything troubling about Solomon Meer? Was there anything—?*
—The lad spent his whole time among the books, man! That's

what he was interested in. The *books*! Spent his whole time reading about Ergarth. Couldn't get enough of the old stories. It was like he was searching for something. He'd stay late, after I'd gone home. Sometimes I think he slept in the shop. He'd found his place.

—*That's interesting. Do you know what he was searching for?*

—Anything to do with the bloody Ergarth Vampire. The Beast from the East. I used to tell him it was some tale made up by the Victorians, but he wouldn't have it. The lad wanted to read anything he could get his hands on about vampires.

Mr Chambers tells me that Solomon was quiet and hard-working. Yes, his appearance was quite dishevelled but he just got on with it, liked to be left alone. Mr Chambers says he does not know and does not care about Solomon's vampire obsession. He says he doesn't want to be drawn into 'all of this nonsense' and says that 'books are hardly evidence of murder', but he does express his sadness for the Bartons.

I feel that there's not much more down this particular path. The link, however, between the legend of the Ergarth Vampire and the circumstances surrounding Elizabeth Barton's death cannot be ignored. I ask Amirah what she knows about the assertion at the trial that Solomon Meer believed that Elizabeth was a vampire. This is something I can find little about.

—I don't know, for sure. I wouldn't be surprised though. He never shut up about vampires in school; he was obsessed with all that sort of rubbish. I remember feeling so happy when we did Frankenstein instead of Dracula in English!

—*Did you hear him mention Elizabeth in connection with vampires?*

—To be totally honest, no. I didn't hear anything about that until after they killed Elizabeth, and even then it just sounded like the sort of thing he would have said at school to sound edgy. You see, that's what it was about: ego.

—*How do you mean?*

—That's why he did it. That's what I think, anyway. It was never about vampires. He just couldn't stand her being more popular

than him.
—*Really? Solomon more popular than Elizabeth?*
—Yeah. That Dead in Six Days video he did…

Solomon Meer's 'Shopping Trolley Sledge' video, which he made and uploaded for the Dead in Six Days challenge, had more views and likes than any of Elizabeth Barton's early videos, but soon enough her channel dwarfed his in terms of views, likes and subscribers. Was this really motivation enough to kill her?

—You know what I think? I think that whole bullshit about a 'prank gone wrong' was just made up by their lawyers to get them a lighter sentence. Everyone round here knows they did it on purpose. She was way more popular than all three of them and for good reason.

Amirah is quiet. She sucks the remnants of her iced coffee through her straw and thinks for a while. I feel our time is more or less up here. A member of staff is cleaning the table behind us rather vigorously and has given us a couple of strange looks.

—Like, I think those three were just jealous, they were the total opposites to Elizabeth – where she was nice and good, they were horrible and evil.
—*I've heard that Elizabeth had begun doing some charity work – setting up a foundation for addicts and the homeless in Ergarth.*

Amirah looks around and beckons me forwards to look at something on her phone: older pictures from Elizabeth Barton's Instagram account.

—Yeah. She was. It was a bit of a secret project she was going to unveil, but she never got the chance. It would have been amazing too; she was shooting videos for it up at the Vampire Tower.

Amirah shows me a short clip on Elizabeth's Instagram. It's filmed inside Tankerville Tower and is dated August 2018. There are only a few seconds: a panoramic shot before whoever's operating the phone turns it back to face Elizabeth, who winks; #somethingscoming is captioned below. I suddenly feel a coldness in my fingers. Muscle memory perhaps; that terrible, fluttering shape.

—She was building up to it, you see. She was so good at this sort of thing. She began with the #givingmondayback appeal. That really took off.

Amirah shows me a number of photographs of Elizabeth crouched down, usually in the doorways of shops, with smiling homeless people. No spice zombies in sight, though.

—This was her whole thing. Like, #givingmondayback was funny because Mondays are shit, you know? But she'd always go out and give what she could to people in need – money, food. I took these ones.

Amirah visibly glows as she shows me more of the photographs: Elizabeth Barton handing over a steaming coffee and a Fellman's pasty into grateful hands, patting a homeless man's dog; it wears a red bandanna around its neck.

—She made a lot of money from YouTube, but she also gave so much back. She was a beautiful soul. People like Solomon Meer and the rest of them would try and bring her down, tell her she loved herself, but they would never have thought of doing something like this.

You see Elizabeth used her popularity and her fame for good. Solomon Meer could have done something after his challenge video got big. But did he? No.

—*And you're saying those three killed her because she was getting the attention they felt they deserved.*

—Something like that. I don't know. I really don't. I think you have to look into them to understand that. None of us knew. None of us who loved Elizabeth could understand why they'd do something like that.

There's a question I have to ask Amirah before I leave. I feel like I have everything I came for otherwise. According to Amirah's account of what went on in Ergarth in 2018, Elizabeth Barton was gregarious, popular and selfless – and in Amirah's view, a local celebrity. Many others share Amirah's belief that Elizabeth could have found herself in the upper echelons of YouTube fame, had her life not been cut short. This sort of popularity did not go down well with three of the town's misfits, especially Solomon Meer, according to Amirah. The missing piece to this view is the obvious parallel between Elizabeth Barton's death and the Ergarth Vampire legend. I want to follow up on this soon. For now, I want to ask Amirah one more question. I write it down on the napkin:

—Why do people think you had something to do with Elizabeth's death?

Amirah slumps in her chair. She looks utterly defeated, and I hope she is not going to burst into tears, as this would attract even more strange looks from the staff and other customers. Amirah seems to hold it together though, and after looking around, swallowing a few times, she finally manages to speak to me, her voice choked.

—My grandma and granddad came to England from Pakistan. But I was born here, in Ergarth. My family are from Ergarth. But even so, when you're the only brown face in a sea of white … it's hard. When Elizabeth let me take some photos of her for Instagram, when I was in her videos, it finally, *finally* felt like I … I dunno, like I belonged. It's proper sad that, isn't it?

When Solomon Meer came along, finally it wasn't me who was the outsider, it was him. But now it's all different again. I just want to get out of here, go to uni, never come back to this stupid little town with its stupid little rumours and stupid vampire story.

But even though I was part of that 'Snowball Fight in Choudhury's' challenge, even though I did it with everyone else, the colour of my skin means my friendship with Elizabeth meant nothing. Look.

Amirah looks around and then shows me another photograph on her phone. It's the outside of her father's shop. Both windows are broken and red paint has been sloshed all over the door.

—They think that because of that challenge, I wanted Elizabeth gone. I guess that's one of the reasons I wanted to talk to you and be on the podcast. I wanted to show how much I loved her, how much I miss her, how I never wanted any of this. It's been two years and I'm still in shock over what they did to her. We've lived in this shitty little place all our lives.

See that? We got up at three a.m. and cleaned it off. So no one would see. It appeared the day after Elizabeth's body was found. That's how fast people turn around here. Like I say, you'd better watch your back.

I ask Amirah who she thinks it was that committed this act of vandalism, but she shakes her head and begins packing up to leave. I understand now why she's no longer active on social media and I wish there was something I could say that would help.

—Are we done now? Do you have what you need?
—*I think so. Thank you so much for your time.*

Amirah makes a hasty exit.

It troubles me that we finished the interview on such a downbeat note. I also wish I could have talked more to Amirah about what she saw in Ergarth Dene; although I wonder whether that would have told me more about Elizabeth Barton's death.

It feels to me that the vampire story has morphed into something else entirely.

School uniforms appear as dribs and drabs of students amble past the fountain in the town square, some on scooters, some scrolling through their phones, some shoving and laughing with friends. I wonder how much the idea of online popularity means to each one of these students. Certainly, everything is online these days and the young have a huge added pressure to curate their lives to an almost impossible ideal. As Amirah says, you never know who is watching.

'Who locked Lizzie in the tower?' I feel the question should really be 'why?'

We know that Elizabeth was hugely popular. From the way Amirah spoke of her, it seemed that Elizabeth Barton was someone to aspire to. She was the perfection that everyone craved. We've also learned about the three convicted killers. George Meldby and Martin Flynn seemed like wayward souls ensnared by Solomon Meer. From the trial and Amirah's interview it certainly seems that Meer was the brains behind the whole operation, which makes me wonder what interest, if any, the others had in killing Elizabeth. Was it about power? Were George and Martin simply 'orbiters', their adoration of Elizabeth Barton manipulated or indeed 'weaponised' by Solomon Meer?

Solomon Meer's motive, though, has never been fully explained. I feels like there has to have been more than jealousy behind it.

What has this graffiti calling card asked of the world? 'Who locked Lizzie in the tower?'

Like Ergarth Dene, there are paths, bridges and impasses throughout this complex case. We may be wandering towards a dead end, a dark corner or a ruined mausoleum.

I have been Scott King,

This has been our second,

Until next time.

Lizzie B

3476 subscribers

In four days, I'm going to die.
A vampire's going to kill me.
I'll be dead in four days' time.

Good afternoon and happy … whoa there, someone's got a loud car engine … There it goes … byeee! Yeah so happy hump day on this Arctic sort of snow-covered, freezing, Christmas-card day in blooming February! I mean, why couldn't this have happened at Christmas, right? It's not a lot to ask for. I mean, Christmas Day was just sort of weirdly warm and a bit grey. Right now, it's like Siberia out there.

I'm wearing all the snuggly cardigans today. I was going to wear this hat; isn't it so adorable? I found it on the sale rail in the kids' section of H&M and I just had to.

I'm staying in the rest of the day now. I went into town for a bit, and I'm still thawing out – my toes are still cold! I was going to buy a load of Christmas decorations in the sale, just, like, to keep this whole Christmas theme going if the weather's decided it's Christmas in February, but it was just too cold and too sad. Everyone's just miserable out there. I texted a few people and they're at work and hating it, so I just thought, like, no.

That's why I'm going to extend #givingmondayback, because we all hate Mondays but those who don't have anything hate it even more, so let's make sure we're giving back on a Monday. If you get a coffee, get an extra one and give it to someone who has nothing!

Oh yeah, I didn't say – the queue in Starbucks today was just like, totally ugh, so I went in this little local place instead. The guy behind the counter totally knew who I was, and he gave me an extra coffee for free for #givingmondayback. So you see, it's working. You can do it too. Have a look at my Insta for the pic!

So thanks for all the love and comments about the last 'Dead in Six Days Challenge' video! So much love, you guys!

'Snowball Fight in Choudhury's' has had the most views and likes I've ever had! Thanks so much guys. It was so much fun! Total chaos, total laugh, lots of smiling, happy faces, and sometimes it's just so nice to do something random like that. My poor hands are still cold. I'm glad you liked the music and it took aaaaages to edit with all the speeding up and stuff, but it was totally worth it, right?

Not gonna lie, ickle bit of the old controversy in one or two comments. Come on, guys, don't bicker. Anyone who's anyone knows I've known the Choudhurys, like, since I was little, and they were all totally cool with it. They loved it, in fact. They've always been nice to me, so you be nice to each other, OK? No one's got this far in the challenge yet.

So that was day two of the Dead in Six Days challenge. Now we're moving on to day three. If you still don't know what the Dead in Six Days thing is, well, I did a whole explanation video, which you can find in the links below, so give it a tinkle and I'll see you in a mo!

I have decided. This snow is not going to stop the challenge. No way. The challenges are going to get harder now; harder and harder, until

I meet Vladlena the Vampire on day six. But you'll all be with me, won't you? I'm hoping to do, like, a Facebook live or something on day six, but it all depends; we'll see.

Let's get to the bit you're all waiting for shall we? Did Vladlena get in touch? Did she send me a new task? Let's find out…

Just looking through my phone here; I need to delete some pictures and stuff cos there's, like, no space at all. OK, here we go…

Oh my God, so I get a sort-of compliment from Vladlena! Wow, thanks, babe, you're so kind! 'Well done', it says, 'but if you really want to die in six days, you'll do something better with the next one … "Liberate the Meat".'

Okaaaay, I think you're getting a little saucy, Vladlena! Still, she's stepped up her game, so I need to step up mine too. This is where I need you too, guys; I need you to like and subscribe, cos this next one is going to need more likes than the other two.

I've already got an idea of what I'm going to do for this next challenge; it's going to be daring, it's going to be something that no one's ever seen before! The stakes are getting higher every time.

'Stakes'; see what I did there? Sorry Vladlena!

So, you know what to do — smash that thumbs-up, subscribe, jangle the bell icon, do it all! Tell your friends, tell your mam, tell your nan. In fact, get your nan to subscribe, and she'll get a notification when 'Liberate the Meat' goes up — and you will too! I don't think I can invite participation for the next one as I need a specialist — in fact, I've got someone in mind…

I've got four days left to live!

See you next time!

Episode 3: Statues and Snowmen

—They were on a conveyor belt. I never thought it would be like that. I saw loads of stuff in there that I'll never forget. Living creatures wriggling and struggling as a fucking rubber-sided conveyor belt moves them forwards like in a factory or something. It's like they're nothing but meat. Honestly, it was like something from a dystopia movie or a Phillip K. Dick book. There was just this fucking brutal juxtaposition of animal and machine. It was a proper powerful image; such a fucking hideous indicator of our species' contempt for the world and the creatures in it.

There were sheep and lambs on that conveyor belt. Mams and kids. They were supposed to be stunned. They had this little pen, a little metal room called a 'stun box'. Ha! That's a joke as well. 'Stunned'. Legally, you have to stun them, unless you're Halal – and don't get me started on that level of cruelty. Here, they stunned one in twenty, if they could be bothered. Their stunning pen was one guy with these giant metal tweezer things chasing around a terrified sheep. Then they'd shove them into a 'restrainer', which was a conveyor belt that squeezes them in so they can't move. Just their little heads sticking out the top.

There was another guy operating the conveyor belt; he'd press a pedal, the belt moved forwards, and the animals would move closer to two guys who stood at the end of the restrainer with knives. Those sheep, the last thing they saw when they went from the stun box onto that restrainer, after a life of grass and fields and wind – the last thing they saw was blood. The last thing they heard was screaming agony as their children's throats were hacked at. Because that's what it was: sheer brutality. They were hacked to death. If those knives were sharp then I'm Matthew McConaughey. Those sentient animals, those gentle creatures that feel fear, that feel pain, ended their lives in terrified agony under the strip lights of that terrible, miserable place. They became nothing but flesh. All that agony, all that fear would become meat that would be discarded if it went off or else picked at by fussy kids around a Sunday dinner table.

That wasn't even the worst thing I've seen. I've seen pigs – animals that are well more intelligent than dogs – living in dark metal pens, chewing the flesh of their dead babies. I've seen turkeys used as footballs; chickens swollen with growth hormones having their beaks ripped off with pliers; baby goats having their horns burned to stumps with no anaesthetic. I've seen men driving tractors into limping mother cows who have just had their newborns taken off them. I've seen dairy workers queuing up to take turns punching a day-old calf in the face. Fish – sentient animals capable of pain and fear – torn out of the sea and suffocated to death, either by lack of oxygen or else crushed under the weight of their dead.

All of this horror, this misery, this fucking agony so we can eat milk and eggs and cheese, and so you can eat deep-fried chicken nuggets and chippy dinner.

That's why I do what I do.

That conveyor belt, those screaming sheep and lambs. That's where it all started for me. Those voices never left me. Those cries for help. That's why I'll never stop.

Welcome to Six Stories.

I'm Scott King.

This is episode four.

In this series we've been discussing the death of vlogger Elizabeth Barton in March 2018. So far, we've begun sketching out a rough picture of Elizabeth from those who knew her. Universally adored; Elizabeth Barton was also philanthropic, as was highlighted last episode. Elizabeth's #givingmondayback hashtag trended on Twitter the week after she died, and searching for it now you'll find a huge amount of people following in her footsteps, posing for pictures of themselves giving food to the homeless. She planned to set up a charity – the Elizabeth Barton Tower Foundation – but sadly she was never able to. It would have made a huge difference in the town.

Elizabeth was murdered and decapitated by Solomon Meer, George Meldby and Martin Flynn during the 'Beast from the East' 2018 cold snap. It is becoming increasingly clear that a toxic mix of jealousy on the part of Solomon Meer and perhaps unrequited adoration from the other two could have been the motivation for this savage killing.

Recently, however, a message was scrawled on the wall of the Barton family house: 'Who locked Lizzie in the tower?' I am wondering if perhaps that message is not questioning who killed Elizabeth Barton, but why?

Today we are going to look at Elizabeth through the eyes of someone who knew her before she became Ergarth's favourite vlogger. We're going to get a glimpse of life with Elizabeth before she began ascending the steps to celebrity. I want to know what made Elizabeth, what motivated her and perhaps gain some insight into what lay beneath the veneer she presented in her videos. Ergarth is a small town and people don't often move away. This gives me the perfect opportunity to scrutinise what, if anything, has not been said about this case, that has perhaps been buried. Perhaps I'll be able to shine some light on the festering resentment that Elizabeth bred in her killers. We'll see.

Jason Barton is Elizabeth's younger brother. He has never spoken to the media before about what happened to his sister. He was living at the other end of the country at the time Elizabeth died. Jason did not return for his sister's funeral, and he has so far refused to take part in any documentaries, interviews and news reports.

'Because I want to' is his answer when I ask him why me and why now?

Our interview does not take place in Ergarth. We're a long way south, at the headquarters of an organisation called Justice for the Voiceless. In Bristol to be exact. Justice for the Voiceless are a group of activists who are dedicated to try and expose, he tells me, the ugly, hidden face of animal cruelty in the meat and dairy industry. It seems like both siblings had causes they liked to fight for.

Justice for the Voiceless often targets slaughterhouses and, despite the distance, decided to make an example of Flynn's Meats in Ergarth. In

2017, their investigation led to the conviction of a number of Flynn's staff on charges of animal cruelty.

—We didn't get any of the Flynns though. That's what we wanted. The workers, to be fair to them, were only the heads of the weeds. We wanted the roots.

I wonder if this was part of Martin Flynn's motivation for helping murder Elizabeth Barton. It's certainly possible. However, the undercover investigation was not mentioned in the trial of Meer, Meldby and Flynn, and it seems that Jason Barton's involvement in it was not common knowledge. It's a tough opener, but I ask Jason whether he feels his actions against Flynn's Meats had any part in what Martin Flynn subsequently did.

—Nah; no one knew I was involved. I made sure of that. I didn't want it to be about me, anyway. It wasn't for *me*. It was for those mams and kids, those animals. They were the important ones.

You see, people don't want to hear it. They don't want to know about the terror and the agony that these creatures endure. They want to put their hands over their eyes and their fingers in their ears, and keep consuming cos they 'couldn't possibly give up cheese'.

However, they like it when we expose what's really going on. That's what's so fucking weird about it. They'll sign an online petition to have CCTV in all abattoirs, to stop live exports, but they still want to eat flesh, drink milk from a tortured mother that was supposed to feed a baby animal. It's fucking weird.

I'm interested to know how Jason's views on animals began. From the little I know about him, he seems very unlike his parents and sister. A black sheep is perhaps not the best choice of words.

Jason Barton utilises every inch of the space we speak in – a bland and basic room in the Justice for the Voiceless offices, usually used for strategy meetings. We sit opposite each other at a large table surrounded by folding chairs. Jason sometimes sits but most of the time he paces up and down, back and forth. I wonder what his reason is for agreeing to this interview. A cynic might say that he's made himself available to me to gain a platform – to get more exposure for his cause perhaps? Jason is young, but he's articulate and focused. There's a fierce intelligence behind his words, which come at me in rapid bursts.

—The first time I saw animals being killed like that was at Flynn's Meats. I was only little, like – eleven, twelve, something like that.

—*How did a boy that age manage to get inside an abattoir?*

—I know, right? You see, I was a wanderer as a kid. I could never keep still. I was always getting in trouble at school for messing about, climbing things, running round. I didn't go round beating people up or owt like that. But I've got ADHD. Schools can be good about that, but they can be fucking stupid about it too. Depends on the school. Let's just say West Ergarth Primary thought that shutting a kid with ADHD in a room by himself was the best way to understand such a fucking complex issue. This is what happens when your government treats teachers like shit. You get shit teachers.

Anyway, like I say, I used to wander, and I used to do it at night. It was the only way I could sleep. Mam and Dad, I used to drive them spare. Imagine being home after a long day at work and your kid is bouncing off the walls until bedtime. They used to get me to go into the garden and see how many laps of it I could do in a minute, trying to wear me out.

I used to wake up at around three a.m. and I was just *awake*. The house was dead quiet and still, and I was good at sneaking. The back door that led out into the garden always had a key in it, so I just slipped it into my pocket and went off wandering. Not far; I wasn't running away, just wandering round the area. It was like magic out there at that time. There was never anyone about. It was like being in a dream, all the silent suburbs, closed curtains, the damp of the dew. I loved it.

It was when I thought I saw … well … I saw something weird, that's all. Something I couldn't explain. That's when I stopped walking the streets.

—*What did you see?*

—Ah, it was nowt; I was just a kid with an overactive imagination. Scared the shit out of me, mind. It was ... like, it was just a person I suppose, but they looked all wrong. I was by the closed-up entrance to Ergarth Dene – behind the old cricket pavilion. I reckon it was a junkie or something, but she ... she just didn't move right.

—*I'm not sure I know what you mean?*

—Neither do I really. It was like, she was walking but it was all jerky, like stop-motion animation. All wonky. She was pale and rake-thin, and her mouth ... man, that mouth. She'll have been a crackhead or something. It was like all her teeth were all broken but she was coming at me, straight at me. I started backing off, then I was running and I could hear behind – it sounded like bare feet on the pavement, and her breath all wheezy and whistling. I was shitting myself!

—*Did she catch you?*

—I didn't look back. I ran back home, hopped the garden fence, straight up the fucking wall and into my bedroom. I could see the Vampire Tower from up there – far off in the distance. And I remember being able to see this big, black *thing* flying towards it, like ... like ... well I dunno what it was like. I was just a kid.

I got under those covers and I stayed there. I was freezing, deep inside my body. I can still remember it...

—*In your fingers and toes, right?*

—Right. Ergarth-style cold. I didn't sleep a fucking wink. After that I just stayed in my room at night; ground my teeth, climbed the fucking walls. Kept my curtains closed. Tried not to look out at that tower. Eventually though, it got too much and I had to go somewhere.

—*Was this when you went to the abattoir. Flynn's Meats.*

—Yes. I had to move, had to walk. So I started going out again, but I avoided the streets – I just crept in the shadows like a fox or a rat or something. And then I started wandering across the fields. I made sure I went west – the opposite direction to the Vampire Tower. It's beautiful once you're out of Ergarth. I mean, anywhere's beautiful compared to that shit-hole. But it was genuinely pretty out there with no one about and the sun's just sort of creeping into the sky. I was wandering along the road, by the dry-stone wall, and I suddenly smelled this smell. It's hard to describe; like burned hair and rot. If you live in Ergarth, you know that smell is coming from the abattoir, but I didn't really understand what the abattoir *was*, so I just followed my nose.

There's all these signs outside the abattoir telling you to stay out and that there's guard dogs, but that's bollocks. I just walked in. It was a fucking shit-tip back then; it still is. Old machinery rusting away, puddles, piles of rubbish. There's this huge, grey, spiky fence around the outside, but they don't even lock the gate. So I just walked in. I climbed up this drainpipe on the side and I was on the roof. The smell – fuck it was hideous. That's when I heard the screaming – it went through me like a blade. And of course when I found this hatch thing on the roof that was unlocked, something inside me was begging me not to, but I had to look.

Jason then describes some of the slaughter he saw at Flynn's Meats. You heard it once … I don't particularly want to hear it again, either.

—That changed me. That changed something inside me, and it became my life to try and help animals. I just wanted to do something about it, you know? I thought I was going to be the next Greta Thunberg. I still want to be. She's fucking great. I love how people fucking *hate* her because she's right. All these pissed-off old white guys getting butt-hurt because they're being schooled by a fucking sixteen-year-old. I love it. She's a fucking hero!

It troubles me slightly that Jason has not yet mentioned the brutal death of his own sister. I am not here to judge him for this or dictate how people are allowed to feel. I do think I should bring up the subject, though. There's no natural way to lead up to it. But I'll try.

—What were things at home like when you were that age?
—They weren't great but who can really put their hand on their heart and say they had a fantastic childhood?
—Now's your chance, if you don't feel you've been heard.
—I didn't have a *bad* childhood. I wasn't abused. My parents …

they just weren't there a lot of the time really. They both worked and they both had a social life. That was their whole vibe – 'having kids isn't going to stop my social life' sort of thing, you know?

— *They weren't present; or they weren't emotionally present?*

—They were … distracted I reckon. Like, they'd hurry us off to bed and go out or leave us with babysitters – various girls from round the area. I honestly didn't know who was going to pick me up from school most days. Mam just forgot once. She was too busy having lunch with her friends – which means drinking a load of wine with a load of insufferable old Tory gossips. You know those NIMBY types? They hate wind turbines spoiling their view of the countryside and don't care that without wind turbines, there'll be no fucking countryside.

— *It doesn't sound great.*

—Don't get me wrong; we got a lot of stuff. It wasn't like we didn't have *stuff*.

— *Stuff?*

—Toys, games, TVs, consoles. I had all the best ones, the PlayStation, the Xbox, and a big TV in my room. So, like I say, it's not like we wanted for things. And if my parents were away for a weekend, we knew that they'd make up for it with presents. It was good, really. That's probably why I've, like, rejected all that sort of thing now and try to live for the day, you know, live in the moment. Sorry, you were asking about the wandering?

— *That's right. Do you think your circumstances had much to do with it?*

—Probably. I was just trying to be seen, trying to get them to notice me, I suppose.

— *I'm guessing it didn't work.*

—You'd be correct. What they noticed was what we won. What we achieved. That just wasn't me, though. That was all Elizabeth.

There's a tense silence. Jason sits down in a chair and stares past me into the middle distance. His shoulders rise and fall, swift and sharp.

—She did all the after-school stuff; the clubs, the sports, all that. And she was the best at everything – always bringing home medals and certificates and shit. Mam and Dad loved all that, bragging about her to their friends.

—*What about you?*

—What about me? I wouldn't do any of that stuff, so they tried to give it to me instead. Footballs; I had about a hundred. I just used to boot them into next door's garden to piss them off. So Dad set up a punch bag in the garage, a proper boxing one, hung it from a chain in the ceiling; got me some gloves.

—*That sounds positive.*

—Yeah, but then he just left me to it, like; didn't do it with me, and that was all I wanted. Mam just bought me more and more computer games to keep me quiet, keep me out of trouble. She said if I was up in my room doing that, then I wouldn't be out causing mayhem. They bought me a guitar as well but didn't ever show me how to play it. I think they thought I would become this musical prodigy or some shit. But that wasn't me. That was Elizabeth.

—*Were you close with your sister, Jason, when you were younger?*

—Not really, no. We just stayed out of each other's way to be honest.

—*Can you give me a snapshot of life in your household when you were little?*

—I dunno what good that'll do. What does that have to do with anything?

—*It's your truth. That's what's important.*

Jason twists in his chair, his arms unconsciously wrapping around himself.

—You see, we have a problem here. I don't imagine you'll want to broadcast what I'm going to say.

—*What makes you think that?*

—Because it doesn't fit. But if you're brave enough to put out the stuff people don't want to hear, fair fucks to you, I suppose.

I'm aware that I'm being goaded. But Jason has controlled the narrative up to now so I'm going to let him continue.

—*Tell me what you want to say.*

—OK, fine. I have memories, but you're not going to like them. You may not even believe them.

—*Everyone should be heard, that's what I believe.*

—Yeah. I'm sorry, of course. Look, I know about what happened to you. Man, that must have fucked you up. I suppose … your story is a story that no one expected. And so's mine. But I don't want to be a fucking celebrity or anything, OK?

—*It's your story I want to hear. That's all.*

—So, I remember when I was a kid – I dunno, six, seven? Me and my sister used to go downstairs on a Saturday morning to watch TV. Elizabeth was about ten and she always got to choose what we watched. That was just how it was. The big TV was downstairs and the big, leather sofa. It was better to watch TV in there. Elizabeth had a DVD of this old kids show from the nineties, *Maid Marian and her Merry Men,* and we loved it. She loved it. She would watch the same episode over and over again, for weeks. I still know the fucking dialogue off by heart.

—*What was it like, just the two of you together. Did you get on?*

—Yes and no. In the way that siblings do and don't. We didn't fight – Elizabeth wasn't like that. But … things happened.

—*Go on…*

—Just stupid things. Kids' games. Nothing important.

—*What sort of games?*

—Like, she was the older one, and she was responsible for me when my parents or the babysitter or whoever weren't there. On Saturday mornings our parents used to lie in for fucking hours, sleep off their hangovers, so Elizabeth was in charge. She invented these games to keep me still, keep me quiet. She had this one called 'statues'. I was up and down the walls you see. I don't think I was even medicated then. We were allowed to eat cereal and Elizabeth was allowed to get it for us. If she came out of the kitchen with Coco Pops I knew we were in for a game of 'statues'.

—*Why Coco Pops?*

—I wasn't allowed them, you see – too much sugar or additives or whatever; and because we had this new sofa and Mam and Dad would lose their shit if I spilled chocolate milk on it. It was so fucking important to them – the telly, the sofa, the carpet.

The game was, when Elizabeth was done with her cereal, she would balance the bowl on my head. A bowl half full of chocolate milk. The game was to see how long I could manage to sit still through an episode of *Maid Marian and her Merry Men* before I moved and the bowl fell. How long before I covered me and the sofa in chocolate milk.

—*I imagine that happened, right?*

—Of course it did. More than once. Then I would spend the rest of the morning frantically trying to clean up the mess while Elizabeth just sat there watching the show. Then, when Mam and Dad came downstairs, I was in trouble.

—*That sounds like a really mean thing for her to do.*

—Right? But it was probably annoying for her, me being such a pain. I guess everyone has their own way of doing things, right?

I feel like Jason is giving Elizabeth a bit of a pass for this. But I can see why; Elizabeth was having to play the role of parent to a youngster with untreated ADHD, without much guidance.

Older siblings have a degree of power over their younger counterparts anyway, and Elizabeth was thrust into a position of responsibility by parents who, by Jason's account, seem not to have been much of a presence.

—Now I'm thinking about it, there were other games too.

—*Really? Are you OK to tell me about them?*

—Elizabeth's games were seasonal. When it was cold, when it was still dark and frosty outside, that's when we would have to play 'snowmen'.

—*How did you play it?*

—So, our living room faced out onto the garden. There was a small porch full of wellies and stuff. Elizabeth would tell me to go and get my hat and gloves from the porch. The tiles in there were always properly freezing. I used to hop in and hop out again. Then she would tell me to go and stand outside in the garden wearing only my hat and my gloves.

—*What would happen if you refused?*

—Hmm … that's a good question. I don't … I don't ever remember feeling that was an option. What she said, I did. If she wanted me to play snowmen, I played snowmen.

I would be allowed to strip naked in the porch so my pyjamas didn't get wet. After the first time, I began to wear underpants so she didn't see me fully naked. When I was down to my underpants, I had to go out into the garden and stand stock still with my arms out, like a snowman. She would tell me I had to stand there for as long as possible, to see how long I could take the cold.

—*That sounds awful.*

—I thought so too. I dreaded playing snowmen, I dreaded it more than statues, but I had to do it. There didn't seem any rhyme or reason. I mean, I must have done something – some crime – to deserve it, but I could never work out what it was. I just remember standing there, my arms out, fingers and toes burning they were so cold. She would be sat there on the sofa. I never knew when she would unlock the door. The click of the key in the lock. I still … excuse me, sorry … I still get a flush of relief whenever I hear the turning of a key in a lock. It's stupid.

—*It doesn't sound stupid to me; it sounds—*

—Abusive? Evil? Like something a terrible person would do? Yeah. I told you, see? I told you you might not like this.

—*I'm not here to pass judgement, Jason. I'm here to hear your story. If that's what happened, then that's what happened.*

—You haven't asked me, but I know what you're wondering – and that's whether I'm glad she's dead. You're wondering whether, when those lads locked her in Tankerville Tower and she froze to death and they cut off her fucking head, I felt like there was some sort of poetic justice to it, right? Whether some little piece of me felt like she deserved it?

—*Is that what you felt?*

—A little. Yes. I'll admit it. It would be weird if I didn't, to be honest. But I mean, man, they cut off her fucking head. That's some fucked-up shit. That's beyond just murder. That's brutal.

—*Why do you think they did that? Do you have a theory?*

—Ergarth's a desperate, bleak fucking place full of desperate, bleak people.

There is a sullen silence and Jason stares at me, his face betraying little. He's sat dead still, waiting for a reaction. I wonder how long he's held this conflict between grief and anger inside him, letting it churn and boil. He tells me that this is one of many reasons why he was not present in the wake of Elizabeth's death, why he stayed away.

—I felt like something would betray me; something in my face or my manner. I was scared that I might accidently say the wrong thing, and everyone would know that I didn't really care my sister was dead. More than that, I was scared that my mam and dad would find out about those things she did.

—*What would have happened if they had?*

—It would have destroyed them. More than her dying. It would have smashed up that view they had of her as this fucking perfect creature, this perfect person.

—*Were you worried other people would find out about Elizabeth's games too?*

—I know, right? Then what would happen? Her little online army would be baying for my blood. That was my main concern, cos that could have compromised what we are doing for the animals.

—*So how did you actually feel – about her dying, I mean?*

—It's … complicated. You should care when something like this happens, shouldn't you? I mean for fuck's sake, I care about animals that couldn't give two fucks about me; animals that, if they could, would run away from me; animals that simply cannot conceive that I am trying to help them. I've even seen what those knives can do – take their heads almost clean off while they're still alive. I care about them, I lose sleep over them, but when Elizabeth was killed … well …

I know I didn't feel good about it. But I do remember wondering if it was as easy to cut off her head as it was a sheep's? Was there the same amount of blood? I guess a human neck is thicker bone, isn't it? I just remember thinking about it; wondering whether I cared; but I just felt … nothing. You're not allowed to feel nothing these days, though. You have to be crying on breakfast TV between adverts for car insurance and fast food. If you don't, you're evil. I knew what the world would think of me if I grieved for my sister the wrong way.

—*Those animals you've dedicated your life to helping, they can't help themselves; they need you. Elizabeth didn't.*

—That's true. Elizabeth could certainly fend for herself.

—*I wonder if you see a little bit of yourself in those animals – a younger Jason, who was helpless, who had no one to stand up for him.*

—I wonder that too.

—*These incidents when the two of you were younger, they're troubling. For me, they seem to go just that little bit further than the usual sibling bullying.*

—You're right, they do. There were other things too – plenty of other things. Is me telling you all this spoiling the image of my sister? Is it tainting how everyone remembers her?

—*Your feelings, your memories are your own.*

—Like, she used to drink tea. Mint tea – we weren't allowed caffeine. Mam would give her the cup with the teabag still in. I wasn't allowed tea because I was too scatty. As soon as Mam was out the door, Elizabeth would tell me to put my hands out and close my eyes…

—*I can guess what happened next, Jason. Did you never tell your parents about any of these things? Did they never see what was happening?*

—No. Elizabeth was smart; good at everything. Well, she was also really good at covering her arse. If Mam and Dad found me crying with burned hands or wet pyjamas, it was my own fault.

I at least got their attention then, I suppose. In some ways I guess I was grateful. That's why I never spoke up, that's why I never told them. At least when they were screaming at me, they were saying *something* to me.

I think Jason Barton is being more guarded than he would like to make out. I almost feel that this whole conversation has been rehearsed. I haven't challenged him on his stance about anything yet; but that's not to say I won't. Underneath the façade of the grungy activist, I feel that there's something very vulnerable. So how I manage this part of our discussion will be crucial to whether Jason stays onside or not.

—When I was around thirteen I was diagnosed, at last, with ADHD – much to the shame of my parents, who took it as some sort of slight. Next to Elizabeth, with her grades and her prizes, I'd always felt like a failure, and the diagnosis didn't help.

So when we talk about these horrible things she did to me when we were kids, it automatically begs a question, doesn't it? Did I have anything to do with her death?

—*I haven't asked that question.*

—You don't need to. It's there, between us. It's hanging over everything; it has since she died. The messed-up little brother. I've never told anybody about the things she did – for that very reason; that question would rear its head. It's like when someone dies and the first suspect is the partner. That's fucked up, but they're also the most likely killer. That's what we are as a species, as a society. We're these strange mutant apes that got too big for our boots and spend our time killing each other. Did I kill my sister? No. I didn't know her well enough to kill her, if you get what I mean. We were like strangers. I rarely visited Ergarth, and she never came down to Bristol to see me. It was like we were colleagues who'd worked together for a few years and gone our separate ways.

—*When was the last time you saw her then?*

—I was actually in Ergarth a few days before she died.

—*I didn't know that.*

—But I didn't even see her, or my parents. I was visiting a couple of old mates. I never said goodbye.

—*Do you wish you had?*

—I wish … I wish more that I'd been able to ask her *why?* Before she died. Just find out *why* she used to treat me the way she did when we were little. What was it I'd *done* to justify it?

Were there times I fantasised about killing her when I was a kid? Yes. Yes, because that's normal.

—*And with what happened, the things she did to you, it made sense for you to have those feelings.*

—Right? But I didn't do it. I didn't kill her.

—*Just to play devil's advocate here Jason, maybe there are some who'll hear this and say that you may have been justified if you did.*

—Funny that, because people justify keeping a sentient,

defenceless creature in disgusting, inhumane conditions before mercilessly killing it then letting its flesh go rancid in the fridge. That's much more horrific if you ask me.

—*People in Ergarth talk about how much good your late sister did. What a positive role model she was. So I'm currently struggling to find a clear motive for her murder.*

—It's funny that you should say that, you know, because I'm not. I'm not struggling to understand it at all.

Jason folds his arms and leans back in his chair. I feel like he wants me to react to this, but I don't. I wait. I let silence permeate the room, hanging between us like a fog, and hope Jason decides to fill it.

Eventually, with a sigh, he does.

—I don't think it was *her* especially who was the problem. But she kind of personified that problem, you know? With her videos and her hashtags and her #givingmondayback or whatever. And she was setting up a charity wasn't she?

—*Wasn't that a good thing – encouraging people to give to the homeless? It's still going, isn't it?*

—Yeah. Of course it was. But think about it: do you remember the last time you gave to charity?

—*Yes. I suppose so. I have a few direct debits. I've put some extra groceries in the food-bank boxes in the supermarket.*

—Right. But did you feel the need to take a photograph of yourself while doing it? Did you set up a charity in *your own* name?

—*No. I suppose not. Why would I?*

—Exactly. You don't need to show anyone. You keep it to yourself. You do something nice and move on. You don't need to tell the world. People only do that for other reasons.

—*I'm not sure what you mean.*

—It's all attention. People want to brag about how great they are – 'look at me giving to charity, aren't I just wonderful?'. I guess it's one way of getting attention. That was one of my sister's.

—*I could think of worse.*

—Yeah? How about this; have you seen her #givingmondayback photos? If not, have a close look; look at the guys she took pics with. They're all pretty Instagramable, they've all got beards and dogs, or one leg or something. She ignored the young lads passed out from smoking spice; she didn't bother with the crackhead mothers with broken teeth. Makes you think, doesn't it? – about why she was doing it. Really. Was it for them or for her?

—*The counter-argument being that doing it, no matter how 'Instagramable' it is, encourages people to do the same.*

—Mate, people know to give to charity. All this is about getting attention. Our parents gave us none so we had to find validation somewhere. Hers was online. I got mine in other ways.

—*Like how?*

—OK – can we rewind a bit? I want to go back a few years. I want to go back to school. That's where Elizabeth became popular. That's when she first started the YouTube channel, her Instagram, this image of herself. That's how she got her attention. The attention we never got from our parents.

—*What do you remember about that time?*

—I started Ergarth High in year seven, when Elizabeth was in year eleven, the year she did her exams and left. Mam and Dad thought she'd be staying on at sixth form. So did I. The teachers too. Anyway, she was the one who was the netball captain, the debate captain, the top girl or whatever shit it was. So when I got there, they all thought I would be like that. They expected me to be like her.

—*Do you think they were disappointed – the teachers I mean?*

—They *told* me outright I was a disappointment. They gave no shits. I was a disappointment to them from day one. I couldn't sit still, I couldn't do their work, I couldn't do one thing I was asked. That's the fucking problem with the school system in this country – they don't give a fuck. Since the fucking Tories took over, it's all been about statistics. If you're a kid like me and you learn in a different way or you have ADHD or a learning difficulty you make their statistics look bad. To get through school, you have to be a certain shape. If you're not that shape, you're the peg that doesn't fit in the hole.

—*So what became of you?*

—I was shoved in with the rest of the square pegs – always in after-school detention. That's how I first encountered Martin Flynn.

As has been mentioned before, Martin Flynn has mild learning difficulties and has been described by many in Ergarth as a thug. According to Jason, the after-school detention system put together pupils from all the year groups for an hour in an empty classroom with pens and paper and dictionaries. The pupils were supposed to sit in silence and copy out of the dictionary.

—If it was Delkyn, the deputy head, you shut up and got on with it. It was shit. But if it was someone like Mrs Brandon, the cooking teacher, it was great. If you so much as moved for Delkyn, you got a phone call home and another after-school. If it was Brandon, you could get away with talking quietly so long as you didn't fuck about and piss her off. The teachers were on a rota for supervising detentions, and you soon learned who you could push and who you couldn't.

—*So tell me about Martin Flynn.*

—At first I thought he was great. He looked like trouble; he was huge, bursting out of his uniform. And one of those faces, like all the Flynns have, like a troll. I thought he was like me, another misfit. But he was a real hard case. Everyone in school knew it – no one messed with him.

George Meldby was always in there too but I never noticed him, no one did, he was small, quiet, weird. He just sat there in the corner, getting on with it.

—*What about Solomon Meer, was he in those after-school detentions?*

—Once or twice maybe, but not really. He spent most of his time in isolation. That was different. A bit more shit. Isolation was for the bad ones; after-school detention was for the little pains in the arse, like George Meldby and Martin Flynn.

Jason explains that he wanted to impress Martin Flynn, so he started showing off in detention. He'd make noises to annoy the supervising teacher, throw things, be a general pain. This behaviour encouraged the others and soon, after-school detention became almost like a game. While Elizabeth Barton achieved exam results and medals, Jason Barton began making his way up the ranks of the troublemakers. What I'm interested in, however, is why that was.

—There was more to it than just trying to impress an older lad. I suppose I hoped that if I could get in with him, maybe Elizabeth might lay off me a bit…

—Her bullying of you was still going on?

—I know what you're thinking. Why didn't I stand up for myself, protect myself? Or tell someone for fuck's sake? I was old enough by then. But I was scared of her. I know how that sounds but I was. She'd had power over me ever since we were little, and I thought that if she saw me with Martin Flynn, that she might be scared. How stupid I was though.

—What do you mean?

—Elizabeth was always one step ahead. Even back then she had Martin Flynn wrapped round her little finger.

This takes us back to Amirah's account of her days at Ergarth High. Elizabeth had more or less everyone in her thrall. Martin Flynn was another of her hangers-on. Jason tells me that Martin Flynn's reputation meant that no one dared mess with Elizabeth.

—And you know why he was always in after-school detention? For fighting. Beating people up. And we all knew who he was beating up and why.

—Who?

—Elizabeth was … popular with the lads, shall we say. But no one was good enough for her. She'd break up with anyone she dated really quickly. No one lasted long. Then she'd lie about them, blame them for everything. Then they'd get a hiding from Martin Flynn.

—On Elizabeth's command?

—Maybe. Maybe not. Maybe he did it of his own accord, because he was another orbiter.

—I've heard that term used before about him. He thought he had a chance with her?

—Yeah. That was her power, see? Martin Flynn, since I started knocking about with him in school, was forever asking me if he could come round, if I could put a good word in to Elizabeth about him. It was pathetic. Then there was the thing with the bat and I realised he was just as bad as her.

—*The thing with the bat?*

—Yeah. Sorry, so I found this bat on the way to school; this little pipistrelle. I dunno what had happened to it; maybe it got hit by a car or a bird got at it, I dunno. I had it in a matchbox. I guess I thought I could nurse it back to health. Anyway, I dunno how Martin Flynn found out about it, but he did. I'm guessing Elizabeth told him. He comes up to me one day at break and just says, 'Empty your pockets, Barton. Now.' So I do and he takes the matchbox. Holds it out in his great meaty hand like a troll and just says to me, 'When am I coming round your place?'

—*What did he want?*

—Elizabeth. Simple as that. If he was in our house, then he was closer to her. I don't think it was more complex than that.

—*What did you say?*

—Stupidly, I told him to fuck off. I guess I thought he might back down. He just looked at me though with this *hate*. Like I was nothing to him. Like I was one of those animals at the abattoir. 'Give us back that box, Flynn,' I said, 'or you'll not be coming round, ever.' That was stupid as well. He just shrugs and crushes the box in his fucking massive hand. Then he chucks it up in the air and shoves me backward, and I go arse over tit in the mud. He just walks off. I remember swearing I'd get him for that. Him and his whole fucking shitty family.

While this was a cruel and callous act, Jason's reaction seems a little extreme to me. Perhaps it says more about Jason than Martin Flynn. But Jason tells me that this is how we've been trained to feel about animals, that they don't matter as much as humans.

—If he'd killed a fucking human baby, no one would have a problem with revenge.

I don't want to get into a moral debate so instead I suggest that Martin Flynn was one of Elizabeth's first 'flying monkeys'. Jason gives a wry smile.

—I saw first-hand how she carried on around him: shrieking loudly when Martin Flynn did something stupid, giggling and flicking her hair and letting her skirt ride up whenever he talked to her. What was in it for her, to behave like that? I have no idea. She was always just too close to him, sitting just out of reach; turning round, smirking, giggling. He was putty in her hands.

—*Why do you think she was doing this?*

—Well at first you know, it was just protection. There was this new lad who started a few weeks after me in year seven. Angry little thing called Sam Roper, thought he was the big man because he came from some estate up in Sunderland. Martin Flynn heard him call my sister a slag and broke his nose with one punch. I was told that Sam's a PT in the gym in Ergarth now. Ripped to fuck, but his nose still has a kink in it.

But there were other things that Martin Flynn became useful for. Years later.

—*Such as?*

—Elizabeth always had to be better than everyone else at everything, and she was, usually. Then the Dead in Six Days challenge came along. And of course, Elizabeth had to be the best at it.

One of her challenges was something to do with animals. 'Free the meat' or something like that. Anyone else would have just chucked a load of bacon into a river, but Elizabeth had to be one step better.

—*I'm guessing this had something to do with Flynn's Meats?*

—Yeah. So they'd had the investigation in 2017 thanks to Justice for the Voiceless, so by 2018, when everyone was doing those challenges, Flynn's Meats was like Fort Knox, not like when I was younger. You couldn't get near it. No one dared.

—*Did you encourage your organisation to go after Flynn's Meats specifically?*

—Let's just say I knew what we'd find there.

—*Was this the revenge you swore you'd have on Martin because of the incident with the bat?*

—Put it this way; no one can tell me that the world's not a better place with him in prison. Anyway, that doesn't matter. We were talking about Flynn's Meats. They were paranoid after the investigation and were as difficult to get into as Willy Wonka's fucking factory. But Elizabeth, of course, managed to get around that. She got Martin Flynn to 'liberate' a lamb and then made out like *she'd* saved it from slaughter and was keeping it in the garden as a pet.

—*And how did you know she wasn't telling the truth?*

—Because I knew her, maybe better than anyone else. Like I say, I've still got mates in Ergarth. They told me one of the trucks delivering some sheep got stuck in the snow. The road up to Flynn's on Skelton is a nightmare anyway but back during the cold snap it was impossible. They just left those sheep to die in the cold. There's photos of it; just these huge drifts of snow and that truck half in and half out of a ditch. After a few hours the whole thing was pretty much covered and the animals had stopped crying out. That's when he did it. The day after that, Martin Flynn's family beat him so badly, he had to stay a few nights in Ergarth Hospital. It made the papers! I saw it because I thought karma had come back on one of the slaughter workers.

I've looked up this story myself and I see why it drew Jason's attention; 'Slaughter House Worker Hospitalised After Accident'. The Ergarth Examiner online article states that 'Martin Flynn (24), son of the owner of Flynn's Meats who were investigated for animal cruelty in 2017, suffered severe bruising, lacerations to the face and two broken ribs after falling into machinery at the abattoir'. There is little else in the story save for a rehash of the investigation and how the abattoir has now been deemed 'adequate' on its last inspection.

—I heard that his family gave him a beating; told him to go and get that lamb back from my sister.

—*And did he?*

—I don't know what happened to it to be honest. Last I heard

of it was in Elizabeth's video where it was trotting through the
snow in my parents' garden. She said she made a home for it in
the shed. I don't know what happened to it after that. Another
disposable life.

It got me thinking though; if it was that easy for Elizabeth to
get Martin Flynn to just bust out a fucking lamb like that, what
else was he doing for her that we didn't know about? I'm telling
you, it's good that he's been put away.

Let's move on to George Meldby.

—Oh, OK. That little shit.

—You hated him too?

—If you'd had someone try to set your hair on fire, your coat,
your bag, as many times as he tried to mine when we were in
school, you'd have a problem with him too.

—Why did George have a problem with you?

—Probably cos I caught him trying to burn down Myrmirth
stables, when we were in year nine. I popped the little prick's nose
for that. There were horses inside.

*—There was an incident wasn't there, back in school with George
and a boy named Fellman?*

—Oh yeah. Everyone knew what happened there. Tommy
Fellman from the grammar school. Elizabeth brought him home
a few times for tea. Mam and Dad fucking loved him cos he did
rowing or some bullshit like that. Him and Elizabeth did some
videos together; their relationship was all over Instagram. People
loved them. There were people, *strangers*, actually crying when they
broke up. It was fucking tragic.

*Jason tells me about the pictures Elizabeth uploaded of her and
Tommy Fellman, now all deleted from her Instagram account.
Grandiose shots of the two holding hands over a waterfall in Ergarth
Dene; sipping from dual straws in fancy restaurants; days out at
Christmas markets, the beach – Newcastle, York, never in Ergarth. All
of them perfectly posed and filtered.*

—Tommy wasn't at our school; he lived out in the sticks, which
meant Martin Flynn couldn't easily get at him when they broke up.

—*Someone else did though, didn't they?*

—Yeah, they did. Who got the blame? George Meldby. He never denied it either. No one in Ergarth could understand that part.

Jason's choice of words is strange here. If George Meldby voluntarily admitted to burning down the Fellman's factory, 'blame' wasn't an issue. Jason shrugs when I put this to him and I get the feeling, not for the first time, that he's building to something. Again it's like he's deciding the direction our interview takes, like he wants me to ask a particular question, go down a particular path.

—Tommy Fellman had been all over Facebook, calling Elizabeth a slag and a cheat, and all that. You've seen Elizabeth's YouTube, right? It's all this nicey-nicey stuff. She'd only just started it back then and she couldn't have Tommy Fellman fucking it all up for her. She was supposed to be a fucking inspiration for anyone in Ergarth. Pretty and successful. Tommy Fellman was ruining it by daring to question all that. Then his family's factory burned down. Worked out pretty well for 'Lizzie B' don't you think?

—*I think it definitely shows a pattern of behaviour surrounding your late sister.*

—Exactly. It shows what people were willing to do for her. Even then. Everyone wanted to be like her, to be *in* with her. They'd do literally anything. I bet if Elizabeth had told people to kill their own nannas to be in her bloody shopping videos, they would have done it.

I saw all this happen from the bottom, from where Martin Flynn and George Meldby were. I saw all of this unfold, all this huge clusterfuck of events. I was there for most of it.

—*So, in your eyes, what was it that Solomon Meer and the other two had against her? Was it this power that they resented?*

—I don't think it's that simple. I think they all just got totally carried away.

—*How so?*

—People like Martin Flynn and George Meldby – I think they loved her, they were obsessed, but knew they never had a chance with her. And she played on that, kept stringing them along until it finally broke them.

—*It sounds like you're saying she brought it on herself.*

—I suppose in a way I am. Honestly, at school, everyone thought the sun shone out of her arse. So everyone started subscribing to her YouTube channel; everyone started following her on Instagram.

—*What was it that everyone was following?*

—I dunno. I don't even get it. All she did was videos of shopping, opening boxes of make-up and clothes. Tours of her bedroom, for fuck's sake. Who watches that shit? I'm younger than her and I don't get it. I know that Martin Flynn and George Meldby weren't interested in what she'd bought from Primark, that's for sure!

Why didn't she use this popularity to show something that *mattered?*

—*Like an exposé of Flynn's Meats?*

—That would be better than looking at the colour of some lipstick, for fuck's sake.

—*What about Solomon Meer? He doesn't sound like he was the same as the other two.*

—I didn't know him at all. All I know was that he wasn't particularly well liked when he first came to Ergarth High. By anyone. Teachers didn't like him because he was always mouthing off. Kids thought he was a scruff and a weirdo. He got kicked out of school didn't he? For starting on Mr Threlfall in assembly. That was pretty funny to be fair.

He was smart though, but cocky. And teachers hate that. Other people didn't like him cos … well, he didn't really fit in anywhere. He was a troublemaker, but he was clever. He got in fights but he wasn't really a bully. Everyone has him down as a vampire-obsessed cult leader. But really, the guy just didn't care for personal hygiene and liked to read about vampires, that was all. For some people, though, that was almost fucking criminal.

I want to move away from the years at Ergarth High and closer to the time that Elizabeth was killed. Jason's told me that he visited

friends in Ergarth not long before her death. I wonder if Jason had
any experience of his sister's killers during this and his other occasional
visits to his home town.

—*Did you ever run into any of the three when you were here? Did*
you see them around?

—I might have passed them in the street, I don't know. I had
better things to do than look for scum like George and Martin.

—*What about Solomon Meer? He worked in a bookshop, didn't*
he?

—Yep. I never saw him either, but then I was told no one did
really. He was either hanging round Ergarth Dene or up in the
Vampire Tower. No one really saw much of him until the Dead in
Six Days challenge started.

— *'Shopping Trolley Sledge'?*

—Yes! That video! That was everywhere. I got sent it a few times
and I suppose it was pretty good. I mean, until Elizabeth hijacked
it and made it all about her.

Solomon Meer has been presented, by everyone I've talked to, as a
bit of a dark soul and an outsider. However, there's been no one who
can offer any real insight into him. The closest we have come is our
account from Amirah in episode two, who has described him as an
attention-seeker and as 'OK' at times. I have gleaned that Solomon
Meer may have already had some underlying problems when he arrived
in Ergarth and being an outsider only exacerbated them.

—*I'm thinking that Solomon Meer took exception to this, as you*
call it, 'hijacking' of his video.

—Solomon and the other two killed Elizabeth because of it.
That's the story, isn't it? They locked her in the tower and chopped
off her head because she was popular on YouTube and they weren't.
She was one of life's winners and they were losers. I should hate
them and should see them as savages, animals – especially
Solomon, because he instigated it all didn't he? He called her to
the tower that night.

—That's what the story is.

—That's what it is so far. Yes.

'So far'. I wish Jason would give me more of a clue here. He doesn't though, and I feel like I'm still scratching around for the right question.

Then I remember something else, something that Amirah told me in episode two, concerning the three killers. It may be nothing. It may be something. It's better than silence, anyway.

—*Do you remember anything about a party? When you were back in school? A girl whose house got destroyed. People blamed Solomon Meer, George Meldby and Martin Flynn for that too.*

Jason is very still for a few moments and I wonder what he's thinking. He finally nods his head.

—Yeah. Yeah, I remember that. It was a few years after they'd all left school. Look, I was at that party too.

—*It's been alleged that Solomon, George and Martin locked a girl in the bathroom. Possibly a precedent for what happened to Elizabeth?*

—Yeah. That's the thing that comes out of that entire story. Like they were practising. Of course there's more to that than most people know.

—*Can you tell me?*

—Yes I can. I can also tell you that the girl who it happened to, Gemma Hines, she's been forgotten in all of this. I guess my question would be: what if she deserved it?

—*What? Deserved her house to be smashed up? A sixteen-year-old girl?*

—I'm not saying she did. The press did though, didn't they? According to them, Gemma Hines was a narcissistic brat who'd deliberately made sure that her party got out of hand so she could go sadfishing on social media?

—*Was that the case?*

—Maybe. Maybe it wasn't. This is the thing about stories. As you well know. So Gemma Hines was actually a bit like Solomon in that she joined Ergarth High from somewhere else; somewhere down south. She had that accent: Essex or Kent or whatever, they all sound the same. But she was totally different to Solomon when she joined.

—*How so?*

—Gemma Hines knew how to play the game; she just fitted straight in; it was like she'd always been there. You had to be though, if you wanted to be OK in school. You had to look good and you had to fit in. You couldn't stand out. That's where she got it right and Solomon got it wrong. Gemma Hines, by year eleven, was just another thoroughly unpleasant creature at the top end of the school food chain. That's what she had to become to survive.

—*She was popular?*

—If you like that sort of thing, I suppose. She hid who she really was behind a mask; all bleached hair and fake tan. Lads went crazy for her. She was pretty I suppose. She was nice as well, at first.

—*What do you mean?*

—She was just a genuinely nice person, at first; loved animals, always hanging around down near Myrmirth stables, feeding the horses. But then she had to change. I watched it – I could see her change. It was weird; she used to smile but that smile turned into a stupid pout or a scowl. She would do that 'Oh my god!' thing under her breath if a teacher ever asked her to do anything. I watched Gemma Hines climb every rung on that ladder to get to the top, and I saw her leave a lot of valuable stuff behind to get there. Shedding all of who she was to become popular.

—*But isn't that just growing up? People have to find their place?*

—I suppose. It just made me sad, that's all, to see what she went from, and then what she became.

—*Which was?*

—By the time she had that party, she was fully fledged. She was one of those who just constantly posted selfies, I mean, like at least ten, sometimes fifteen a day. All the same, duck pout, with captions like 'felt cute might delete xx' that sort of thing. It was just for her to get likes and comments off lads – that's all that seemed to matter to her. It didn't matter what the attention was, so long as it was attention. Hence the party.

—*What are you saying?*

—I'm saying there's more ways to get attention than just taking selfies. As I said – I was at that party. And what happened to Gemma – everyone there said she did it willingly. And she let Solomon and the others call their mates because it was going to go online, the video of it. It didn't matter if she looked stupid or ridiculous, the whole party was going to be massive online, and that's all that mattered to her.

—*You're saying that Solomon, George and Martin took Gemma willingly to the bathroom, locked her in and then trashed her house. But she wanted them to. To what end? To film it and get more 'likes' than Elizabeth?*

—To me, it just looked like chaos; it looked like someone had it in for Gemma Hines. It's fucked up isn't it? I don't know for sure. What I do know was that people will do anything, I mean *anything* to get 'internet famous'.

—*That's sad.*

—Yeah. It really was. It is. That's all some girls lived for, most of the lads too! Likes and comments. Nothing else seemed to mean anything to them. I hated all that, I still do. It's like poison, it's like an addiction; it *is* an addiction. People are just obsessed with themselves, with validation. That's why so many people are hooked on their phones, constantly checking their social media. I saw that start at school, and now adults are doing it. It's fucking tragic.

—*That seems more Elizabeth's world than Solomon Meer's though.*

—I think Solomon Meer posted his 'Shopping Trolley Sledge' video just for fun. I think he had no idea it would go viral. But then Elizabeth wanted a piece of that.

—*The three at the party though: Solomon, George and Martin. They were acting together, right?*

—That's the thing. That's what everyone thought but … I don't know. I just didn't see it like that.

—*Really? How did it seem to you?*

—Like, Solomon Meer didn't really *do* anything. A few people said that George Meldby and Martin Flynn locked *Solomon* and Gemma in the bathroom. Solomon Meer got the blame for it all, because … that's just what happened to Solomon Meer. He got the blame. A bit like me I suppose.

—*That's interesting. It raises something else I'd like to ask you about.*

Something I'm struggling with is why would Elizabeth have gone to meet Solomon Meer on the night she died? Can you offer any insight?

—She would have gone to meet anyone if she thought there was something in it for her. If she could get something out of it. That sounds really harsh, doesn't it? That's why I've never really spoken up. That's why I've never told anyone about who Elizabeth was, what she was like. Statues and snowmen. People don't want to see her that way.

—*I've found there's often several sides to every story.*

—Yeah. I know. That's why … Listen. There was one other thing about my sister and Solomon Meer. I can tell you, but there's not much I know about it. I think you'll just be frustrated.

—*You never know…*

—I mean, no one knows about this … except my parents. And Elizabeth of course.

—*Go on…*

—It's a pretty weird one. I dunno what to make of it all. I was down here at the time, but apparently, just a few days before Elizabeth was murdered, Solomon Meer was at the house. At my parents' house.

—*What? Really?*

According to Jason, his parents woke up in the middle of the night to strange noises. Thinking they were being burgled, Mr Barton went to investigate, armed with a cricket bat, and came face to face with Solomon Meer who was trying desperately to escape through the front door.

This is something that has never surfaced before, as far as I'm aware. I'm genuinely shocked. Jason nods and sits back. This feels like his trump card. Again, I get the impression that I need to react in the correct way to this revelation. My question has to be the right one. This feels like my last chance.

—*What happened? Did they call the police?*

—No. I never could understand why not. According to my dad they'd 'dealt with it there and then'

—*Dealt with what? What was Solomon Meer doing in the house?*

—They would never say. They said it was 'dealt with' and that was all I needed to know. That was my parents all over. They knew best. But then Elizabeth was killed a few days later.

There are no police records that I am aware of, nor anything else that relates to this alleged incident. It's impossible for me to know if it is true. This has been the hook behind Jason's lure. Now I need it to pull me in the right direction.

Jason shrugs and tells me that's all he knows about it. He tells me it was this sort of attitude from his parents that made him move as far away from them as he could.

—I think they were too bothered about how it would make them look. They didn't want to associate with someone like Solomon. They put that above their own safety. And Elizabeth's I guess.

—*What I don't get is why on earth your parents didn't call the police. Especially after what happened.*

—Not gonna lie. I think my parents preferred stories to what was really going on. They were good at telling their own. About us, about me and Elizabeth – the black sheep, the good daughter. I've got a feeling that this might have scuppered that story.

—*But why?*

—My guess is as good as yours.

—*And what is your guess? Are your parents to blame for Elizabeth's death?*

—I know my parents and my theory … well … it's just a theory, like. I think there may have been something going on there, something my family didn't want Ergarth knowing about.

—*Between Elizabeth and Solomon Meer?*

—Like I say, your guess is as good as mine. But let's just say my parents liked to be seen in the best possible light and associating with Solomon Meer would have been their worst nightmare. They were that superficial.

—*Jason, I need to know more about this.*

—That's why you're here though, isn't it? To find out who locked Lizzie in the tower? I couldn't find out anything about what happened that night, but maybe you could? If you ask the right people.

—*OK, I'm asking you right now; why didn't you tell the police that Solomon Meer had been in your parents' house a few days before your sister was killed.*

—It's almost like you haven't been listening. Elizabeth was the one with the power in that house. Not Mam, not Dad, least of all me. You're not asking the right question – the question is why *Elizabeth* didn't want anyone knowing Solomon Meer was in the house. There's a story there that needs telling and you're the one to tell it.

Something suddenly clicks and I prepare myself for Jason to shut up shop and terminate our interview.

—*Jason. Who wrote the calling card on your parents' wall?*

He smiles and puts a finger to his lips.

—I'm Elizabeth's brother so I can tell you one thing about her: all her actions fed and nurtured one thing: herself. It's hard to see it from the outside, but I lived it, and I lived through it. I saw her every day. Every single thing she did was thought out, planned, and devised to make her look better or make someone else feel worse. The day I left home, when I realised Mam and Dad wouldn't see it, I swore I'd devote my life to protecting those who can't protect themselves from people like my sister. Who locked Elizabeth Barton in the tower? Lizzie B did.

I've told you some of the story. I think you need to find out some more. I think you need to know everyone's story. You know all about stories. You were told a story about your life. You never questioned it. Not until your hand was forced. Force this story too. You've got three more episodes to find out why I kept my mouth shut about Solomon Meer that night too.

Jason stands up. I begin to ask him to stay for one more question but stop. He won't. He's said his piece; shattered the image of his late sister and is now leaving me to pick through the shards.

So where next? I feel like there are some significant questions about Elizabeth and her killers that need more perspectives, that need answers.

Were Solomon Meer, George Meldby and Martin Flynn on some warped righteous mission to rid the world of narcissistic young women? Was the incident at the party with Gemma Hines a trial run? What on earth was Solomon Meer doing at the Barton house? I initially subscribed to the vague theory that some type of online rivalry between Elizabeth Barton and Solomon Meer might be at the heart of what happened. But now, I feel I've drifted even further from the truth.

In this episode, I feel like I've learned more about Elizabeth Barton than Jason. I've learned that some stories don't get told and that there are two sides to every tale. I want to put the differing views we now have of Elizabeth in context, because she no longer has a voice.

That's where my path leads next.

I have been Scott King and this has been Six Stories.

Until next time.

Lizzie B
3,689 subscribers

A nip and a punch for the start of the month,
I've only got two days of this one left,
Cos in two days I'm going to meet a vampire,
In two days, I'm going to die!

Hey everyone! It's March and it's still snowing. *Yay, I'm so unbelievably happy. Can you tell from just how happy my voice is? I love being constantly cold and everything being shut. It's so great.*

Can I just ask that everyone keeps up with the giving; not just #givingmondayback, but Tuesday and Wednesday too — all the days, because it's just horrible *out there and people are suffering!*

To be fair, I'm suffering too! Look guys, I'm wearing gloves! *Indoors! It's that cold, really. I just can't get my fingers warm.*

*Thank you so much for the love for the last challenge! Look at these bee-*yootifal *flowers! You guys are so kind!*

No, I'm not going into how I did it, but isn't he just totally adorable? I can't get enough of his little face. I promise we'll go and see him in a minute.

Right now we're on day four of the Dead in Six Days challenge and I tell you something, Vladlena the Vampire's got her work cut out because I'm smashing it. Big time!

So I'm now just getting his milk together – he needs to drink this formula stuff, so that's just here. Just giving it a shake. It's got to be warm, too. Listen … listen to that … can you hear him? Oh my God, I'm going to die of cuteness. He knows I'm coming with his milk, bless his little face.

So just before we go see him, I need to tell you all that the votes are in! No, he's not going to be called Sheepy McSheepFace, even though that name was a close second. We're going to call him … Billy! Billy the Lamb, or Billy the Baby Ram I suppose! He's just so totally adorable, so fluffy and cute and … there you go … you can hear him make that lovely little bleating noise!

Look, I'm going out into the garden and … oh my that's cold. Billy! Billy! Come here!

Look, here he comes. Aw, here you go little guy, here's your milk. Oh my God, I'm totally never eating meat again … can you believe this little guy was going to slaughter? Thanks guys but I'm really not a hero at all. Just gonna put it out there to say it's lucky he was rescued and, of course, I may or may not have had something to do with that!

Now he's safe and warm and … OK … OK I'll stop.

Yeah, so my parents weren't best pleased that their garden shed is now a home for Billy the Lamb. Mind you, it's not like they're ever here. If you want to see how I turned the garden shed from a grimy, spidery place to store the lawnmower into a little lamb heaven, the link is below, give it a clickaroo and I'll see you back here in a bit.

So task number three has been the most popular one yet. If you follow me on Instagram, I'm Lizzie B there too, and you can see a lot of photos of Billy. He's Internet famous already – he'll probably need his own channel soon!

Anyhoo! That's enough about the little fluffy one. So cute! So, so cute!

Now down to the nitty gritty; it's time for the penultimate Dead in Six Days challenge! Yes, of course, here we go … the lovely Vladlena has been in touch. You'll see that her next challenge is a little … obscure, shall we say?

'Rob from the Rich, Give to the Poor' … I mean, it doesn't sound particularly interesting, does it? I'm getting a whole Robin Hood vibe going on here. But I know you, Vladlena, I know all your tricks! You like some stealing don't you? What's that word? A kleptomaniac, you are, or else you're just trying to get me into trouble! Either way, we need to get more likes and more subs for this next one.

I'm a little bit dubious about live streaming this challenge as the snow and the weather are really messing with my Internet. Connection's not great to be honest and I don't want to disappoint you guys. So watch this space!

Sub-to-the-scribe, smash the likes, hit the bell icon and that way you'll know when the next video of Billy the Lamb goes up – I swear, you'll want to sub just for him!

Oh and I've got three days left to live!

See you soon!

Episode 4: Old Photographs

—Your honour, my name is Harold William Barton. This statement represents the thoughts of myself and my wife, Mildred Ethel Barton.

When our lovely daughter was taken from us so savagely and prematurely, it decimated our family. Our grief is impossible to describe. Elizabeth was our first child. We watched her grow from a beautiful, cheerful baby into an ambitious and driven young woman. All we have left now are our photographs and memories of our child.

Elizabeth was a beautiful and successful person, she saw her life as a challenge and strove to master whatever was put before her. Horse riding, gymnastics, football, debating, tennis – Elizabeth took all of these things on and the medals she won are testament to her competitive nature.

Elizabeth worked hard and never took anything for granted. From a young age we instilled in her a belief that hard work pays off and that life did not give hand-outs. Elizabeth achieved top grades in her studies as well as her extracurricular activities. Elizabeth's bedroom, still painted in the pink of her childhood, is festooned with medals and rosettes, reminders of all she had achieved and wished to achieve in life.

Although a grown woman, Elizabeth was not ready to leave home. Maybe we took for granted her presence in our house – her laughter, the sound of her voice and the familiar *ding* of her phone. It's now silent and we are poorer for it. There is an empty space at our kitchen table, an empty space at mealtimes where Elizabeth would sit and talk to us about her days of school, her interests, her hobbies and her activities. If Elizabeth's younger brother, Jason, who she loved like only a big sister could, was here today, we know he would share our thoughts.

I would like to tell those who denied us another day with our daughter – in such a callous and devastating way – that it is hard for us to forgive them. We are only human. I wonder, as you snatched our daughter from us, if you knew what it was you were doing.

What you have taken from us is our reason for being, the reason for our existence. What you have given to us is emptiness, silence and endless questions.

All we wish for you is that someday you see – and more importantly are able to feel – the true weight of what you have done. For you have not only taken our little girl from us, you have punched a hole in our very being, a hole that we will never fill.

Please think about this, your honour, during your sentencing: the road to rehabilitation begins with acknowledgement of the weight of a crime. But that is only the first step on a long journey. We, in our grief, are unable to begin our journey. There is no recovery for us. Our pain will last our lifetime and into the next.

Welcome to Six Stories

I'm Scott King.

What you've just heard is the impact statement from the Barton family at the trial of Solomon Meer, George Meldby and Martin Flynn. The statement was read to the judge before the sentence was imposed on the three young men.

Harold Barton has kept a copy of the statement and the weight of its words lies heavy across the living room where we sit for this episode's interview. Mr Barton is stoic as he reads, the pain in his eyes and on his face, betraying the power of his voice. This is only the second time that Mr Barton has read this statement out loud and when he finishes it, the resonance of it hangs in the air between us.

Harold and Mildred Barton were not satisfied with the sentences handed down to the three killers but would any punishment have been enough?

—I don't believe in the death penalty. What is it they say? – An eye for an eye leaves the whole world blind. Ghandi, that was, wasn't it? He was right, of course, but it's hard. It's hard to think like that after what happened.

I cannot imagine how this must feel for Mr and Mrs Barton. I have come to meet Elizabeth's parents with a thousand questions, but really, I want to let them speak. I want to see Elizabeth through the eyes of those who loved and cherished her most of all.

—No parent should have to bury their child. No parent. There's no coming back from pain like this.

The Barton house is set back from a main road and is enclosed by a wall and wrought-iron fences; in the garden there are trimmed rose bushes and neat shrubs. The graffiti on the wall has been cleaned off.
The house is modern, built in the 1990s, perhaps: three floors with stone stairs up to the front door – faux Victoriana. Inside it is simple, modest. Clean and comfortable. Despite it being not far out of Ergarth proper, the difference in the class of people who live here is obvious. The paintwork is neat, and there are framed photographs of the family in happier times and a crucifix on the wall. A sloppy brown spaniel snores on a rag rug before a coal-effect fireplace.
Mr Barton is sitting on a large leather sofa.

—This is Sammy. Lazy thing. We got him from a breeder last week. Beautiful, isn't he?

At the sound of his name, Sammy's ear twitches and his back leg moves in a slow-motion scamper. Our attention shifts gratefully until Mildred Barton, a slight woman with black hair and wide blue eyes, comes in with a teapot and mugs. Harold tucks the statement he's just read to me into a brown leather folder, which he places on a side table.
Mrs Barton sits down and turns her eyes on me. She smiles, her face creasing. There's no joy in the expression.

—No one's been interested in Elizabeth. Not really. They only ever want to talk about what those lads did to her. That's the thing we can't understand. That stays with us now; it'll never go away. The knowledge of what they did to our beautiful girl. So savage. So inhuman.

It was Harold who identified Elizabeth's body, he tells me.

—After that, I drove through Ergarth, my home, and I looked around. I looked at the place like I'd never looked at it before. Everything was still frozen; the roads had been gritted and there were great piles of slush everywhere. The verges were spattered pink and the sky was a soulless grey. The cold was relentless, unending, uncaring. I even went out to that tower; drove past and just stared at it. It was freezing – that cold that gets into your fingers. That was about the only thing I *could* feel.

I drove around the town faster and faster, something inside me praying I'd slip. Because all I could see in my head was what they did to her. All I could feel about this entire town was that it didn't care. There was no heart, no community, no compassion. Just endless grey. That's what we brought our Elizabeth into. An endless grey.

All anyone has to say is that they wonder why they did it, those three. That's how it is these days. The killers become the story. The criminals are more exciting than the victims. We're the ones left behind in all this. No one wants to know about us, what we have to say.

—*I'm only here to talk to you both about your daughter, Mr Barton. As much as you want to. We can start where you like and we can stop whenever you want. But I'm here to listen.*

Mildred pours the tea. It's begun raining outside, and the slight patter of the drops against the windows is soothing. There is no awkwardness between us; just a reverential solemnity. Mrs Barton leans forwards and pulls a photograph album from underneath the coffee table. She turns the pages gently, touching only their edges. I have questions that are burning inside me, especially the one about Solomon Meer being here, at the Barton's house, a few days before Elizabeth died. I've been wracking my brains to come up with a possible reason. Was this an early attempt on Elizabeth's life? If so, why didn't anyone call the authorities – straight away, or at some point after Elizabeth's death?

Or was he invited here? Or here on other business – on the command of Elizabeth, or someone in her family? If so, what business? Jason Barton told me to 'force this story' about the death of his sister. I can only hope I've chosen correctly.

I want to dive in straight away, get this question in the room, but it would be tactless to be so abrupt, right after Harold Barton has shown me a little of his anguish.

Mildred sighs and turns another page in the photograph album on her lap.

—We don't look at these very often, Mr King. Only on special occasions, so they don't become too familiar. There's always something new to see when I turn these pages, something I've forgotten or some new memory. One day, there won't be. Hopefully I'll be gone before then.

It's heartbreaking to see the couple look through the photographs of their late daughter, savouring them like chocolates. I feel wrong being here at all. I feel like I'm intruding on their moment. But the Bartons agreed to an interview, they even welcomed it. If they don't feel like they want to speak about her death or those who caused it, I have made it clear that is fine. The last thing I want to do is exploit these people's grief.

However, some of the things Jason told me about Elizabeth are also humming at the forefront of my mind, and I feel that they must, at some point, be addressed.

—We read that article in *The Times* about you Mr King.

Mildred Barton's eyes are wet with tears.

—About what … happened to you when you were young. I don't know why, but it feels like, if anyone could understand our pain, it would be you.

We're all damaged somehow. It's a strange one; since the revelations about my past unfolded in front of the world, people have felt like they can relate to me; they can connect. It was a reaction I was not expecting. In some perverse way, it feels sometimes as if the darkness inside me gets me into places I may not have had access to before. But that access comes with its own guilt. Am I using my own trauma as a way in? Am I being disingenuous? The way I justify it to myself, is that if someone feels they can relate to me, that I might understand them, then that's OK.

The photograph album is a nice way to begin. The Bartons tell me that they are aware that for me, there is no album of baby photos. And for my part, learning a little about Elizabeth Barton as a young child is somehow comforting.

According to the Bartons, Elizabeth was an intelligent baby; inquisitive and well behaved, she slept well, and exceeded all her developmental targets. I recognise Mr and Mrs Barton in the photographs, yet there always seems to be a different face holding Elizabeth. Mildred Barton explains.

—We both worked a lot. We both worked hard. Enough to give our children everything they wanted. Unfortunately that meant we were not always there as much as we wanted to be. These women are nannies, babysitters and the like. Lovely women, all of them. But they were young, always temporary; we could never find someone who would stay with us long term, unfortunately.

Mr Barton chips in, wagging his finger.

—Mind you, there was always plenty of food in the cupboards and a roof over their heads. Elizabeth and Jason never wanted for food and shelter. Never. We provided for them. Not like our parents did for us.

I don't want to stray too far from the subject, but I think it's important to know where both Harold and Mildred Barton are coming from. Both grew up poor, the son and daughter of a shipbuilder and a trawler man, respectively. 'Dirt poor' are the words they both use. Harold Barton continues.

—Both our fathers were hard men, wouldn't you say, my love? Hard workers. Hard drinkers too. That's what it was like back then. There wasn't much in the way of work. The shipbuilding was all but gone from the North-East, the trawler men made little and were away a lot. We were both … disappointed … when we were children. There was never much on birthdays and Christmas. Sometimes nothing. We didn't want our children to grow up like that. So we made sure they were never disappointed. With anything.

Mildred and Harold Barton were both high achievers academically, escaping their modest childhoods by way of work. Harold went from a delivery driver to being a trustee on the board for Hylux – one of the biggest UK haulage companies. Mildred was regional director of the Pinston boutique hotel chain. They had their children later in life and both are now retired.

As Elizabeth grew into a toddler, she was plied with toys and books. There are many photographs of the youngster amid piles of cuddly toys. The Bartons, however, began to show some concern over Elizabeth's interactions with other children.

Mildred Barton shows me a photograph of a chubby-faced Elizabeth at around three years, sat amid a tight circle of cuddly toys while two other children play together on the outside of the ring of stuffed animals. It's a poignant image, not lost on Mildred Barton.

—That was all her doing, Mr King. She would surround herself with toys, sat in the middle, orchestrating the tea party. That was Elizabeth. She was always happiest when she was in charge, when she was calling the shots. But when she started going to nursery or the crèche at the church hall, that's when we thought something might be amiss.

There wasn't a problem as such, it wasn't that she couldn't play with other children, she just preferred to be alone, lost in her little world by herself. It seemed, to us anyway, that when other children joined in Elizabeth just…

—They just didn't understand her, did they, my love?

—We never saw it as a problem. That's just who she was. Her personality was emerging, that was all. I told the nannies and the childminders to take her to all the baby groups while we were working. It wasn't like she wasn't socialised.

—*Did this introversion ever become a problem, when she was older, or was it just a little-kid thing?*

—No, it was always a part of who she was. She was never unhappy with others, she just preferred her own company.

—*What about when she started school? Did things change?*

—I feel like that was when we started to lose her. I know how that sounds; it was so early, but it's true. Primary school just seemed like a big competition: who had the best toys, who had the most things. We couldn't be there to pick her up but there was always a present waiting for her when she got home … we always made sure that she wasn't the one missing out…

Mildred Barton has begun crying. It is silent, just tears down her cheeks, a hairline crack in her voice. I pause for a moment, let her compose herself. There's a word in here that has felt to me like it is a cornerstone of this case: 'competition'.

A snore from Sammy breaks the tension and Mildred passes the open photograph album to her husband.

Even from a young age, Harold tells me, Elizabeth was a hard worker. She loved to achieve. As you heard in the statement at the beginning of this episode, they still keep all her trophies and rosettes pinned to the walls of her bedroom – which is now, like so many bedrooms in the aftermath of a tragedy, a shrine.

—Look, Harold, do you want to explain about this one? The Sunday Club?

Mr Barton takes the album from his wife and points to a photograph. The inside of a church hall, a group of children stand before a trestle table; all of them look around eight to ten years old. They are muddy, smiling, some of them have brown stains around their mouths.

—That was the Ergarth Explorers group. The Sunday Club I thought that it might help her with … with the others … Look, we'd just been building a camp fire that evening down the Dene. It was a cold one that night. All the children were warming up with some hot chocolate. It was a lovely evening. Magical. There's Elizabeth there.

A young Elizabeth Barton grins, gap-toothed at the camera. Harold runs his finger along the row of children, naming names. Behind them there is a frieze on the wall – a giant whale and a little boat: Jonah and the Whale in cut-out card. Green see-through-plastic seaweed. He continues.

—It was just a little thing I helped out at when she was little. I thought it would make up for me working all the time. I did it when I could, helped out with the seven- and eight-year-olds. Just for the church. We didn't call it Sunday School and no one preached to them. It was something to do – making things, listening to stories, singing. Campfires and marshmallows in the autumn. Elizabeth and her school friends. She invited them all, and look at who came, look how many of them wanted to join in. It's heart-breaking really.

There is only one set of photographs from this particular event, which suggests to me that it was only this once that Harold Barton helped out. Elizabeth and two others are the only children there. Harold doesn't need to tell me how he feels he failed his daughter. He tells me he was hugely relieved when Elizabeth's popularity soared in her later years. This is a huge conflict in Elizabeth's life that cannot go unnoticed.

Mr Barton's finger points out a third child I did not notice in the photograph. A small boy standing just off from the others. He's pale, his eyes on the floor.

—George Meldby. There he is.

There is a pregnant pause and I feel the atmosphere in the room tighten. Harold's finger stays below the pale boy and he looks past me, out of the window. Mildred gets up and drifts away into the kitchen. I say nothing. Eventually Harold speaks.

—Even when they're that age, you can tell how they're going to turn out. There's the talkative ones, the shy ones, the naughty ones. It all starts emerging at that age. George was summer-born, one of the youngest in the year. His mother was ... well, she was a funny one, with all her dogs and the house full of junk and tanks of lizards. We all knew that, and we all felt a bit sorry for little George. Everyone did. He was an odd one even then. They caught him trying to set a fire in the girls' toilet. And when he was caught, he tried to blame our Elizabeth for it! Said she told him to do it! I mean, I ask you. Everyone knew the Flynn boy as well. We kept our daughter as far away from his lot as possible. He was a nasty little thug from the off.

I'm glad to say we have no photographs with him in them. They kept themselves to themselves up at that terrible place on Skelton Road. I imagine he was taught how to kill things from a young age.

—Were he and Elizabeth and George Meldby all friends?

Harold Barton sighs and a look passes between him and his wife. Eventually Harold clears his throat and puffs out his chest.

—Like we said, Elizabeth found it hard with other children when she was little. We just didn't think associating with George Meldby, considering ... er ... how he was, how his family was, was a very good idea. We discouraged the association, let's say. But the lad wouldn't leave our Elizabeth alone. What could we do? We had words with that bloody mother of his down on the Prim – the Primrose Villas estate. When we drove down there, I thought the car would be stolen, if I left it too long. I told her in no uncertain terms to keep him away from our Elizabeth.

Harold Barton shows me another couple of photographs from the Sunday Club night. George Meldby always sits just on the outside, his wide eyes staring at Elizabeth as if posing some eternal question. It sends a shiver through me, so I cannot imagine how the Bartons feel I wonder why they keep these particular photographs. Everyone grieves in their own way, though. Everyone has their own way of bearing such trauma. I'm not going to question the Bartons'.

Mildred takes over and flicks through more of the album until the page comes to rest on a photo of Elizabeth in a school uniform. She is stood straight-backed in the porch. Sun pours in through the coloured glass. Mildred sighs. The difference in Elizabeth's appearance is striking. Her face is almost stern, her mouth a line and her eyes serious. She looks significantly older than her years.

—This was her first day of year seven. She was twelve. Elizabeth … developed … quite early on. She certainly had a growth spurt. But she also grew academically as well.

—*Were her high-school years better than in primary school?*

—Yes. So much better. It was at high school that she really started to flourish.

—*What do you think was different for her there?*

—It felt like a new start. She had matured physically, of course. And it was easier for her to achieve things in high school. She was part of everything, all the sports teams, the after-school clubs and she won in all of them. That in itself brought new friendships and new opportunities. It was like she left the old Elizabeth behind in primary school. This was the new version.

—*What about at home? Did the two of you notice anything different about her?*

There is an odd moment when the Bartons look at each other, puzzled. Harold Barton takes over.

—They're hard at that age, teenagers. Want nothing to do with you. Want to be shut away with their computers and their phones and everything, don't they? The times we were here, Elizabeth was busy with her videos and things, wasn't she? We couldn't get our heads around all that, but we made sure she had the best of it. The computer, the phone, the lights. Look what came of it: she was making a living from it in the end, wasn't she? She was forever off in that car of hers, working with the down-and-outs, making her videos. Doing good work, not like some of them.

—*So Elizabeth fitted in socially at Ergarth High, is that right?*
—Oh yes. She was really very popular. It was like she'd been a little cocoon all this time and was just spreading her wings. Her beautiful new wings.

There's another look between Mr and Mrs Barton. Mildred nods pointedly at her husband, who sighs and shifts in his chair. I pretend I haven't noticed and wait for whatever this niggling thing is to come out. Eventually, a red-faced Harold Barton speaks.

—There was something else. Yes. From the start of school. Something Mildred and I just … I mean, we're not old stick-in-the-muds. We're not prudes but…

Mildred picks up the tail end of this thread.

—Elizabeth always had a lot of hangers-on, little followers. But in high school, it was different. The other students, you see, they were from all over – there were a lot of different sorts of people at that school. Older people, people Elizabeth didn't know and they were very eager to … well…
Are we talking male attention here, boyfriends?

Harold lifts a hand and takes over.

—Truth is, Mr King, our daughter was trusting. Sometimes too much so, and there were people who would take advantage of a beautiful young girl like that. Especially the older ones.

Harold sighs and I can see the pain in his face as he ploughs on, staring down at his slippers. Mildred holds his hand.

—They grow up so fast. In the blink of an eye they're suddenly so far away from you. You see, we found out Elizabeth had been … she'd been, she'd not been telling us everything.
—*What sorts of things hadn't she told you?*
—There'd been boyfriends. More than we knew about. But

some had been older, much older. Elizabeth was only young. She was a little girl. How could she have known what to do?

—It's not like I didn't try to tell Elizabeth about the birds and the bees and everything. We were both very progressive, I think they call it, about all that. It's better if these things are out in the open, isn't it? A mother and her daughter should talk about these things rather than suppressing them? That's when things go wrong, when things are left unsaid.

—*I agree. How did Elizabeth respond when you tried to talk to her?*

—She was … cold; that's a good word for it. She would sit and listen to everything I had to say; not wide-eyed, not shocked, just with a sort of acceptance. Then usually she would just nod and say 'OK Mam' and that would be it.

—*Did she never have questions? Did she never confide in you?*

—No. On both accounts. Never. I would sometimes ask her about boys, expecting her to go red, to try and bat away my questions but … her actual responses were worse somehow.

—*How do you mean?*

—They would just be so matter-of-fact. She dated them for a little while and then it was over. No more than that. I remember once we were shopping in town for some new school clothes. Making an afternoon of it, coffee and cake and stuff. Elizabeth was so well behaved. She never rolled her eyes or moaned; never coveted new phones or trainers. She just went along with me. We were in JD Sports, looking at trainers, and I saw these lads looking at her. I mean she would only have been about fourteen. Anyhow, you can tell when someone's staring and they're pretending not to — and these boys kept shoving each other and giggling. It was quite sweet, really.

—*How did Elizabeth react to that?*

—It was like she hadn't even noticed. I never understood it. She had so many of them following her round with their tongues hanging out, but she just seemed … indifferent to them all. If she had noticed, she just didn't care. I tried to bring it up with her afterwards, but she shrugged it off. It wasn't like she had low self-esteem … she just didn't know how to connect her emotions with that sort of thing. I don't think there was anything wrong; that was just who she was. That summed up her approach.

    —*Did you ever meet any of Elizabeth's boyfriends?*

    —There was only one that Elizabeth ever decided she would share with us.

Harold Barton directs me back to the photo album. He flicks through the pages, past pictures of Elizabeth holding more awards and rosettes. As we work through her school years, I see a girl starting to change even further; the serious look of the year seven on her first day giving way to make-up and fake tan. As fashion changes, Elizabeth keeps up; her clothes, her hair. She grows taller too. Harold stops at a photo that is unlike all the others. This one is a close-up and appears to have been taken candidly. Sunlight shines on Elizabeth Barton's face. Behind her is a crowd of other children in coats and rucksacks on a cobbled street. I'm guessing she is around fourteen or fifteen. She is laughing, her eyes slits. In one hand she holds a crepe that oozes chocolate sauce. In her other, she holds her phone, in a rubber cat-shaped case. Beside her, mimicking her mirth with an equally joyous expression, is a boy of around the same age. Maybe a little older. Harold sighs.

    —I'll never be able to tell you why, but this one always gets me. I think because she didn't know it was taken, because that laughter in her, that joy was utterly natural … it came so rarely to her after that time.

    —*Where was this taken? It looks different from the others.*

    —Yes, quite. Neither my or my wife's poor camera work here. No. This was one that came from school. It was a trip to France at the end of year nine. Only those who had got the very top marks and the best attendance in the school were allowed to attend. By all accounts, they had a wonderful time; they visited the war graves, the markets, art galleries. All with others like them. It was a wonderful experience for her. At least that's what we thought.

    —*Something went wrong on the trip?*

    —You know how young people are, especially at that age. Everything matters to them. It wasn't so much during the trip that anything went wrong, it was afterwards.

—*What happened?*

—It had something to do with the boy in the photograph – Tommy Fellman. They'd met in France and become … close.

This is the same Tommy Fellman we've heard about before – son of Horace Fellman, of Fellman's pasties fame. The French trip was organised jointly by Ergarth Boys' Grammar School and Ergarth High.

Mildred Barton re-enters the conversation, one hand on her husband's arm.

—When Elizabeth came home from France, she seemed different. In a good way. She was bubbly, shiny, more smiley than usual. She kept mentioning the name of this boy and how they'd had such fun … Well, we wondered…

—I just want to say I'm not that kind of father, Mr King. I never had a problem with our daughter having a boyfriend. I'm not an old fuddy-duddy killjoy. I was pleased for her. I hoped that she had found someone worthy of her.

Elizabeth was more open than she had ever been with her parents about anyone before. Tommy Fellman was a boy who was similar in ability, a high achiever. He was a few years above Elizabeth, part of the sixth form at Ergarth Boys' Grammar School. The Bartons found the gap in age a little troubling, but decided that they'd let it slide; they were simply happy Elizabeth was being so candid with them. They corroborate what Jason told me in the last episode – that Tommy Fellman attended dinner at the Barton household a few times. Harold Barton recalls this.

—He was perfectly well-mannered too. Polite. We actually felt a lot better about the whole thing when we met him. He was certainly the sort of boy we hoped Elizabeth would associate with, not like the rubbish who flocked around her at school.

It was a few weeks into this relationship when something went wrong. The Bartons say that Elizabeth never told them what had happened, but they got an inkling all wasn't well when Elizabeth's demeanour changed. She had gone from quite jolly to suddenly quiet and brooding. Elizabeth spent a lot of time up in her bedroom or else glued to her phone. Mildred Barton recalls that time:

—We were invited to the school not long after that; all the parents had, to an awards assembly of some kind. Elizabeth was to receive special commendations from the head for her overall performance and behaviour on the French trip. Elizabeth refused to come. We were taken aback, as she would usually jump at another award. Harold and I went dressed in our best and sat with the other parents in the hall. We couldn't not be seen to be there!

The head began displaying the photographs from the trip on the overhead projector. To our dismay and embarrassment, whenever a photo of Elizabeth appeared, there was a number of...

—Cat-calls, Mr King. Whoops and whistles from the children – it was like a building site. It was hugely humiliating for us and we were very glad that our daughter was not present.

—When that photo of Elizabeth and Tommy Fellman went up, there was a cheer, but like Harold says, not a nice one, it was like a football ground. The head was furious. He apologised to us afterwards but the damage was done. It was horrible. A horrible way to treat a young girl. All the older ones were joining in as well.

—That's when we started to hear things – gossip and slander about our daughter.

—*What did you hear?*

—I mean it was ridiculous. Horrible really. Heartless things that people were saying about her. It was all on Facebook apparently. Tommy Fellman was accusing Elizabeth of horrible things. He was calling her a cheat and a liar and worse. Others were joining in too. All sorts of boys were saying disgusting things about her that I will not repeat. They were calling her a cheat as well; calling her a liar. To be honest it was the first time we'd ever seen Elizabeth disappointed. All those years we'd kept such negativity from her, and this Tommy Fellman ruined everything.

This all happened online and to such a degree that Elizabeth's parents decided to intervene.

—We spoke to the heads of both schools, and they both told us this sort of thing was 'not acceptable' and 'things would be put in place', but nothing was ever done. By either of them. Our daughter just had to get through it, wait for it all to blow over, which it did. Eventually. No thanks to the schools, I may add.

—*But it did eventually stop?*

There is a rather awkward pause. The Bartons look at each other with guilty expressions. I think I know what is coming.
Harold Barton clears his throat.

—Yes, it did. Yes.

—*Was this after George Meldby burned down Fellman's factory?*

—Yes. And we saw the link just like everyone did; we didn't bury our heads in the sand. Elizabeth assured us – *swore* to us – that it was entirely coincidental. And we believed her. We still do. George Meldby burned it down of his own volition. If he was doing it to stand up for Elizabeth – well, that was his choice, not Elizabeth's. I do know Elizabeth felt sorry for George; she was that kind of girl. You could see that in her charity work. She'd always looked out for him in primary school and, well, he must have taken it the wrong way. He would have done anything for Elizabeth. There were a few like that, she was very, *very* popular.

This remark corresponds with Amirah Choudhury's – when she was describing Elizabeth's fans: her 'flying monkeys' as Amirah put it.
There's something that has been rankling throughout this series and I think this is a good place to try and find the next path, to at least get a balanced view of Elizabeth. You see, I feel like all I've ever heard about her so far is negative. Sure, there's the charity work and the popularity online, but Jason Barton has painted a very unpleasant picture of his older sister, and Amirah Choudhury … well, I'm starting to feel that fear played more of a significant role in her relationship with Elizabeth than I thought. Of course, Elizabeth's parents are going to have a positive view of their daughter as all parents should. This is why I ask the next question.

—*I'm interested in talking to any of Elizabeth's close friends after this. The people she would have confided in, told things she couldn't tell either of you. Do you know what I mean?*

The Bartons look at each other and shrug. Mildred asks me to clarify.

—*I mean proper 'friends' — people who were always over at the house, people who she would go and meet.*

Mildred Barton gives a laugh and shakes her head.

—Well, it's all online these days isn't it? She was never off her phone. I imagine she did it all on there. If she had people over to the house, which I imagine she did, then it wasn't when we were here.
—You have to let young people do their own thing don't you? We couldn't be prying and poking into Elizabeth's business.
—Like Mildred says, she was always on that phone of hers. So she must have been talking to *someone*! I mean, what else could she have been doing?
—*Did you ever ask her about her friends.*

Another of those looks. Harold clears his throat.

—Elizabeth was … let's just say she made it very clear about her personal … barriers. Her room, her phone. She was an adult and we treated her like one. All that stuff was *hers* and if we wanted to know anything, that was *her* decision.
—That was healthy. For her to be headstrong like that.
—*Did Elizabeth ever want to move out, or was she happy at home?*
—I know she was looking for a place, when the money from her videos started rolling in. Of course, we didn't want her to leave us with an empty nest, but you can't stop them can you?

I think of Jason again, leaving Ergarth as soon as he could. I also remember him saying it was Elizabeth who had the power in the Barton household. But is he telling the truth? It's clear that Jason has

his own agenda. Right now, I want to turn my attention to Martin
Flynn. Harold Barton's face clouds over when I ask about him.

—Yes, well, I have to say I never approved of Elizabeth's
association with Martin Flynn. I told her no good would come of
it. The boy wasn't right. He was a nasty thug. He certainly wasn't
a friend. In the month before Elizabeth died, he had taken to
hanging around here at night. That was something that troubled
me. Prison is the best place for someone like that. And now we see
why.

The Bartons tell me about numerous occasions when they looked out
of their windows at night to see Martin Flynn skulking around in the
area. The Barton House is on the other side of Ergarth from the
abattoir and the Flynn family home. Harold tells me they once called
the police, but because Martin Flynn wasn't actually doing anything
wrong, there was little they could do about him.

—He technically never 'harassed' Elizabeth, never knocked on
the door or anything, nothing like that. It was almost as if he was
some kind of guard dog. Or an addict. It was certainly not normal.
Again, Elizabeth was an adult; she told us she would deal with it.
She was up in her room making her videos. She didn't have time
for all this nonsense. She assured us that the Flynn lad was no
bother to her and we believed it.

'Guard dog' and 'addict'; these are both interesting terms to use, and
I wonder if this is the right moment to ask about Solomon Meer. I
don't want to ruin the rapport we've built up. Both Harold and
Mildred are opening up about their daughter and I want them to
continue.
I turn their attention to the years after school; the years closer to
Elizabeth's encounter with Solomon Meer. Harold is the one who
answers my questions.

—*When Elizabeth left school, did she want to go into further*
education?

—No. It always puzzled us, that one. I'm afraid I got rather caught up in it all – you know, arranging visits to open days, that sort of thing. Elizabeth, bless her, humoured me for a while, came along but never showed a lot of interest.

—*So what did she want to do?*

—Some of them travel, don't they? We suggested that too, but that wasn't Elizabeth either. I think she just didn't know. She was suddenly rudderless, you see. School had been everything and now she was almost cast adrift.

We bought her a car and driving lessons, to get herself about, to give herself mobility, to make her more employable. She loved that thing, always kept it sparkling clean. And she just went out and got herself jobs. One minute she was at home, the next she was working in a pet shop. We didn't even know she'd had an interview!

It was this time when Elizabeth's YouTube channel started becoming popular. Mr and Mrs Barton said they noticed the amount of parcels that were arriving in the post. Make-up, clothes. The Bartons had no idea what to make of it – this was a world totally unfamiliar to them. Mildred smiles as she recalls Elizabeth's sudden fame.

—I have to say it was a little bit like being the mother of a film star or a singer. People would come up to me in the supermarket and tell me they'd been watching Elizabeth on the Internet! They were full of compliments. It was all very exciting, I must say.

It was her charity work that really got her noticed in the end, and we were so proud. We were proud that we'd raised someone so giving. Elizabeth was such a positive influence in people's lives, and the work she did with the homeless really exemplified that. She was using her popularity for good, that was Elizabeth. I know that just before she was kill— … before … what happened, Elizabeth was working on a new project for her channel. She was looking into setting up a foundation to help the most vulnerable in society. That was who she was. A beautiful soul.

A cloud passes over Mildred's face.

—But all that brought with it some problems, of course. As soon as your name is known, there'll be people who are jealous. It's amazing isn't it, really? Someone wants to do good, and there are those who hate them for it.

—There were people in Ergarth that actively hated Elizabeth? That must have been hard.

—Yes, well, luckily, we didn't have much trouble from them. We both worked a lot. We knew Elizabeth could handle it like a sensible adult, which she did. These people are cowards, Mr King. That's what you have to know.

—Did you know of anyone specifically who hated her?

—There was a girl, wasn't there, Harold, do you remember? Some little so-and-so … a little ne'er-do-well from Elizabeth's old school. She was a spiteful little thing who tried to exclude Elizabeth; didn't invite her to a party or something like that. I remember Elizabeth being very put out. But, of course, these things were really passing us by, by then. We had other things we had to worry about.

I am only assuming this 'so-and-so' is Gemma Hines, who deliberately didn't invite Elizabeth to her party, as Amirah and Jason have both told me. The Bartons are not able to recall much else about this incident. In fact their focus had shifted quite significantly away from their daughter just as her YouTube channel was beginning to see its first real spike in popularity.

—I hate to say it but someone was in the way of us getting to know our daughter's new world; stopping us from celebrating her new success. I know how this makes me sound when I say it. I sound like a bad mother.

—You don't, my love, you—

—I do and I want to say it because no one is perfect. None of us. We did our best. My parents were never interested in one single thing about school; they had to work. We did what we could for Jason as well as Elizabeth. we did our best. But back then, when Elizabeth started with her YouTube, it was Jason, her little brother, who we had to turn our attention to.

This is their first mention of Jason Barton, save for the impact statement at the top of the episode. Taking a quick look around the room, I see no photographs of him save for one showing a younger Barton family, posing awkwardly. Elizabeth is about four, gazing wide-eyed into the camera; a tiny bundle is in Mildred Barton's arms.

I accept more tea and ask to hear about Jason Barton. I wonder if I should mention that I've spoken to him. I leave it for now but if they ask, I'm not going to lie.

There's a stock image of Jason Barton the press use when they bother to mention him – a blurred photograph of Jason at seventeen years old, face red and creased with rage as three police officers in high-vis jackets physically restrain him. It seems that this is the summation of Jason that the world has accepted – including his parents. Mildred sighs, and there is a sadness in her voice as she talks about her son.

—Jason was a difficult birth and a difficult baby. That's the long and the short of it, I'm afraid. He was fussy, he wouldn't sleep, and the whole family were like zombies for about a year from the lack of sleep. He used to fall over a lot, get himself hurt, and it was always Elizabeth who managed to save him. So when Jason was very little and he'd just started to walk, he used to follow Elizabeth around like a little lost puppy. For a while anyway.

Mildred Barton puts a hand over her mouth. Mr Barton, who has been sitting patiently, turning over the pages in the photo album, comes to her rescue.

—Elizabeth was just indifferent to Jason. From quite early on.
—*Did she ever show any feeling toward him?*
—She did when she had to. She would accept a cuddle, a kiss from his jammy face. She would go through the motions but she would never choose to interact with him.
—*You mentioned Jason's problems…?*
—He was the polar opposite of his sister. We used to say he was a changeling – a joke, of course. Oh gosh, I'm sorry Mr King. A slip of the tongue.
—*Please, it's OK.*

—He was very needy as a little boy – always running to us for a cuddle, always wanting reassurance. He was accident-prone too – always leaping off the sofa, walking into things, falling over. If you heard a crash in the house you could almost count – one … two … three – and then Jason would start wailing.

He was scared – always full of nightmares and worries. Real things, imaginary things; Jason was in and out of our bed, while Elizabeth slept like a log, all night from the age of about one!

We gave him as much as we gave Elizabeth; toys, games, clothes. He was never happy with any of it. The babysitters and the nannies were always calling us at work because Jason was playing up. It was because of Jason that half of them never stayed.

I wonder if this is true and I also wonder if it was this that seeded resentment toward Jason in Elizabeth. Mildred carries on telling me about Jason's early years.

—His problems continued into school. With his erratic behaviour, at first we were worried that he was being bullied. And sometimes there were even bruises. His hair singed and burn marks on his clothes. But he assured us he was fine – and always explained them away – a fall here and there, playing football. Messing about with Bunsen burners. He blamed Elizabeth a lot too, but we knew that was probably just jealousy, Jason vying for our attention.

He was forever asking to be taken to the woods, the seaside; anywhere there was wide, open spaces. He was never happier than when he was splodging around in his wellies in the mud. Of course, we were at work a lot and the babysitters weren't prepared to do that. We got rid of one who let him wander off once. He was nine years old!

—*Did you ever find out what was happening with Jason, why his behaviour was extreme?*

—We know now that it was that ADHD, but back then we didn't. We asked his teachers, of course. They told us Jason needed attention. I remember getting quite cross and telling them exactly how much we gave both children, how many toys and video games Jason had. He never wanted for anything, neither of them did!

Harold Barton clears his throat. Anger furrows his brow.

—But it was the *lying,* Mr King. That's what we could never get on with. Jason was forever making things up. Most of the time to try and get his sister into trouble. We think that he was jealous. Elizabeth was achieving, she was on every sports team, and the only thing Jason was getting was detention.

I'm surprised at the lack of empathy the Bartons have for their son. For me, his behaviour suggests a child who lacks loving attention. However, I'm still not sure that Jason has been one hundred percent truthful with me. I ask Harold to elaborate about Jason's lies.

—Oh it was constant. He was jealous of his sister and would make her out to be some kind of monster. If he hurt himself, it was Elizabeth's fault. If he went running off outside in the cold, it was Elizabeth's fault. If he spilled food all over the brand-new sofa, it was her fault. At school, Jason was always challenging authority, arguing with the teachers. And if it was bad before, his behaviour took a real nosedive. I blame the people he started associating with too: older lads, trouble-makers George Meldby and Martin Flynn, to name two very specific examples. Jason was forever in after-school detention with those two. Jason had his own issues but he was better than that.

Harold Barton's voice has risen with the colour in his cheeks as he talks about Jason's association with his sister's two killers. I feel like I detect a degree of blame in Mr Barton's tone. I cannot imagine the conflict within him and the pain it must bring.

—Maybe I should have been stricter? Maybe I should have forbade him to go near those two.
—*Do you think that would have stopped him or perhaps driven him closer to them?*
—I suppose you're right. The more we objected, the more he would have pushed us away

Harold sighs and flicks back through the photograph album and opens it at a photo of Jason at around eleven years old. Jason is wearing a raincoat. It's smeared with dirt, as is his face. His eyes are wide and happy, and a smile is spread across his whole being. He looks up into the camera, a piglet in his arms.

—Animals. The blessed animals. I want to say that's where it went wrong with Jason, but it wasn't really wrong, I suppose. Oh I don't know. This picture is from year seven, when he started Ergarth High. It's from a school trip to some sort of organic farm affair up in Northumberland. After that Jason became absolutely obsessed with animals. The babysitters would tell us he was forever bringing home injured birds; putting out food for hedgehogs; he even made a great big hole at the bottom of the garden fence for the things!

I remember the day after the pig farm. Jason was wittering on about it. He asked me why the sows had tags on their ears. Well, I told him, as gently as possible, of course, that these animals had been bred for meat. I'll never forget what he said to me:

'Even the piglets, Dad? Even the little piglets?'

Well, I couldn't lie to him, could I? That's not right. I had to tell him that yes, even the piglets, once they were old enough. Well, he was distraught – I mean really cut up about the whole thing, bless him. Refused to touch meat from that day onward. Wouldn't have it. Things only went downhill from there.

More photographs: Jason getting older, taller; his face seemingly setting into a scowl. Jason's dress sense changed too, as did, his father tells me, his friends and his attitude. He would deliberately flout school rules to provoke a reaction; dye his hair and wear trainers or jeans. He would lie to teachers, telling them he had allergies to his uniform, but telling his parents it was a charity non-uniform day. These lies only increased in frequency. Jason became a bit of a class clown at this point, performing dangerous acts for the attention and amusement of the others. Mildred remembers being called into school to see her son swarming up the side of the main building and leaping into the branches of a nearby tree, in front of a crowd of crowing children. He

*told her he did it because he thought he'd seen a cat stuck up there.
There was another, even more disturbing incident when Jason walked
away from his father after an argument straight into a busy road,
where he dodged three oncoming cars before doing some sort of dance
on the pavement on the other side. Unable to communicate with his
son, Harold begged his wife to try and talk to him.*

—I tried my best but it was impossible. Jason was just so full of
anger; he would say over and over again how much he hated
people, just the human race in general. I couldn't understand where
it was all coming from – none of us could. He would slam his
bedroom door, smoke cigarettes, hang around with those ... with
those *boys* ... anything to provoke a reaction.
—*What did you think was the matter?*
—I wish we knew. I think it was the ADHD. I still don't know.
I mean ... we haven't seen Jason for so long ... I wonder if he
would tell us now?

*Jason Barton is effectively estranged from his family – his choice, his
parents tell me. All they know is that he lives as far away from Ergarth
as possible. I feel a sudden pang, knowing exactly where Jason lives when
his parents don't. I wonder if I should tell them. Jason didn't, they say,
attend his sister's funeral nor has he been in touch since her death. Both
of them find this difficult to forgive. Jason told me he was in Ergarth a
few days before Elizabeth was killed. Something does not feel right here,
I feel like I have an idea why Jason's behaviour was so extreme, but
it's not for me to tell the Bartons. It also seems as if they have no idea
about Jason's wanderings – around Ergarth, across the fields, and up
to Flynn's Meats.*

—Harold and I have no idea why he didn't come to say goodbye
to Elizabeth. We'd like to think that maybe it was too hard for him.
Everyone deals with death in a different way – there's no right or
wrong way to grieve.

*By sixteen, Jason had dropped out of school and was barely in the
house.*

—He'd taken up with quite a militant bunch up in Northumberland. He would take buses up there, be gone for days. They were some sort of animal-rights group; they would go out into the hills and sabotage fox hunts. He was only a young lad but he was forever being brought home by the police. Sometimes he would show us the footage from the sabotage. Don't get me wrong, neither my husband or I approve of killing animals for sport, it's a barbaric practice. The hunters themselves were horrible people, charging their horses and swinging their whips at Jason and his friends. Honestly, I had no argument with the saboteurs, I was just worried about my boy – worried he'd get hurt or sent to prison. That was all either of us was worried about.

Jason didn't stop, nor did he care what his parents thought. Jason has allegedly done many things in the name of animal welfare, none of which are pertinent to this case. Save for one.

As I mentioned to Jason himself – it is alleged that he was part of the group that secretly recorded undercover footage of animal cruelty at Flynn's Meats in 2017. Jason won't admit to being part of this incident but Justice for the Voiceless have taken credit for the footage, which saw two members of Flynn's slaughterhouse staff given suspended sentences.

This incident could possibly constitute motivation for Elizabeth's murder on the part of Martin Flynn, but to me it seems a tenuous argument; it was never mentioned in court, and there was no evidence put forward to support it. I ask Mildred about her views on Martin Flynn, in the years before Elizabeth's murder.

—If you'd have asked me back then, I would have told you that, despite who he was, he wouldn't have hurt a hair on Elizabeth's head. It all started getting worrying when he was hanging around the house at night, but Elizabeth, she told us it was nothing. She was good like that; she told us to imagine that Martin Flynn was like a guard dog or a burglar alarm. She said she took him with her when she went out to do her charity videos. Sensible, if you ask me; you don't know what you could be letting yourself in for. I remember her saying that we could leave our doors open at night

– no one would have dared get past him to steal something. I don't think he would have hurt her, not unless he was … coerced into doing so. George Meldby was the same. Bear in mind, Mr King, these two boys grew up with Elizabeth, they both knew her since they were all very young. That's why it was so shocking; especially what they did to her.

I want to ask about the incident with a lamb from Flynn's Meats a few days before Elizabeth died. Elizabeth apparently kept it in the garden.
Mildred shakes her head.

—It's amazing what sort of stories people make up isn't it? For attention. I don't know where you've heard of all this, Mr King. But I can tell you now, it wasn't nearly as interesting as you are making out. It's not the story you've been told.

Harold Barton joins in.

—No. Exactly. I mean, I was away in Frankfurt that day. Elizabeth was looking after the house. The snow had closed off all the roads. Nothing could get in or out of Ergarth. She was hardly going to go walking around the fields, now, was she? She wouldn't have dreamed of doing something so ridiculous. Yes. There was a lamb in the garden. I've seen the video. But it was all for Elizabeth's YouTube; it was just a stunt. Any idiot would know that. She was making a lot of money at that point, saving for a deposit on a flat and she obviously paid one of the farmers to bring around one of the lambs for a while.
—*So she didn't 'liberate' it from Flynn's Meats?*
—She wouldn't have done something like that. And certainly not in that snow! Not Elizabeth. And if Martin Flynn did it, he did it of his own volition. Elizabeth would never have asked him to do something like that. Elizabeth wasn't *friends* with Martin Flynn. Their relationship was entirely business however much he wanted it to be more. I wish people would understand that.

I think of the newspaper report – the injuries to Martin Flynn. Elizabeth's YouTube video surrounding the incident, in which she claims she 'rescued' the animal from a truck that got stuck in the snow. In Elizabeth's 'Liberate the Meat' challenge, we only see the animal bounding through the snow in the Bartons' back garden. The 'rescue' itself remains ambiguous.

I wonder who is telling the truth right now. Is Jason Barton the liar his parents make him out to be? Was Elizabeth making up a story online to get more popularity? Are Harold and Mildred Barton in denial? I think the truth lies somewhere in between.

Mildred sighs and stares down into her empty cup for a good thirty seconds as if reading the leaves. She takes a deep breath and turns to me.

—I wish we had something in the way of answers. This is the thing that we cannot get over. There's no answer to what those three did to Elizabeth. The savagery of it. Elizabeth was popular, she was clever, she was beautiful. What anyone could have against her, I just don't know. All I do know is that wretched tower needs knocking down, demolishing. Its ashes need raking into the sea and the place forgotten about.

—*I can imagine it's a constant reminder of what happened.*

—It's not just that, Mr King. It also reminds us about the ridiculous rumours and stories in Ergarth – and how things like that get blown out of all proportion.

—*Stories like those about the Beast from the East – the Ergarth Vampire.*

—Exactly. You see how a silly folk tale can be perpetuated. Even when we were young, people said they'd seen her … Everyone had a vampire story.

I'm desperate to ask for more, but I'm aware of how unwelcome questions about vampires would be right now. Instead I stay silent. Harold Barton takes a breath.

—Listen. This is a good example of the sort of rubbish that Ergarth's been plagued with. When I was a boy – twelve, eleven –

I used to wander around and explore places where I shouldn't. Including Tankerville Tower.

As Harold begins this story, Mildred shakes her head, lips thin and eyes closed. Eventually she leaves the room. I don't blame her.

—My friends and I had clambered in, as you do. There were none of those drug addicts there then. But the place was still unpleasant: it smelled bad, and there was just a terrible feeling in there, in the dark, where all you could hear was the sea smashing on the cliffs. There's no light in that tower, just wet earth. We didn't dare go up that staircase into the top. No one was brave enough. Plus it was freezing cold. Our fingers were numb.

Anyway, we were prodding about with sticks, you know, as boys will, and we came upon something in there, something terrible, half buried in the earth.

—What did you find?

—There will have been a perfectly rational explanation of course … We came upon this sack, one of the large ones for animal feed. Heaven knows why, but we kept digging, pulling out this bag. It was huge and there was something in it; lumps and bumps. We used our sticks to lever the thing out, and when it did there was a smell so terrible it nearly knocked us to our knees. Harvey Brown was sick, I think.

—What was in the bag?

—Pigeons; there must have been twenty of them or more, stuffed into that bag. All of them without heads; half rotted, their insides hanging out. It was as if something had been at them. I still dream of it sometimes. I sometimes wake up still smelling that smell; seeing those dusty feathers, their bones, the places where their heads had been.

—What on earth was that about? I mean who had done that?

—It will have been pest control, I imagine; someone doing it on the cheap and dumping them in the tower. At the time, of course, a ludicrous rumour went around about something in the tower.

—What do you mean?

—Just a silly story. People were saying they saw something in the sky around the cliffs at twilight. Something huge.

—*Who saw it?*

—Like I say, it was just silly stories. People heard about what we found and then turned seagulls into giant bats with their overactive imaginations. As Mildred says, the sooner that place is demolished, the sooner everyone will sleep better in this town.

Harold tells me that after he and his friends found the bag of dead pigeons, the stories of something 'big' flying around Tankerville Tower at night spread. Others said they heard something scratching at their bedroom windows, and there was a spate of family pets going missing. All these things, Harold tells me, are typical of the Ergarth rumour mill. All it takes, he says, is one silly thing to start it off again. I wonder if it was this sort of insular Chinese-whisper effect that began the legend of the Ergarth Vampire in the first place. I think of the shape I saw out there, and the biting cold I felt.

I tell the Bartons that I'm now going to ask about the perpetrator of their daughter's death we haven't yet discussed: Solomon Meer. They tell me they understand. It's almost like they've braced themselves for this moment.

—But I think you may be disappointed, Mr King.

Harold shakes his head. They both look tired, spent. I don't want this to go on for much longer.

—Elizabeth never even mentioned the boy's name to us. Not even once. Since … what happened … we've come to find out that he was in some of her classes at school. I mean, that's it. That's all we know. We know he hated her, but why? Because she was everything that little toe rag wasn't. He wanted to be popular and he killed our daughter to do it.

As he speaks, the emotion finally cracks and tears trickle down the hollows of his cheeks.

—She was beautiful where he was scruffy and savage, she was smart where he was insolent and stupid, she was talented where he had nothing! Our daughter was everything Solomon Meer wished he was; she had everything he wished he had. What he did to her after she was dead – we'll never understand that sort of butchery, never!

Mrs Barton dissolves into tears beside her husband. Harold is shaking with rage and grief, and I feel that we may be drawing to the end of our interview. Harold takes a huge, rattling breath and prepares to keep going.

—*Can I ask what you know about the whole 'vampire' angle on this? Solomon Meer was obsessed with the story of the Ergarth Vampire, wasn't he?*

—All that was something we only discovered after the event. We heard Meer was found down in Ergarth Dene with some others, conducting Satanic rituals. I heard he was trying to bring the vampire back from the dead. That's what people have told me. He wasn't right in the head, was he? There was something deeply wrong with that young man, but he was clever with it – a manipulator, a sociopath.

—*He worked in Ergarth Books, didn't he?*

—That place is about as welcome in this town as Tankerville Tower. No wonder Meer turned out the way he did, reading all that nonsense.

—*Do you think Solomon Meer coerced the other two into helping him do what he did to your daughter?*

—He had the gift of the gab. People with minds like his, they know how to convince people their delusions are real. That's how he managed to coerce those other two into helping him with his plan. Those two weren't the brightest buttons – Meer spun them some yarn about Elizabeth being a vampire and they swallowed it. It all made sense after that – Martin Flynn hanging around the house at night; George Meldby harassing Elizabeth at work. He was the one who took advantage and made those two help him. Then what they did to her after she was dead. It was just … it was beyond the pale. It was beyond inhuman.

What I'm saying, Mr King, is that whatever you do, however much you achieve, there's always someone out there who wants to bring you down a peg or two. I've learned in my lifetime that achievement breeds resentment, jealousy and there's nothing you can do about that. That's what I told Elizabeth, when she started to win things, when she started to achieve – I told her that there'd always be someone who wouldn't be happy about it. I told her to rise above them, to tell herself that it was a problem inside them, not an issue in herself.

—*Solomon Meer maintained your daughter's death was an accident, that it was a prank gone wrong.*

—Maybe it was. We'll never know for sure. But if that is the case, why did he play the prank in the first place? That's the issue here. To be popular? To get everyone to look at him and like him? That's the sign of someone who's damaged. Why our daughter? What did she do to him? It just doesn't make any sense.

I feel we're coming to the end of the Bartons' patience. I'm not sure how much more of this interview they can take.

The Bartons tell me they simply didn't understand the Dead in Six Days challenge until after Elizabeth's murder. This is something I find very hard to believe. It even made the local newspaper. This bothers me and maybe I'm wrong, maybe it's unethical of me to say, but I just don't believe them. They are certainly older; having Elizabeth and Jason much later in life but is that really an excuse?

Harold Barton tells me that it must have passed them by: 'We're old people, Mr King,' he repeats, 'we cannot be expected to know every little silly craze that is going on at all times.'

The Bartons have had little to say about Elizabeth's online success, save that they were pleased about it. I wonder what would have happened if they'd taken more interest. Harold and Mildred Barton knew Elizabeth was popular online, yet it seems this was all they saw. Maybe, for them, it was all they needed or wanted to see. The finer dynamics of social media seemed to have passed them by.

I simply cannot leave without at least trying to get an answer from the Bartons concerning Jason's claim that Solomon Meer was in the Barton house a day or two before Elizabeth was killed. Something else occurs to me as I think about this, something that, for some reason, has not entered my mind until now. I curse myself for not realising and asking Jason Barton outright.

Jason Barton lives in Bristol. How on earth could he have known if Solomon Meer was there or not? Unless someone told him? Or he was there too? Something's missing here.

—Mr and Mrs Barton, I want to ask you one last thing before I go.

Mildred lets out a sob, and Harold Barton waves his hand at me. He tells me that they've had enough of my questions now. They've said all they can. Perhaps it's unkind of me but I finally disclose to the Bartons that I've spoken to their son. Harold Barton's face colours but he expresses no anger. He only slumps in the sofa, his face sags, eyebrows furled in disappointment. I wonder how many times Jason saw this exact look.

—And I suppose he told you what terrible parents we were, didn't he? I wonder if you bothered asking him why he didn't come to Elizabeth's funeral. What on earth she had done that deserved that?

—What Jason said about you was that you both provided well for both him and his sister. You did your best.

Some of the disappointment and suspicion in Harold Barton cools at this.

—Well that's true at least. A roof over his head, food on the table. Even if it was that vegetarian muck. Neither of them wanted for anything, Mr King.

I think of Jason's night-time escapes, his poor behaviour in school. His desire for something from his parents that they were not giving him.

Jason told me a story. About Solomon Meer.

Harold and Mildred exchange raised eyebrows and now a wry smile plays over Harold Barton's mouth.

—Yes indeed. *Stories.* That's our Jason's area of expertise. Always has been. What did he tell you?

—He told me that a few days before Elizabeth was found in Tankerville Tower ... Solomon Meer was in your house. In the middle of the night.

There is a terrible silence. The smile falls from Harold's face. Mr and Mrs Barton look at each other. For a moment, I think Harold is going to order me from his home. He opens his mouth and Mildred places her hand on his knee. She looks up at me, tears still wet on her cheeks.

—We've held it in for too long. All of that.

—My love…

—No, Harold. Enough. Just tell him. Let's let it go. It'll help us … to let her go too.

I feel for the Bartons, I really do, and in some ways I wish I could take back what I've said. But whatever it is that they've held on to for so long will surely be better gone. With a heaviness, Harold Barton takes over.

—They found her on the Sunday. This would have been Friday – the middle of the night. I'd got back from Frankfurt and I couldn't sleep. Too much travelling. I'd got back late because of the snow. Had to take a taxi from Newcastle Airport all the way to Ergarth. I nearly didn't. I nearly stayed in a hotel.

At first I thought it was the snow; something to do with the pipes. I don't know. I woke up and heard footsteps on the landing. Whispered voices. You know your own family don't you? You know their noises, the sound of their footsteps. You know when something's not right.

—You thought there was a burglar, didn't you my love?

—That's right, a burglar. So I got out of bed and—

—You picked up your cricket bat, didn't you?

—Yes. I picked up my cricket bat and went out onto the landing, only to come face to face with that piece of work, Solomon Meer.

—*What was he doing?*

—Well ... he was on his way out wasn't he, dear? You weren't face-to-face with him; you saw him in the hall, downstairs.

—Correct. And none of it ... none of it made any sense.

—*Go on...*

Harold Barton is becoming more and more flustered. Mildred is still on hand, prompting him on the finer details.

—Solomon Meer was in the hall...

—We had no idea what on earth he was doing.

—I must have caught him in the act, before he took anything.

—It was actually Elizabeth who saved the day in the end.

—*How so?*

—She was down there too ... but she had her phone out. She was filming him. We had all the evidence we needed, he was bang to rights!

—That's why we didn't call the police in the end. That's why we left it at that. Our daughter was ahead of the curve. As always.

—*I think what I'm struggling with is why you didn't call the police.*

—Sometimes, Mr King, you have to take the initiative. You have to sort things out yourself. Make no bones about it; I told that boy to leave our daughter alone. I told him I didn't want to see him ever again, and if I heard a peep out of him, we'd give the police the film.

Let me tell you now, there's not a day that goes by that I don't regret it. What I didn't do. What I didn't do will stay with me forever.

The whole thing was entirely my fault.

Harold Barton finally breaks. It's like he collapses in on himself and his whole body is wracked with sobs. It makes sense — they didn't speak out about this incident; they didn't go to the police. If they had,

Solomon Meer would have been placed in custody for long enough not to be able to do what he did to Elizabeth the following night.

I feel that not all of this frankly bizarre and convoluted story is true, but I don't challenge them on it. The Bartons are clearly consumed with guilt and my sympathy for them knows no bounds. But I am utterly perplexed about why they failed to mention this incident to the police after Elizabeth's death; why they went through the trial without speaking of it. Surely it would have shown premeditation on the part of Solomon Meer?

—I have to ask you: why was it that you decided not to mention this to the relevant authorities during the investigation into Elizabeth's death?

Pain spreads across the Bartons' faces. Harold draws himself up and wipes his eyes. His breath shudders in his chest.

—I'll tell you the truth, Mr King. It was on Elizabeth's request that we didn't take the matter further.

—Elizabeth?

—Yes. She begged us, she implored us to leave it – to let the matter rest there and then.

—What were her reasons?

—Elizabeth was the sort of person who saw the good in everyone – to her own detriment in the end. She had the video evidence of Solomon Meer in the house, she said. That was all she needed.

—I still don't understand. Did he break in? Why was he there?

—Elizabeth felt sorry for him, I think. Him, of all people. My guess was that he was like the others – she'd been kind to him, she'd taken time to speak to him, to do something caring. Perhaps it had something to do with her foundation, her new project, those videos – that's why she didn't want us to do anything.

—Elizabeth made us promise not to mention it and we obeyed her wishes. We gave her everything she wanted, we made sure she was not disappointed. She stretched out a hand of kindness to that man and look what he did. That sums the whole thing up. That shows us who is wrong and who is right in this whole terrible affair.

—Whatever he was doing here, it doesn't matter anymore does it? That's not what I think about when I remember my daughter.

—*What about afterwards? Surely it would have played a part in helping to convict the three of them? They were all trying to get reduced sentences weren't they? It would have showed premeditation.*

I wonder if I've gone too far. Harold and Mildred Barton close their mouths and look at each other with glassy eyes. They've moved closer together on the sofa and taken each other's hand. I can't press them any further. The question remains though: why did neither Harold, Mildred nor indeed Jason say a word about Solomon Meer being right here, in Elizabeth's house?

There's also Elizabeth's 'new project' – the Elizabeth Barton Tower Foundation. We know that Elizabeth was working with Solomon Meer on something to do with YouTube videos; was this it? Now Elizabeth is gone and Solomon Meer is in prison, why can't it come out?

Frustratingly, it's time for me to leave. I extend my deepest sympathies to Harold and Mildred Barton. It is they who will have to live with their decision the night before Elizabeth was killed. How they will live with themselves is beyond the realms of my understanding.

I actually feel like I now understand some of Jason's anger toward his parents. He knew about this incident – perhaps it was them who told him about it. It makes sense that he hasn't seen them since. Maybe he feels like the apple of blame for his sister's death doesn't fall too far from the tree.

For the Bartons, Meer, Meldby and Flynn's motives are something they may never understand. For now, the place where their daughter was is an empty hollow where their memories are forever echoing until one day they'll fade.

So what have we learned from a pair of grieving parents? I don't want to say nothing, but I do believe there is more to the murder of Elizabeth Barton than we see on the surface. I want nothing more than to explore in greater detail the motivations of those that took her life. Whether each of them had their own axe to grind with Elizabeth and fate flung them together, or whether they came together through some eldritch belief in vampires, I still don't know.

What does seem clear is that the links between Elizabeth and her killers are beginning to emerge. Ergarth is a small place, and George Meldby and Martin Flynn were certainly friendly with Elizabeth as they grew up. In fact both seemed to have developed a rather unhealthy obsession with her. Was unrequited love enough to drive them to force Elizabeth into Tankerville Tower, leave her to die and then remove her head? What was it about Solomon Meer that overruled their adoration and invoked such brutality?

Solomon Meer remains enigmatic in all of this. Meer was indeed the antithesis of Elizabeth Barton, but was this enough to kill her? And were Meer's powers of persuasion strong enough that he could convince the other two that Elizabeth Barton was the second coming of the Ergarth Vampire?

Next episode, I want to get closer to those convicted of killing Elizabeth. Especially Solomon Meer. There are not many who knew the three personally, but as I am swiftly learning, every page of this story needs turning in order to judge it properly.

This has been Six Stories.

This has been our fourth.

I'm going to meet a vampire tomorrow,
That vampire's going to take my life.
Tomorrow, I'll be dead.

OK guys, I'm sooo sorry. I know you've all been waiting for the 'Rob from the Rich, Give to the Poor' task. I know I haven't done half of it and I just … I'm really sorry, OK?

Thanks so much for all the love for the compilation video. The comments are totally amazing and you're all so lovely. I really enjoyed visiting the Ergarth Foodbank and meeting all the guys there. Hopefully that video gets loads of likes and views and stuff! I know that's only the second half of the challenge.

Truth is, yeah … it's like, I just can't do it! I can't steal! Who am I going to steal from? Like, I don't know any proper rich people, at least no one who deserves to be stolen from. I don't want any of you guys doing stuff like that either. Sooo, I'm pretty stuck.

I think you've got me, Vladlena. I think you may have won … sad face!

But there's something else I need to tell you guys about. Things have been getting really weird all up in here and … let's have a little walk … through my room … because something happened last night … oops, just move that a sec … hang on.

So last night I was in my bed – just here. I was all snuggled up, fast asleep, you know? I hear this noise. I wake up and it's freezing – the heating wasn't on. My breath was in actual clouds. Like in that movie: 'I see dead people!' But, you guys, that wasn't far from the actual truth!

So I go out on the landing … just here *and … duh, duh, duhhhh!*

Yeah. So there's nothing here now. *But last night … let's have a look at some weird stuff, OK? So like, here is this little window on the landing, and it's closed now, but last night it was* open. *That's why the house was so frickin'* cold!

You guys know the Ergarth Vampire story, right? She was this beautiful, like, witch from Siberia and they brought her to Ergarth as a hostage in, like, Victorian times. But she conjured up this snow and this ice, and people were dying. They said she could turn into a bat or into fog … and she would come into people's houses and drink their blood at night.

Ooky-spooky, right?

Well, last night, when I got out of bed and went out on the landing I saw this figure. Just standing there in the dark. It wasn't a burglar, cos, like a burglar couldn't get through that window, plus if we look here, you can see they'd have to climb up the side of the house. Plus they didn't take anything.

I think the vampire was in my house. I'm not even joking, guys.

Vladlena, if that was you, I'm sorry, OK? I'll do the rest of the task, I promise. I just need a bit more time and … hang on, what's that?

Look, oh my God, guys, she's been in touch, Vladlena's sent me a message. *I swear, this is live, this is totally not a set-up. Let's have a look ... What does she say? ... oh my God, you guys, look at this:*

'I'll accept you completed your task. Just. Last night was your warning. Tomorrow night, you will receive one more task. Pass it on or you will be mine for evermore. Tomorrow night is when I will decide your fate!'

Oh my God it feels like I'm in big trouble!

But it's also kind of exciting, right? No one's ever got to day six before and I've managed it by the skin of my teeth!

So this is gonna be a total cliff-hanger, but it's only a matter of hours until we all find out what happens on day six of the Dead in Six Days challenge.

Hit that like, hit that subscribe with everything you've got. I'm still trying to work out some logistics for live-streaming tomorrow. Whatever happens, make sure you've rung the notification bell so you can find out the moment *I upload what happens tomorrow with the vampire and the final day of the Dead in Six Days challenge.*

Bye for now, you lovely people!

Episode 5: The Lost Boy

The wind howled. It wasn't the sound of a tortured dog, but a hungry wolf. Simon could feel the pain and suffering burrowing deeper and deeper into the very marrow of his bones. That's all Simon was these days, skin and bones. He smoked cigarettes and drank endless cups of black coffee; pushing away all need for food.

Simon didn't sleep well at all on the filthy mattress in a corner of the ancient house that had no electricity. The voices in his brain were as bad as the suffering and gnawing in his bones; the physical and the psychological terrors and gut-wrenching misery clung to him like soaking wet clothes.

'Kill them all, Simon,' the voice said. That oh-so familiar voice. 'Kill them all, but especially her. The cause of all this pain. If you kill her, you will be free.'

'Noooo!' Simon screamed as he sat up in bed, his throat raw like he'd swallowed glass. His screams mixed with the howl of the terrible wind that had woken him. All he could see was her, all he could think of was her.

Simon lit his first cigarette of the day and swallowed the dregs of a bottle of vodka by his bedside. It was all just a dream, just a terrible dream. Everything was OK. They were together, she was his. She was never going away.

'Well, that's what you thought, Simon,' said a voice from the shadows.

Simon jumped, goose pimples standing up all over his skin. The shape that hung in the dark rafters of his room slid down the wall and sat at the foot of his bed.

'You're not real, you're not real!' Simon begged hopelessly.

But it was very real. The pale skin, the long fingers, that voice that flowed over its terrible fangs like water over razor-sharp rocks.

'It'll only be pain for a moment, Simon,' the vampire told

him. 'Just a moment, and then you will be in heaven for the rest of eternity. No more pain. Those who pick on you, who ridicule you, you will have the power to smite them with a flick of your little finger. Oh such power I will bestow upon you…'

Simon took another swig of vodka and gazed into those fathomless eyes. The creature had come to him in his dreams and now was sat here, bold as brass at the end of his bed.

'But I can't,' Simon begged, 'I can't do it. I can't become like you. What will become of her?'

The vampire laughed and it was the sound of terrible bones clattering against a stone floor.

'Her – the girl who pretends to everyone that you don't even exist? Why she will mean nothing in the end, Simon. Once you are one like me, mere girls will become echoes; echoes of a life long ago, echoes of a life, long snuffed out.'

—Not bad, is it? Not bad at all, considering. I was impressed. I was thinking of selling it on eBay. I'm joking of course, but really, it would get quite a lot, I imagine? Of course it's totally unethical for me to have kept old students' work…

Solomon Meer could have done something creative, if he'd got the help he needed. That's what I'm saying, I suppose.

Welcome to Six Stories.
I'm Scott King.
This is episode five.
There is no question that the murder of Elizabeth Barton in 2018 was committed by three young men from the North-Eastern town of Ergarth. Solomon Meer, George Meldby and Martin Flynn were all convicted of murdering Elizabeth by locking her in Tankerville Tower on the night of the third of March 2018. Temperatures dropped to nearly minus 10°C as that exposed part of the North-East coast was assaulted by the freezing, Siberian winds of a polar vortex known as The Beast from the East.

The evidence presented at the trial included fingerprints and DNA from all three young men, taken from the grate that was placed over the entrance to the ruined tower. It remains unclear which of them decapitated Elizabeth's corpse after she passed out and died from hypothermia.

Digital evidence showed a text message from Solomon Meer's phone, asking Elizabeth to meet him at Tankerville Tower that night. No reason for the meeting was given and Elizabeth did not reply. However, it appeared that she did, of her own accord, go and meet Solomon Meer, George Meldby and Martin Flynn at around ten p.m. on that fateful night. The only explanation the three offered for the killing was that it was 'a prank gone wrong', apparently corroborated by a video clip from Solomon Meer's phone that shows Elizabeth's body with Meer's voice repeating, 'What have we done?'

All three men are now serving prison terms. Over the previous four episodes, a couple of possible motivations for the killing have emerged: the first is a combination of jealousy and unrequited adoration of a gregarious young woman who was moving up the ladder of celebrity. The second is that the vampire-obsessed Solomon Meer coerced the other two into believing Elizabeth Barton was undead.

So why do I find myself here in Ergarth, investigating this case? I have been drawn here by a slogan painted on the wall of the Bartons' house – apparently a message from Elizabeth's younger brother, Jason:

'Who locked Lizzie in the tower?'

To this question, I have received some answers as regards to who. That was never in question. 'Why' is what I really want to know; and 'why' has also proved the most difficult to answer. Elizabeth Barton had power in this small town; power over hearts and minds. I have heard conflicting accounts about Elizabeth. Speaking to her parents and her younger brother, I have two differing pictures of her. One, from her mother and father, is of a hard-working, sociable and high-achieving young woman; the other, from her younger brother, is that of a manipulative and narcissistic bully. Could I put this down to sibling rivalry, two children vying for attention from parents who were absent much of the time?

There is also a new question. What was Solomon Meer doing in the Bartons' house the night before Elizabeth was killed and why did none of the Bartons tell the police?

In this, our penultimate episode, we are going to speak to a woman who has asked to use a pseudonym. I'll call her Jo. Jo was a learning mentor at an educational unit for eighteen- to twenty-five-year-olds who were at risk of prosecution by the police, or worse, prison. The now-closed Leighburn Educational Unit was often used as a 'last-chance saloon' and at-risk young people could be referred to the unit by the court rather than face a custodial sentence or the prison system. The stipulation was that attendance was mandatory.

This was quite a novel scheme and was successfully piloted in Ergarth until its funding was cut and the unit closed in early 2019. Jo taught GCSE-level English at Leighburn and tells me she saw many people who had left school with nothing, and were in trouble with drugs and crime, manage to leave, proud of themselves for getting some qualifications, but more importantly, with the knowledge they could achieve something.

Unfortunately, not a great deal is known about the four or five years after Meer, Meldby and Flynn left Ergarth High School. What we do know is that Solomon Meer was permanently excluded in his final year for attempting to assault the headmaster. George Meldby was excluded a year before that.

From what I gather, each drifted for those intervening years; Martin Flynn working at his family's abattoir, Flynn's Meats, Solomon Meer working at Ergarth Books, and George Meldby collecting benefits.

All of them, however, in a coincidence that would prove disastrous, were referred to and attended Leighburn Educational Unit in September 2017.

—Our place was another option – for those who were on the dole long-term or else they were looking for a new start. Most of the time, to be fair, they weren't. The majority of them had no interest in being here; the job centre would sometimes refer them to us. It was about getting back those qualifications they missed out on when they were at school, you see. They had to want to work too; if they showed up but only pissed about they were gone.

Most people, most teachers, when they think of Leighburn, think of a monkey house: chairs being chucked across rooms, that sort of thing. In all honesty, it was a pretty calm place. It had to be. The young people here were people, not animals, and we treated them like people. They were adults now, too. It wasn't school anymore. There was no punishment and detention. If they threw a hissy fit and walked out, we didn't stop them. It took a little longer for some of them to get used to that. When you show them that you're not going to start throwing your weight around, when you show them a little bit of respect, you get it back.

Jo has worked in alternative education provision for most of her career, she's in her fifties and she's fazed by very little. Right now she works at a specialist pupil referral unit for some of the most violent youngsters in her area. Jo no longer lives near Ergarth. She still loves her job.

—It's safe to say that ninety percent of young men are the same: big, scary, tough, and yeah, they're intimidating, but it's all front. The few truly scary ones don't act like thugs – they don't need to.

I'm interested in Jo's insight into the three killers and what she has to say about the narratives that surround the young men: that they were driven by jealousy – that Elizabeth's status and popularity represented something they couldn't attain, so they took out their frustration by killing her; or else it was about a prank gone wrong, part of a craze in Ergarth at the time known as the Dead in Six Days challenge.

Elizabeth Barton posted several YouTube videos every day, documenting her shopping trips, her thoughts on issues and of course her participation in the Dead in Six Days challenge. By successfully 'curating' her online persona, she became Internet royalty; but with royalty comes resentment. As I know full well, if you stand up, there's always someone who wants to shoot you down. Often, this sort of trouble occurs when the online version of someone does not correspond with reality. Was this what drove the three men who killed Elizabeth?

There is another theory about why Elizabeth was killed, and while it is the most unlikely, it is the one that has caught the public's imagination – the idea that Solomon Meer was under the bizarre belief that Elizabeth Barton was a vampire. To be fair, this has never been reported as actual fact, but the rumour clings to this case like a bad smell. But why? It seems to have the least substance behind it, but I suppose it is the better story.

So where am I with this one? I find myself questioning all of these explanations. None of them offer enough to really get behind.

So far we've talked a lot about Elizabeth Barton. The common view of her is a benevolent and charitable young woman. Yet there were detractors from this view. Even Elizabeth's family paint hugely differing pictures of her – the high-achieving and popular vlogger so revered by her parents; and the elusive and allegedly abusive manipulator whose own brother took himself as far away from her in the country as he physically could. Who do we believe? Which Elizabeth was the real one? Or was there more to her than we can ever know? Amirah in episode two, I feel, was vague about her relationship with Elizabeth, and her parents struggled to come up with any answers when I asked whether Elizabeth had close, real-life friends. Jason Barton, however, has provided me with the most intrigue. I feel like after speaking to him, after he told me to 'force this story', I'm searching for the right path in a difficult maze.

So I thought maybe I'm looking in the wrong places. Perhaps the way to solve what exactly happened to Elizabeth Barton is to take a different path. An indirect route.

—They come and they go. I've seen the same surly lads a hundred times over – they've had a bad start, you see: chaotic home life; a lack of boundaries. More often than not, there was exposure to trauma at an early age – emotional abuse, violence, lack of role models, nearly always no father figure in their life. In every single child – because that's what we're talking about here, children – inside every child I've seen pass through the system, is the same lack of self-esteem. That doesn't change when they get older, either, they're still fighting against everything. And what has school taught them? That they're useless. They've left with nowt, and there's nothing for them anymore but the streets.

It's funny isn't it? You don't think of hard lads and lasses from rough estates like that do you? They're thought of as egotistic, arrogant. But it's all a front. All behaviour is communication. Why are stray dogs vicious? Because they're scared, so they'll bite you before you bite them.

It's the same with the people I work with. There are very few exceptions.

Solomon Meer was one of those exceptions.

What you heard at the top of the episode is a piece of creative writing penned by Solomon Meer while he was attending Leighburn Educational Unit, and being taught by Jo.

It is raining hard in Ergarth, where Jo has kindly offered to meet me. We conduct our interview in Jo's car, parked up outside the old Leighburn unit. It's now an unremarkable community facility with a nursery and office space, meeting rooms and various support services.

Around the unit a few crumbling terraced streets lead off into the distance; pebble-dashed walls, grimy windows with thick net curtains. A few young mothers share a chat on the corners, babies asleep in prams. Traffic-calming measures in faded paint fill the roads around here, most of the bollards broken off and the signs tagged or cracked. I hate to paint such a bleak picture, but there are signs of a community just clinging on, constantly trying to heave itself back from the brink. Just along the road is Ergarth Food Bank, alongside a new community cafe. Jo tells me it's a project tackling food waste; everything made in the kitchen is 'surplus food from supermarkets that would have been otherwise thrown away. 'Pay what you feel' is written on a large chalkboard outside, and a huge man with a face full of tattoos carries his twin daughters on his shoulders through the doorway. All three are shrieking with laughter.

—I'm glad we're here.

—*Outside the old unit? Does it bring back memories?*

—It does but you also can't see Tankerville Tower from here. We're facing the wrong way. I hate that place, I always did. Gave me the creeps. It's even worse now, after what happened. Wherever you are in Ergarth, you can see it; just this nasty black shape that you can't look away from – like a crack on the screen of your phone. It's also so bloody cold on that side of town. It gets right into your bones. Takes ages to get warm again. No, we're much better here.

—*I suppose there's added poignancy to the tower now, right?*

—It's just a sad place really, like a dead tooth in someone's mouth. That tower sums Ergarth up, really. Half forgotten, crumbling. No money to maintain it, no money to get rid of it. I see it in my dreams sometimes, still. Just that tower; falling snow. And ... *things* flying in and out. I can never get to sleep after one of those dreams. It's weird.

Jo shivers slightly and turns the heat up slightly in her car. She presses both hands against the vent, her fingers red with cold.

—*You taught English to Solomon Meer a few years ago, that's right isn't it? I'm struggling to find anyone who had any first-hand interactions with him.*

—I knew from our first session together that there was something deeply troubled about Sol – and believe me, I know about trouble, I know about damage. I've worked alongside damage my entire career.

—*Can you tell me about the Solomon Meer you knew?*

—Sol was the first of the three to end up here; the other two, I already knew. When his name appeared on my mentee list I had that bit of anticipation you always get with a new client: what are they going to be like? Are they going to tell you to fuck off? Are they going to be that exception – the one that you won't ever be able to reach? There's been a few of those in my career, but I honestly never thought that about Sol – or the other two, if I'm honest. Not until I found out what they did to Elizabeth Barton – the details of it ... the ... her *head.* I honestly never thought any of those three capable of that. I wonder if that's why Ergarth's been on my mind recently, why that tower keeps popping up in dreams.

—*So you met Solomon Meer when he first came to Leighburn, you were his mentor?*

—Yes. The system was quite good here – management really got it. There's a really delicate dynamic in classes like these; you can't just chuck a load of angry young people together and hope it works out. In alternative provision, your classes are no more than six, but in reality you'll only be ever teaching around two or three at once. Most classes are relatively calm. They know that if they mess on here, they're out, and then it's prison. They can be surly. They want to come in, get their head down and get out again. The introduction of the wrong type of person can fuck up that dynamic. So here we were careful. Every mentor had a few mentees. Outside lesson time you'd chat to them, give advice about careers, be an ear to listen if they wanted you to.

I'd actually read Sol's behaviour log from when he was at school, and I wasn't expecting a scared young man to be sitting there. You know what his first question was to me? 'Has anyone ever been really badly beaten up here, miss?' *Miss?* He was twenty-four! My first instinct was to hug him…

—*What had you expected him to be like?*

—I read about the incident with him squaring up to the headmaster when he was at school, and I won't lie, I was a little nervous. Is 'nervous' the right word? No. Apprehensive is better. I don't know what I expected really: in Ergarth, you didn't get a great deal of variety. Maybe a thug – a Martin Flynn?

The reasons for Solomon Meer being referred to Leighburn are not particularly noteworthy. Meer was excluded from Ergarth High when he was in year eleven. He stopped education completely, and began working in Ergarth Books full time. However, when Solomon began getting in persistent trouble with the Ergarth police for petty offences – drugs, vandalism, drunk and disorderly – he was sent to Leighburn to try and get some qualifications and make something of his life.

—*What was it about Solomon Meer that was so different from the others?*

—With the new ones, they'll often say hello, shake your hand, no bother. Then there's ones where it's hoods up, arms folded, defensive. Then there are the ones who won't look at you, who won't even acknowledge you – that's quite rare and you know that's where you're going to get trouble. Sol was none of those. He was sat at the desk, staring up at me with these big, wide eyes. I could tell he was on the verge of tears. That look was desperation – a desperation to please.

—*What was his work like?*

—One of the first pieces of work I do with the new intake is about heroes, just to have a look at their English skills, a free-writing piece about someone they admire. The usual is sports stars, actors or musicians. Very rarely it's members of their family. Most of the people who come to Leighburn had a terrible time at school, and lots of them had lost hope. There's a lot of problems with drugs and drink here. Most were from broken homes, they'd grown up amid chaos, often with no role model, no one to look up to. Now they were adults with their own chaos; cos that's all they were used to. Chaos.

Sol's piece – I don't have it anymore, in fact I submitted it as part of some evidence to try and get him some help – it was strange.

—*Who did he write about?*

—It was a *what* not a *who*. Sol wrote about a demon.

We're off to an interesting start. According to all reports and accounts about the young man, Solomon Meer was obsessed with vampires and the occult. Honestly, I was not expecting something so ... obvious.

—It had a funny name: *Pazuzu.* The demon from *The Exorcist*, the one that possesses that little girl. Sol knew a lot about this demon, called him the 'God of the Winds' – that phrase stuck with me, I don't know why.

The famous Mesopotamian demon Pazuzu was the son of Hanbi, the demon king of the underworld, a representation of the south-west wind, personified as a human with the head of a lion, talon-like claws and a scorpion's tail. Pazuzu was thought to be the bringer of famine, raging storms and locusts.

—Sol's piece was very well informed. He wrote about how this demon was good as well as bad, how he was destructive but also protected people from other demons. It was an odd piece, rather long and rambling with no real point. I don't recall exactly what it was that Sol liked so much about the demon. I mean, at the time, I thought he was just trying to be edgy. Like a teenager.

I have been compiling and reviewing what I know to be facts about Solomon Meer, free of speculation or hyperbole. It's not a lot. He was from Nottingham in the East Midlands. There was little to report from his previous school in terms of poor behaviour, but when his parents separated, he moved with his mother to Ergarth.

Jo speaks with a distinct fondness when talking about Solomon Meer, and I decide to challenge her on this right away. She bristles.

—I can see why everyone now thinks he's the personification of evil. A devil-worshipper who killed a young woman. This demon stuff probably doesn't help. I can only say what I saw in front of me – and what I saw was not evil at all. The demon knowledge – well, anyone can know about that sort of thing by listening to a podcast; it doesn't make them evil. It doesn't make them a killer. What I saw in Sol was a very disturbed young man who needed help.

Solomon Meer worried Jo from day one, she says. He was quiet and withdrawn, unwilling or unable to mix with any of the other young people in the unit.

—That whole devil-worshipper thing, he'd constructed as armour; it protected him from the world. Underneath that façade was a sad, scared young man with a lot of issues.

Solomon Meer is a figure shrouded in myth. A rather overexuberant series in the states named Teenrage: When Kids Go Psycho *portrayed Meer using a six-foot-tall actor with raven-black hair down to his shoulders, wearing full goth regalia – leather trousers and white make-up, sat snarling and carving pentagrams on his desk. But the photographs of Meer in the media show a pretty normal-looking young man in his early twenties – average height, skinny with mousy curls that hung over his eyes. In court he wore a suit, his head had been shaved roughly, giving him a rather odd appearance. Despite this, Solomon Meer's obsession with the occult has followed him wherever he goes. Even Rob Karl in episode one accuses Meer of being a devil-worshipper. But burning flowers in Ergarth Dene seems to be the only actual evidence anyone has that could remotely back up this claim.*

I'm starting to understand, though, that Meer used this perception of him to perhaps 'curate' his own life – but unlike Elizabeth, he did it in a negative way. Perhaps he did this to protect himself in a small town where he didn't fit in. Jo tells me she thinks it came from somewhere deeper.

—*You describe Solomon Meer as 'disturbed'.*

—Yes. He had a lot of issues: depression; crippling anxiety. He told me so many times that his brain was 'rushing' – that was the word he used: 'rushing'. He was always so apologetic about it, always so sorry. Some days he would come in late, looking like he hadn't eaten, hadn't slept. He would say he was having a bad day, couldn't get out of bed, couldn't think straight.

—*Was he getting help? Counselling? Medication?*

—That's honestly hilarious. Mental-health provision for young people in somewhere like Ergarth is more or less nonexistent. Sol was on a two-year waiting list for therapy. It's ridiculous. No one goes for help until they're at the end of their tether, in crisis; and then they have to wait two years? And he was scared of being medicated. He'd read about the potential side effects of antidepressants – he was frightened he would commit suicide. My heart went out to him, it really did. I could see him getting worse, and there was nothing I could do about it. In a town like Ergarth, a place that's been stripped to its bare bones by government cuts, then forgotten about, there was no hope for him. None at all.

—*So how did he fit in at the unit? As I understand, it's not a place that specialises in mental health or special educational needs.*

—Right. We weren't qualified to deal with people who had a diagnosis past mild learning difficulties. Our speciality was social and behavioural issues. We simply didn't have the facilities or the staff to deal with someone like Sol.

—*So how did it work for Solomon at Leighburn?*

—I think, when Sol first came here, he just wanted to do his time and get it over with. He didn't want to stick out, and I didn't blame him. There was no uniform there, obviously, but Sol always wore very plain clothes, just basic, no logo hoodies and jeans, not the sportswear that most of the lads and lasses wore. Sol just wore anonymous stuff.

—*Why was that, do you think?*

—Because he was terrified of the others. He was a petty criminal: graffiti, broken bottles, drinking, stealing chocolate bars from the newsagents. He thought he'd be eaten alive in Leighburn, he thought it was going to be like school.

—*It's going to be hard for people listening to understand this. Especially after he did what he did.*

—Yeah, OK. I see what you're saying. But even to this day, when I think about Sol, I don't think of him as a cold-blooded killer. I'm not trying to deny or excuse what he did. It's just … It's that cliché isn't it? It's always the quiet ones.

—*I want to talk about George and Martin briefly, but right now, let's stick with Solomon Meer. It seems like people knew a lot more about the other two than him.*

—It sounds a bit unkind to say it, but I will. You see, most lads who come to Leighburn, despite their social issues — there's not a lot going on between the ears. I'm not being funny but it's true. Ninety-nine percent of them come from a background that lacks order. They come from damage since they were little. Kids *need* order as they grow up. They need routine. Just stay with me for a moment; back when these lads were in school, lads like George and Martin, they don't often understand the work and didn't want to be called 'thick', so it's much easier to kick off, mess about, get sent out the room. Then it escalates and they get kicked out of school. So they've never had to face the work they didn't understand. Then they often spend their lives repeating the same cycle – they're now grown adults with no real skills, getting in bother rather than getting a job. It all comes from a place of fear.

Sol wasn't one of those lads though. There's plenty of smart kids came to Leighburn for other reasons: school didn't suit them, other problems at home. A lot of them have grown up a bit, realised they want more from life, they want to turn things around. Sol was one of them. Like I said, rare for Ergarth; he had a brain in his head, he just didn't like having to use it for such trifles as school. He was likeable, funny, he read a lot, had a vast imagination, loved writing stories. But there was always this darkness behind it all, his mental health was like a black cloud that sometimes overshadowed his entire life, sometimes just peeping over the horizon.

—*When Solomon was at school, he tried to assault his headmaster, Mr Threlfall. I've spoken to an Ergarth volunteer fire-fighter who says Solomon Meer caused a lot of petty trouble in town. It might not have been mugging old ladies, but he was no angel.*

—Well, yes, I suppose that's true. For the record, I don't think Mr Threlfall's story was exactly accurate, though.

—*Can you elaborate?*

—I have a few friends who worked at Ergarth High at the time. I'm not going to stitch anyone up here, but the word in the staffrooms in this area was that Mr Threlfall was throwing his weight around, trying to be the big man, and Sol just snapped. In my eyes Sol was more the victim in that situation.

—*So once Solomon had got over his initial fear and settled down at Leighburn, did you get to know him better? Did he open up?*

—He did rather quickly, actually. We used a lot of techniques that come from alternative provision. So, for example, we used to have 'mentor time' on Friday afternoons where we'd have an hour one to one, to discuss the week, play board games, chat. It sounds a bit babyish for lads and lasses who are in their twenties, but I'm telling you, if they didn't like it, they wouldn't do it. A lot of the Leighburn lads have never had an adult to share their feelings with, they've not really had someone who'll just spend that time. It's good for their social skills. They all pretend they hate it, but they never miss a mentor session. You'd be surprised how many of them who're in a bad situation want to open up. I had a lot of board games in my cupboard here, and sometimes we would sit and play, just chatting about nothing really. Those were the moments when you'd get them disclosing to you. It was hard sometimes, it really was. They'd tell you about what they get up to – I often had to tell them to keep the drug talk to a minimum. But I've had a few occasions where we've been in the middle of a game of Boggle and a young lass has offhandedly mentioned some horrific sexual assault when she was a teenager. I've had lads quite matter-of-factly tell me about the things they've seen at home when they were little – stabbings, drug deals, domestic violence, the lot.

—*What sort of things did you and Sol talk about?*

—He opened up a little bit about his family. He went through a lot when he was a little boy; he saw violence in the house. He was the victim of a few beatings by his father before they moved. How true that is, I'll never know, but he told me these things and I had no cause to disbelieve him.

He told me about someone he was seeing, too. A girlfriend, of sorts.

—*A girlfriend? Was this someone from Ergarth?*

—No. This was someone he was talking to online. Sol was very guarded about her. The only time he'd mention her was when he was making a point about something.

—*What do you mean?*

—So if Sol was talking about something – it was usually to do with vampires – he'd make a point about some characteristic. For example he told me that Polish vampires sleep with their thumbs interlocked; this mystery Internet girl had told him it, so that was that. It was fact. I saw that as symptomatic of Sol's utter lack of confidence. He needed strangers on the Internet to tell him he was valid.

—*Why do you think Sol opened up to you in the way he did?*

—We built up a lot of trust you see. The intake is always a bit sparse at the start of the academic year. Sometimes there was only Sol and one or two others in the class. This was a good few months before George and Martin arrived.

I also encouraged Sol to do a lot of his talking through writing. I think he found a degree of solace in writing creatively. I encouraged him to turn his difficult feelings into stories. Before those other two arrived, I actually thought Sol was doing better. The black cloud had retreated a lot. But it came back when those two arrived at Leighburn. Sol really started going downhill.

George Meldby and Martin Flynn were referred to Leighburn Educational Unit at around the same time. What interests me is Jo's assertion that the relationship between the three was the exact opposite of how it was portrayed in the media. It also conflicts with what everyone else has told me about the three.

—How those two behaved toward Sol had an absolutely devastating effect on his mental health. I was amazed when they were portrayed as a trio – as if they associated with each other.

—*You're saying they didn't?*

—Of course not! George and Martin and Sol? Never. Not in a million years. Not in Leighburn anyway. Sol was scared stiff of the pair of them. That's what always bothered me the most about this entire affair; what on earth were they all doing *together* at the Vampire Tower, that night. It made no sense to me whatsoever. Sol seemed terrified and fascinated by the place at the same time. He used to tell me he saw shapes flying in and out at night. That's where my dreams came from, I suppose.

—*What were your impressions of George and Martin?*

—I'll start with George. He was a funny one. You'll have heard that from a lot of people, I imagine, and it's true. He was small, quiet, kept himself to himself. He wasn't one to raise his head above the parapet, was George.

—*You were aware of his fire-setting?*

—Who wasn't?

—*George Meldby had been excluded from school, had a stint in a pupil referral unit and then nothing, is that right?*

—George was your typical rudderless drifter, happy just to pick up his benefits and let life pass him by. He was in a dream world half the time, that lad. I think there were a lot of issues with him as well, what with the fires and everything. He could have done with help too.

This much is true. George Meldby lived at home with his mother, claiming benefits and doing very little after he left school. There's no real record of him doing much of anything, and he wasn't much of a trouble-maker. There's no record of violence with George, save for the

Fellman's factory arson attack. George was referred to Leighburn because he'd shown no inclination to get a job. Sending fit-for-work benefits claimants to better themselves was part of the scheme that was piloted in Ergarth. For a lot of people, it gave them a purpose, it helped them back to work. Not George.

—*Was fire and setting fires ever mentioned while George was with you?*

—Yes and no. There was a lot of sniggering and nudging and silliness with him and Martin. George was like a little ghost, just passing through. He gave very little away; some staff said he had a slyness to him. I think I only saw him being remotely aggressive – overtly so – once. When he threatened Sol.

—*Really?*

—Oh, it was an empty threat really, I think, but there was one incident when I caught the tail end of an altercation. It was handbags at dawn, really, but George was telling Sol, 'I'll burn your fucking house down.' I remember telling George he needed to be careful with threats of that particular nature and he slunk off.

—*What was the altercation about?*

—I did ask Sol, but he said it was nothing; told me to forget it.

—*What about Martin Flynn?*

—OK. So Martin was your bog-standard Ergarth thug. I'm sorry to say it, but he had no real redeeming qualities. Martin was hard, like you'd expect – he was a Flynn after all. He also had a mild learning difficulty. Mind you, that was never officially diagnosed; his family didn't really engage with support services. So long as he could work in the abattoir then that's all they cared about.

—*Do you know what it was that Martin had actually done to land himself at Leighburn?*

—To be honest, Martin would have done better going to prison. Sounds harsh doesn't it? But Leighburn wasn't for him. It was some minor assault charge. We never really got to know.

—*To me, it seems coincidence that the two were referred to Leighburn like that at the same time.*

—I think it was, yes. The thing with Martin was that he'd grown up learning to solve problems with his fists. Sometimes he'd turn up to my classes and say he couldn't be bothered and put his head down on the desk. I have to say that I always managed to get *something* out of Martin on those days, however little.

—*When did they start victimising Solomon Meer?*

—They never left Sol alone from day one, those two. I'll never understand what on earth it was about him they hated so much. They never did enough to get them kicked out though. They were smart about it. I used to do what I could – keep Sol behind at the end of lessons, give him a place to read at lunch times. But this wasn't school. These were all grown men. Young, yes, but still adults. I couldn't fight Sol's battles for him.

Despite all this, I will say one thing about those two; something that pulled on my heartstrings: whenever they were caught, they never denied it.

—*They were unrepentant?*

—It wasn't that. It was more like … I think Martin Flynn actually summed it up rather well once. He once said to me when I was ticking him off, 'There's no point me saying nowt is there? No one ever believes us. Never have. Never will.' George actually wrote something about it in a piece of creative writing.

—*Can you remember it?*

—I can. That's another one I wish I'd kept. It was about fire, of course – it was always about fire with him. I'd asked him to write a piece about a strong, childhood memory; first day at school, something like that. George was quite articulate in his writing, I'll give him that. There was a story about a boy in a primary school; how a girl who he was in love with had tried to set fire to the toilets and the boy got the blame. She got commended by the head teacher for ratting the boy out. That was fairly self-explanatory.

—*It was the incident from George Meldby's school days? I wonder who the girl was.*

—Right. He did another one about a ghost burning down a church. We were doing ghost stories for Halloween, you see. In the story, the ghost makes the boy promise not to tell and he'll get a reward. From year seven to thirty years old, it's always what most lads want to write about; ghosts and blood and guts.

—*What do you think this story was really about?*

—George had this whole victim complex going on – that no one believed him. Martin Flynn was the same. I found it rather sad at the time, and I remember asking him why he thought that was and he just shrugged. Grunted. Walked off.

—*You said George and Martin had a detrimental effect on Solomon Meer?*

—Correct. He was starting to open up until those two came, and then he just retreated, the shutters went down. Instead of talking at mentor meetings, he'd just curl himself into a corner with one of those blessed vampire books.

—*Vampires. That was Solomon Meer's obsession.*

—It was. It probably still is.

—*How did it manifest itself when you knew him?*

—It was all Sol talked about. He'd read everything; all the Anne Rice, Poppy Z. Brite, K.J. Wignall; for Sol vampires were everything, and everything was vampires. That's all he would talk about as time went on. At first, it was more like a literary admiration, but it became an obsession very quickly.

After a while, during mentor meetings, when Sol wasn't reading, he was ranting. When his mother had moved him to Ergarth, he made a connection in his mind to the Beast from the East vampire legend, became convinced it was his 'destiny' to be here. He would say that a lot. That's the thing with a disordered mind – you can see it flailing around, making connections to things that aren't there. I asked him to write his thoughts down, turn them into stories. I thought it might help.

Jo reads me the story you heard at the top of this episode. She tells me the vampire it features appeared in many of Sol's creative pieces, always muttering seduction to his protagonist, always plaguing him with the temptation to kill, to become immortal.

—Sol told me he heard voices, you know. He mentioned it a few times, but I never knew if he meant it or not. I wondered if I should refer him to a hospital or something. He wasn't acting out enough to be sectioned, unless he did it voluntarily, and he wouldn't take medication. I think Sol personified what he heard in his head with this 'vampire' entity in his stories. It would tell him that it was going to come for him one day. It told him he had to 'find it', and I think he spent his spare time doing just that – searching for something. I cannot imagine what that must have been like. Horrible. Just horrible.

There'll be more than some who take real umbrage with Jo's sympathetic portrayal of Solomon Meer and say that he was lying to get attention. Lest we forget, Meer was deemed fit to stand trial for the murder of Elizabeth Barton, something Jo describes as 'typical'. I don't want to challenge Jo's view of Solomon yet; every angle has its own value in helping us understand what happened to Elizabeth Barton.

—Is this why the 'vampire' idea was brought up by the prosecution? It must have started somewhere.

—It would have started with Sol, that's my guess anyway. When they were all here – it was only a few months before what happened – he never stopped talking about vampires. He kept telling everyone that the Ergarth Vampire was going to return. The other two found this hilarious, of course. They just made his life even more miserable. Sol began wearing this amulet around his neck; he said he used it to attract vampires. He said that this person online told him how to make it. One of the others – George or Martin – took it off him, apparently. Broke it. For no other reason than they knew it would distress Sol. That sums up what they were like.

—Were there consequences to this? Were George and Martin punished at all?

—It happened off the premises, and it was their word against Sol's. Of course, they tried to get themselves off the hook – they told me that they were concerned about him, but really they were trying to stitch him up. They said he had this messed-up idea that the Ergarth Vampire was lurking somewhere in the town. They said they were worried he was going to do something daft. Maybe I should have listened to them.

—Did anything come of Solomon's vampire search?

—I usually walk my dog over near Myrmirth stables; over where there's the fields and stuff. It was early in the morning, before work. December, still dark. Snowy. Horrible. I never went near the tower, or the coast; the wind was brutal. Problem was, all the fields and paths were clogged up with snow. So I had to take Nicky over by the Vampire Tower where you could actually walk about a bit. I was quick though, I wasn't wanting to stay around there very long.

—*I'm guessing you were wary of the people that were in there?*

—Well yes. Of course. Nicky, my Doberman, he looks scary but he's not much protection – he's soft as anything. And there's the gulls up in the tower as well. They're almost as big as Nicky and they're aggressive. They'll swoop right at you, like they want to attack. Anyway, I throw the ball for him and he won't go, starts whining and I think, *Right, time to get out of here.* It wasn't just the addicts, it was the tower as well; such a horrible place, poking up through the snow like a middle finger. Anyway, I can see something. A flash of light; again and again. There's someone up ahead, they're all curled up on the floor in the shadow of the tower. I wanted to just get back in my car but, I thought, what if they're dead or something? Anyway I go over, and it was Sol.

—*What?*

—He was lying in the snow with his shirt off, shivering. I thought he'd been beaten up or taken something, you know? Then I see he's got his phone in his hand. He's not even seen me.

—*What on earth was he doing?*

—This was when I really started to worry about him, I really got concerned. He was lying there with all this – I mean I thought it was bruises but it was make-up – all this black around his eyes, fake fangs in his mouth, lipstick all over his lips, like blood. He was taking photos. Lying there taking photos of himself. The lad was almost blue with the cold.

—*What did you do?*

—I honestly didn't know what to do. It felt wrong. *I* felt wrong. I felt like I was intruding on something very private. It also … well, yes, it scared me. Something in his face, in his eyes. I … I mean I don't know what I could have done. I just backed away. I went back to my car. He wasn't doing any harm, I suppose. Then a few months later … he did what he did…

—*What was it for?*

—I never asked. I wish I had but I felt like if I'd have brought it up, he may have … I don't know. I didn't want to betray his trust, I suppose. I think everything had gone wrong inside his head – this vampire stuff; he loved and hated it at the same time, and it was all starting to blur with reality.

Jo tells me that this was when Solomon's famous video, 'Shopping Trolley Sledge', went viral – a couple of months before the three killed Elizabeth Barton.

—Oh yes, I remember the video. Sol actually garnered some sort of minor celebrity status for that. I remember thinking that maybe it was a good thing for him, some positive attention at last. It seemed to lift him, temporarily. I think maybe the photos with the vampire make-up had something to do with it as well?

The video meant Sol ended up getting attention from the last person in Ergarth he'd have expected it from: Elizabeth Barton. I ask Jo to elaborate.

—Everyone in Ergarth knew Elizabeth Barton. That shiny red car of hers, with the eyelashes and stuff; you'd always see it around Ergarth. Lots of times, she'd be parked up near the food bank. But no one dared touch that car. All the boys wanted her, all the girls wanted to be her. George and Martin had known her a long time, hadn't they?

—*Since primary school.*

—That makes sense. It felt like those two had become part of her entourage, her private security firm.

—*You know the story about the Fellman's factory, I imagine.*

—Of course. We all did. When George came here, everyone told me it was him. I never mentioned it and neither did he. Like I said before, nothing was ever George's fault.

—*What was Solomon Meer's view on Elizabeth? Did he ever mention her?*

—Only after she visited.

—*I'm sorry, what? As far as I know, there was no record of Solomon Meer and Elizabeth Barton ever being in touch save by phone – a single message the night she was killed.*

—Oh really? No, she came here a few times – to the unit.

—*Why?*

—No idea. She simply turned up one day, out of the blue. I saw her arrive outside in her little red car. Sol nearly had a heart attack, bless him. They talked. She drove away. The same thing happened fairly regularly after that. Sometimes he would get in the car.

This is a huge detail that I can't believe I've not heard until now. Jo tells me she was never asked to give evidence in court and never reported it to the police in the wake of what happened.

—I didn't know what was going on. It wasn't my business. I assumed everyone was aware that Solomon and Elizabeth knew each other. Everyone knew everyone in Ergarth; they'd been to the same school, after all. These were adults, free to make their own decisions. All I can say is that she was smart. She never showed up when George or Martin were there.

—*Why do you think that was?*

—I think she knew very well that it would only get them up a height. They'd start showing off, wouldn't they? Making fun of Sol to impress her. She wasn't daft.

—*What did Solomon say about these visits?*

—He was as you'd imagine: rather chuffed. His mood certainly got a bit better. Then it turned again. Back came all the vampire stuff; the poor lad was up and down like a yo-yo.

—*What do you think their chats were about?*

—Well, I can only imagine it had something to do with those bloody Dead in Six Days videos. Both Sol and Elizabeth did them, didn't they? I banned all talk of that challenge from my lessons. These were adults, not children – and they were passing round these ridiculous challenges like they were still in primary school.

—*A common theory is that Elizabeth wanted a piece of Solomon's sudden Internet fame; his 'Shopping Trolley Sledge' video had done considerably better than all of hers.*

—Yes. I did ask him once or twice about that – whether the two of them were doing some sort of collaboration. Sol kept saying everyone had to wait. 'Just wait,' he would say over and over. Now I realise what he meant. I understand now what that final challenge was. It was Sol, wasn't it, who told her to come to the vampire tower that night?

Jo trails off a bit, dabs her eyes.

—I had no idea – no idea at all that he was going to do what he did to Elizabeth Barton. That level of violence, I never saw it in him. The other two as well; it was so … I don't know. Maybe it *was* one of those ridiculous challenges that went wrong – like they said in court. Sol lost track of reality? I don't know.

—*Who was setting the challenges, do you think? Who was behind it all?*

Jo gives me a rather severe look.

—I very much doubt there was a nefarious online vampire, if that's what you mean. That silly challenge wasn't about vampires at all. It was about one-upmanship and popularity; getting the most likes, the most views – to be the most famous for five minutes. Was anyone being controlled by some dark figure? I'm dubious about that. As you already know, Sol's video started it all off. Then Elizabeth Barton got a hold of it. That's when it became more than a silly challenge.

Jo proceeds to give a long and heartfelt explanation of the pressures on young people online. She tells me it's easier for people who didn't grow up with every move, every bad-hair day being scrutinised and rated by an endless jury of your peers. She says people like us used to play outside. But I know if I had the access to the Internet that young people today have, I would have spent my entire life staring into that abyss. Jo says it's easy for us to dismiss the young as vapid and vain – preening into their phones, posting endless selfies; it's easy for us to dismiss their eternal quest for validation. But for many of the young people she has worked with this is the only validation they have.

—A lot of youngsters nowadays grow up being parented by devices. Parents try and fix all their children's problems by giving them *things*. A lot of the older generations, the baby-boomers, grew up with very tight rules, very dictatorial parents, and they wanted to change that. So it swings the other way, those parents don't want to see their children disappointed. Ever. That's not healthy either, not allowing your child to feel disappointment, to *want* something and not get it.

I think of Harold and Mildred Barton. I think of Elizabeth in her bedroom, Jason with his consoles and big television. Their desperate need for attention.

—The young people I work with – young men and women, *adults* for God's sake – this idea of being liked online is the only validation they've ever had. We call them 'emotionally impoverished'. If you've grown up when Mam and Dad aren't available, you have to get validation somewhere else, don't you?

Jo tells me that for the young people she works with, everything about everyone's lives goes online. People post Instagram stories at memorials of their dead relatives, read poems at funerals that they'd found on Facebook. Jo tells me that she sees this every day, it's certainly not limited to Ergarth.

—I'd say it's even worse now. I was working with a woman just the other day who found out her beloved grandfather had passed because a cousin had posted about it on Facebook. That's how she found out. Honestly, it's true. The cousin was totally unrepentant. She had no idea what she'd done wrong.

Maybe it's our age? I don't know. I think we have to look at why there's this need to curate your life, to overshare. Where does this need for attention come from? That's why this Dead in Six Days thing was so important to everyone. To do well at it was to be someone. In the week before Elizabeth Barton was killed, it was all anyone ever talked about. Elizabeth Barton had made that challenge her own.

In the days running up to her death, Elizabeth was posing videos of herself participating in the Dead in Six Days challenge – defiantly refusing to pass any of the tasks on – in order to meet her 'death' at the end. Jo shares the idea that Solomon Meer resented the fact that she'd effectively taken the one thing he'd had positive attention for and made it her own.

I ponder Jo's term 'emotionally impoverished', and it makes me think of what Jason told me – about the things he and his sister were given, about the various babysitters and nannies, their absent parents. Did he contact me – summon me by painting graffiti on his parents' house – to be validated. Was the fact that I responded as validating for him as the likes on his sister's YouTube channel were to her?

At this moment it feels like there were three, rather than one case of emotional impoverishment: two siblings vying for validation, and the lost boy in all of this – Solomon Meer.

—Whatever happened between Sol and Elizabeth seemed to have cooled off by March. He wasn't saying we had to 'wait' anymore. I have a feeling she used him for something and then dropped him. But I don't know for sure. Whatever happened, I think it finally broke him, if I'm honest. I think everything became distorted in Sol's mind. I have no idea what on earth happened at Tankerville Tower that night, but we all know the result, don't we? I'll never be able to get my head around it. I just hope that Solomon Meer gets the help he so desperately needs.

—*The narrative is that Sol resented Elizabeth's popularity online.*

—Is that what we've come to? Someone can die over who gets the most likes online?

—*There are still things that don't add up for me in this story. What on earth was going on between Solomon Meer and Elizabeth Barton?*

—I don't know for sure. He never said. I will say that George and Martin were really on his case around this time, they simply did not let up.

—I've spoken to Elizabeth Barton's family and they told me that Solomon Meer was in their house the night before Elizabeth was killed.

Jo flinches, as if she's been hit.

—Yeah. Yeah … I was wondering if you were going to mention that. It was one of those – was it true or not? I'd heard about it too – Ergarth's such a small town. Maybe there was something between them? I don't know.

—Maybe it had something to do with the Dead in Six Days thing? Or … and I really don't like saying this but it's out there … could she have been exploiting him? The way Sol was back then, it might have been possible. Maybe she wanted to video him and he lost it? It goes around and around in my head sometimes, like the dreams about that tower. Maybe we'll never know exactly.

There is something else that has been bothering me throughout this interview, something I feel Jo can help me address.

—George and Martin were Elizabeth Barton's self-appointed 'protectors' weren't they? What do you think turned them against her that night?

—I'm not saying anything conclusive. I'm not an authority, an expert, anything. All I do is try and help young people with little hope try and make something of themselves. I'm giving you my opinion, that's all. I just want to make that clear before I answer you, OK?

—Understood.

—And my opinion is that I don't believe that Sol or the other two killed Elizabeth Barton of their own volition. There. I've said it.

—Are you saying that it wasn't their idea?

—I'm not talking from a place of expertise. I'm giving you an opinion. I may be completely wrong. But I say what I saw, and this idea that Sol was some sort of leader just isn't true. He wasn't. Sol was well read, intelligent, but ultimately very ill. If anything he would have been a follower. Just like George and just like Martin. He certainly wouldn't have been able to convince those other two to do something like that.

—*So what happened at Tankerville Tower? What brought these four together on a freezing night in 2018?*

—I don't know. They all said it was a 'prank gone wrong' in court didn't they? Maybe in the end that was true?

Jo sighs and looks down at her feet. Leighburn Educational Unit never recovered from the association with Meer, Meldby and Flynn, and I understand now why Jo wanted her identity kept a secret.

—There's not a day goes by that I don't allocate some blame to myself for what happened to Elizabeth Barton. But how was I to know? Was it my fault? I have to tell myself it wasn't. I did all I could to try and get Solomon Meer the help he needed, but there was only so much I could do. If I'd had any inkling of what they were going to do, I would have told someone. I would have done. I know it.

—*It must be hard to have to carry that burden.*

—I just … I never saw it coming, I never did. I've been working with bad 'uns for so many years. Sometimes you can see it in them, that lack of empathy, that deadness behind the eyes. By God, I've taught a few of them. I've been in rooms with lads and girls who I would never like to meet again; lads and lasses who put me in fear of my life. Sol just … wasn't like that at all. Whatever it was he was putting out there, it was bravado – it was battle armour. The whole devil-worship thing, he said to try and make himself sound dangerous, to make people leave him alone. But in the end it probably helped convict him.

It's all so confusing – so hard, so awful.

—*If it wasn't a prank, could it have been an act of anger? Or an act of distorted love? Solomon Meer was caught burning flowers in Ergarth Dene only a few days before he killed Elizabeth.*

—Was he? Well, that's actually rather interesting. Burning flowers was one of Sol's motifs, you see. He used to write a lot about it.

—*Really? Why do you think that was?*

—I'm probably reading too much into it   that's the English teacher in me – but Sol wrote about a character burning flowers on his father's grave. Maybe it signified an end to something? Flowers symbolising love, perhaps? I don't know.

—*There was another lad with him apparently.*

—Well … that doesn't sound right.

—*Why not?*

—A couple of reasons: one; you don't do something like that with company do you? Unrequited love is a very solitary thing, don't you think? Also, I don't remember Sol having *any* friends, not really. Who was he?

—*I don't know, the person who caught them didn't either. The boy was younger than him apparently.*

—I suppose that makes sense doesn't it? Everyone around Ergarth saying that Sol was a manipulative cult leader. I imagine this lad was some other lost soul like him.

—*I've been told that he burned them where the Ergarth Vampire, the Beast from the East, is supposed to be buried.*

—Interesting. There's a lot you could read into that, I suppose. Or it could be a coincidence.

I feel that this sums up the case of Elizabeth Barton rather well – reading a lot into something that could just be a coincidence. Were Solomon and an acolyte deliberately burning flowers over the ancient vampire's grave, plotting to kill? Or was a damaged and lovelorn young man acting out in a town where there was little hope? Is there anything we can read into this? Every time I feel I've found a thread that takes me to the heart of what happened that night, it splits. Jason Barton's sentiment about forcing the story comes back to me. But it's a mess. Jason's story still lingers – the abusive and tyrannical side to his sister. Was it this that Solomon Meer saw, and in his distorted mind, made a connection with an old story?

I think there's another story that emerges from this interview, one shaped by the new information we have discovered. Most significant is the relationship between Meer, Meldby and Flynn. If what Jo is saying is correct, and I have no reason to doubt her, the three were not some sort of coven, but enemies. I also think that the mental-health issues that Solomon Meer was experiencing are significant. They can't explain his actions but may have distorted his thinking. We're left then with two huge questions – what was Solomon Meer doing in the Bartons' house, and what were Meer, Meldby and Flynn doing together on the night Elizabeth died?

In this episode we've seen another side to Elizabeth's killers. However, I am still struggling to understand the real motive behind what the three young men did. Maybe they finally found something in common that day – a shared resentment towards Elizabeth Barton – someone none of the three would ever have a chance of really getting to know.

I admit to Jo that I'm still conflicted and ask if there's anything else she can tell me that might help with where to go next. I tell her my repeated requests to interview the three have been ignored. I'm starting to feel at a loss and wonder if perhaps there actually isn't anything more to the case of Elizabeth Barton.

Jo's theory that none of the three convicted were acting of their own volition is one that I've not entertained and neither, it seems, has anyone else – perhaps because it doesn't seem to have much behind it either, save for a hunch. In court, Solomon, Martin and George made out that what they did to Elizabeth Barton was an accident, though I suspect that was prompted by their legal counsel, in an attempt to reduce their sentences.

Then there's the removal of Elizabeth Barton's head. This is the one thing, I think, that truly ties the idea of vampires to the murder. A deluded Solomon Meer, obsessed with the Ergarth Vampire, may have been convinced Elizabeth was one. But the question remains: how on earth did Solomon Meer manage to coerce the other two into helping him do this to someone they both adored?

If, however, Solomon Meer, George Meldby and Martin Flynn were indeed following orders, who was giving them?

Maybe that's what we need to ask when we conclude this series. Until then, this has been our fifth, and I have been Scott King.

Until next time.

Lizzie B

3,689 subscribers

Today has been my last day on earth
Tonight I'm [......................] vampire,
[......................] I'm doing something no one has ever done before
Tonight is the night of my death
[......................] dead [......................]

Oh my GOD, guys! What is this SNOW? Look, look at it! It's like a ... blizzard or something. Like, there's no way I'm going to be able to livestream. My internet is absolutely terrible up here. Guys, I don't even want to go out there!

It's stopped. Sort of. Look. Look at my windows! If I open them, there'll be like a snowdrift in the house. I cannot imagine what it must be like for homeless people out there tonight. I feel so bad.

OK, *feeling a bit better now, and as you can see, I've got this brand-new coat on and my lucky penguin hat! I'm even wearing thermal underwear! Bringing sexy back, right here guys!*

Two pairs of socks and I'm ... gonna ... make ... that ... three. There we go.

I [......................] them! I can't even get my boots on!

So I got a message from the lovely Vladlena. She says I've got to go and meet her in Tankerville Tower, and we all know what that place is all about.

So, like, someone told me that [......................] of the Ergarth Vampire story, the proper *version. You know, like the Grimm Fairy tales aren't the proper versions. Like, the proper versions are much more grim. See what I did there? [......................] funny bunny!*

So tonight I suppose I'd better say my goodbyes. You know, just in case! Sooo, thanks to Vainglorious of course for all your lovely make-up; thanks to Chirrup for your clothes – oodles of unboxing videos on my page if [......................] a parcel from Vainglorious waiting at the post office cos of the snow!

[......................] lovely things [......................]

Happy girl [.......................]

Chocs and treats and stuff and as soon as the vampire's gone and the snow melts, I'll unbox all your delights.

I wonder if, like, Vladlena's doing her own channel – like vampires do unboxing on people's throats?
    Yeah, I'm [.......................] I? Delaying the inevitable. Tick, tock. Oh my God, I'd better get going.
    You guys, I'm pretty scared; I wonder how many of you [.......................] me? Just in case … it's dark out there!

    OK, here I am, at the front door. Gonna say bye-bye to Mam and Dad.
    Mam? Dad? Bye!
    Oh what a surprise, [.......................] leave them a note shall I? Some flowers? What shall I write? Dear Mam and Dad gtg, vampire to meet.
    Hopefully […] some of you […] Tower!
    I mean [.......................] if I don't come [.......................] them! Ha-ha!

OK. This is it. This is the last day of the Dead in Six Days challenge – this is as far as anyone's ever got. I'm off to meet Vladlena at Tankerville Tower. I'll do another video while I'm there and upload it as soon as I get back. For those of you who can't make it!
    Promise!

OK, so smash that like, hit that subscribe if you want to know what happened on the final day of the Dead in Six Days challenge. I promise you it's going to be good. Let's see if we can make this the most views ever!

If I come back that is.
Oh my gosh it's cold!
See you guys there, I [......................] of you!
Byee!

Episode Six: The Quiet One

—I'll never forget how it felt when they found me. 'Miss!' one of them said. 'I've found that little girl. She's hiding in the bin!' I'll never forget it as long as I live. All those teachers, the dinner ladies, the other kids who didn't even know my name before, they were all around me, hugging me. Everyone at school suddenly knew who I was, everyone was telling me it was OK, everyone was telling me I was lovely, that they liked me, that I was pretty. I got to sit with all the popular girls at lunch. I was first in the queue and the dinner lady let me have extra pudding. Custard and cake. She called me a 'pretty little bobbin'.

There was a special assembly the next day, all about including people, all about being nice to people who don't fit in. Kids who are *different*. I remember sitting there in the front row in my brand-new skirt and tights that they'd bought me. I was wearing a jumper that didn't smell of grease or mould. It was like there was this light that I never knew was there had suddenly turned on inside me. That light was shining out, and everyone could see it. Everyone knew that the special assembly was about me.

The day after the assembly everyone wanted to play with me; everyone wanted to hold my hand in the yard, wanted to let me play with the best toys. Even the boys were asking me if I wanted to play football with them. I'd never felt like that before and I've never felt like it since. It must be what supermodels and celebrities feel like. I couldn't wait to go to school after that. Sometimes I didn't do any work in my lessons and the teacher wouldn't say anything about it. People fought and argued to sit next to me and help me.

I had gone from being nobody to being the queen of the school. The centre of the entire world.

Then we moved house.

Just like that. I'd been the star of the week – I had my certificate and my green sticker with my name on it, and Mum was waiting at the gate with all these suitcases.

'Quick,' she said, and I had to pull this huge suitcase along. I dropped my certificate – it was raining and I watched it soak into a puddle. No one dared to stop us or say anything to Mum, but they were all looking as we pulled those stupid suitcases all the way to the bus stop. I stuck my green sticker on the back of the seat on the bus. I didn't know where we were going, but if we ever came home, this would be my seat on the bus.

But we didn't go back. I don't even remember where that was.

We went on a train after that for hours, and then another bus that made me feel sick until we ended up at a house on an estate somewhere. It smelled. The bathroom had a carpet that was always wet and my clothes got mouldy in the wardrobe. I started going to a new school that was much bigger than my old one; it was loud and it was crowded, and I was totally lost. I didn't know anyone and the kids were all louder with an accent I couldn't understand. So I started hiding again, but this time there was no special assemblies or kind teachers. This time, some bigger kids found me and they told me I was a weirdo and a tramp, and chased me. That happened every day. I hid but they would find me and chase me, and sometimes they would hit me. I got put in a bin one time; it stank and I was sick.

Then we had to move again. I was glad. A flat this time, then another one. More trains and buses and suitcases, and I always thought about that green sticker that said my name and I wondered if I'd ever get that bus home again. There were no more star-of-the-week certificates or green stickers, just fists and bins and running; chewing gum in my hair. Spit all over my coat.

So I learned what to do when we moved. I learned to forget about certificates and stickers. I learned to forget about old cuddly toys black with mould in the corners of bedrooms. I learned how to keep everything I needed, everything precious, in one bag, ready to move. I learned how to look after myself, how to steal food from the shop when I was hungry and how to turn Mum over onto her side so she didn't die in her sleep.

On the outside I learned how to blend in. I learned how to be like the rest of them. More importantly, I learned who to be seen with. I learned that so long as you're with certain people, no one sees the dirt on your clothes or the flea bites on your legs. I learned that the people at the top got there because they stepped on others, because they are monsters, because they're dead inside.

I learned that the people at the top, the people I needed to be with get there by drinking blood.

Welcome to Six Stories.

I'm Scott King.

Over these last five weeks, I've been treading the much-trodden paths that lead through the case of Elizabeth Barton. I've spoken to her family, the people who knew her and a few who knew her killers: Solomon Meer, George Meldby and Martin Flynn. There is still no doubt in my nor anyone else's mind that these three young men were responsible for her death. The exact details are still sketchy. Maybe we'll never know which of them removed Elizabeth Barton's head or why.

This is a fresh and rather grim grave we're raking over.

There are still questions that lurk around this case; the motives of the three killers have always been unclear. And what was going on between Solomon Meer and Elizabeth Barton? I still feel like there is some integral part of this case that's missing.

I'm slowly coming to the conclusion that everything – every rumour about an ancient vampire that haunts Ergarth Dene and about a deadly Internet challenge – all these things have a grain of truth to them, but these grains are buried under conjecture and gossip.

So where to go next? We need to end up at the truth. Who locked Lizzie in the tower and why?

Unfortunately, it looks like speaking to any of the three convicted for the murder of Elizabeth Barton is going to be impossible. My requests to their families and to the prison service have been ignored. I felt like I had reached an impasse and that maybe three young men killed a young woman for little to no reason, that maybe I should leave it at that.

However, things have changed.

I received a text message from Jason Barton, Elizabeth's brother, telling me that I'm looking in the wrong places. The actual wording was: 'You're very cold right now'.

I feel like I'm being herded; placed in the position of being able to tell this story, the correct gate open somewhere before me. And now I have someone snapping at my heels to hurry me towards it. Someone wants this story told in a certain way.

In the last episode, I feel we saw a side of Solomon Meer that has, until now, been hidden. A vulnerable, malleable side. Does it absolve him of what he did? Certainly not, but it does beg questions about the death of Elizabeth Barton. Were he and the other two solely responsible for what happened?

Jason Barton's text message suggests to me that there's something I'm missing. If I am, why didn't he tell me this when he and I spoke? It feels like Jason is starting to take control of the narrative here. Is this something he's been trying to do since the start?

Is he more like his sister than he would admit?

Again, that question, 'Who locked Lizzie in the tower?' pecks and presses with increasing persistency.

So I packed up and left Ergarth again to travel south west. To Bristol. To meet Jason Barton.

Again.

We'll come to whose voice is permeating this episode soon, I promise.

—I learned a really important lesson in school that had nothing to do with maths or science or fronted adverbials. It was a lesson about being beautiful. I watched loads of other girls try and be beautiful. Some of them were; some girls didn't need make-up and fake tan; they were just beautiful. But that's not how to be beautiful. Not really.

Maybe 'beautiful' isn't the right word. Because there were loads of beautiful girls that didn't get anywhere. Maybe I mean 'powerful'.

Yeah.

If you were powerful everyone would tell you you were beautiful. Everyone would inbox you if you were powerful. If you were powerful, you didn't need to be beautiful. But if you were both...

Well, that's not right. No one is both.

In the school I was in before Mum moved us to Ergarth, there was a girl called Mercedes Yaxley. She was beautiful and she was powerful. Honestly, I don't think I've ever seen someone more perfect than her. Her hair, her skin, her body, her face.

I became her friend almost immediately. By then I knew how to, and you know how I did? By crushing the competition. I became friends with Mercedes Yaxley by humiliating other girls, fighting, spreading shit and bitching about anyone who raised their pretty little head and tried to get anywhere near me.

I became Mercedes' best friend, her second in command. I dated her cast-offs and commanded a little army of nasty bitches.

But I didn't know her. No one did. Because I realised soon enough that she wasn't human.

This is something I realised about power and beauty and all of that stuff. No human can have both. It takes another type of creature to be both powerful and beautiful.

I arrange to meet Jason Barton again at a cafe in St Nicholas Market, in Bristol city centre. Bristol is on the opposite coast and opposite end of the country from Ergarth – some three hundred miles. It's a bustling place, and as we've met before, I knew I'd recognise him. However, our time to meet came and went.

Frustrated, I attempted to call Jason on the number he gave me, yet it rang out. Had this all been a waste of time? If this was a stitch-up, what was the purpose of it? I drank a couple of cups of coffee and decided to be on my way. But what did Jason mean by me being 'cold'? There was definitely something to find here; maybe I wasn't looking hard enough.

As I was getting up, a woman sat at the back of the cafe caught my eye. She was in her mid-twenties, average height, wearing a hoodie pulled up, her face in shadow. She hurried away, head down, looking at her phone.

As I was walking back toward Temple Meads train station, my phone buzzed with a message: We were just checking you'd come. Meet at Arnos Vale Cemetery. 2pm. Jason.

This was all becoming a bit cloak and dagger – my resolve to look monsters in the eye, not to hide, to meet people face-to-face, was being tested. So I took a bus across the city to the vast Victorian cemetery that sprawls out not far from the centre.

On the way I connected to the bus wifi and received another notification. This was a link to a selection of videos; each of them lasted no more than a minute. All of them were filmed in and around Ergarth; by now, I easily recognised the place. The videos had no sound, and were the same scene shot from various different angles. Elizabeth Barton walking down Ergarth High Street and stopping at an alleyway between two betting shops; a huge council refuse bin looming from the shadows. The most striking video was taken from inside the alleyway; from what appears to be a lower angle. Elizabeth approaches the camera, a look of concern on her face. As she gets closer she smiles once, before her face collapses into a scowl. She reaches for the camera, teeth bared. The video ends. I texted back, presuming it was Jason, but received no reply. What he was showing me, I was not sure.

Arnos Vale Cemetery is an impressive place with winding paths and hills among reams of sepulchral towers and monuments, many of which are claimed by undergrowth and ivy. It's huge; forty-five acres, a former country estate, sloping upwards through surprisingly dense woodland. Slender trees lean over the paths, creating a cool canopy; the curls of old iron fencing is visible through the foliage. Shrouded in a respectful quiet, Arnos Vale is both a public place and a working cemetery. The day was pleasant with sun dappling the paths through the leaves. I certainly did not feel under threat. So I stood at the entrance gates, between two huge walls with the sound of the road behind me and the stillness of the graveyard in front.

Then she appeared again. The woman from the cafe. Still hooded, emerging from behind a towering obelisk. She beckoned me up the path and I followed. The air became cooler, the sound from the road almost nonexistent here. I turned on my recorder.

—Who are you?
—I know who you are. You're looking for the Ergarth Vampire.
—I've come a long way, hoping to know more about the murder of

an innocent young woman. Personally, I don't believe vampires really have much to do with it.

—Well let's see shall we? I'm Gemma by the way. Gemma Hines. Nice to meet you.

Gemma's voice is the one you heard at the top of the episode. Our recording was actually rather good quality. There's the occasional tweet of bird song, our feet crunching on the gravel of the path. Arnos Vale was more or less empty; we had the place to ourselves.

Gemma Hines, of course, is a name I've heard throughout this series. She was a girl who had a party back when Elizabeth, Solomon, George, Martin and Jason all lived in Ergarth. Gemma and Jason were pupils at Ergarth High at the time. By this point, Elizabeth, Solomon, George and Martin had all left.

All of them were apparently present when Gemma was supposedly locked in the bathroom by Solomon Meer. From what I've been told, this was Elizabeth's revenge for not being invited to the party. Gemma tells me not to worry, we'll get to that night soon. First, I tell her, I want to know why Jason Barton called me here and exactly where he is. Gemma tells me all will become clear, soon enough.

—The thing about the story of Elizabeth Barton is that no one wants to hear from the quiet ones.

—Ones like you?

—Like me. There are other stories that no one wants to hear.

—I'm here now, aren't I? Halfway across the country.

—So can I start?

—I'm listening.

—Mum moved us to Ergarth when I was about twelve or thirteen. We were running from something. We always were running from something. Something or someone. I imagine that it was a debt most likely. I knew all about debts by then and the sort of people who collected them. High-interest loan sharks. Blood-suckers.

—Vampires?

—You're getting it. Vampires have to move with the times too. They can't have cloaks and fangs anymore. They have other, more modern ways of operating. They're everywhere. It's an epidemic.

Gemma tells me the stories you heard at the top of the episode. Her early years were all about survival. Always moving, always running. Gemma Hines had to work hard to fit in quickly wherever she went. She uses the word 'vampire' a lot.

There is so much I want to ask here, especially about the strange videos I've just been sent, but I think it's all going to come out as we walk through the paths, past rows of guinea graves – the cheapest burial option for Victorian paupers ... three coffins stacked on top of each other below the surface.

—Mum used to invite them in. That's how a vampire gets inside your house, isn't it? You have to invite them. A few of them asked me to call them 'Daddy'; one of them said it in a way that made my fucking toes curl. When *he* stayed over I used to sleep with two pairs of knickers and leggings on.

But he didn't last long.

None of them did.

I still don't know who my real father is, my real daddy. I might try and find out – ask my mum for my birth certificate, but I don't imagine she'll know where it is. It'll have been sold for crack. Is a birth certificate worth anything? Who knows? Who cares, because he'll just be a name won't he? What closure will it give me to see his name? I might look him up on Facebook, see if he's posting Brexitty shit on Twitter.

Or I could just leave it alone.

—*I'm sorry that you had to go through that, Gemma.*

—Me too. But I'm not after sympathy. I want you to know that I know vampires. I know how to identify them.

—*I understand.*

—I also know how to beat them. How to get rid of them.

We'd moved north. We'd been somewhere near Derby before, and now we were in Yorkshire. Doncaster I think. It was worse up there cos of my accent – they all called me a cockney. They didn't know nothing. I started this school, year seven, halfway through the year. I still had a black eye from some shithole in Stoke and everyone was scared of me.

There was a teacher. I can't say his name; let's call him Mr Smith. I got put in his form. He sat me at the front right next to this freak girl who wore lace gloves and dyed her hair black. There was something not right about Mr Smith. I could tell that straight away. It was the way he looked at you; his eyes were like little ghost-hands all over your tits. I swear you could feel him looking at your arse when you had your back to him. He made my skin crawl. There was something else too; it was the way he made you feel. It was like he sucked all the energy out of the room. Being near him made me tired.

There were some real bad eggs in Mr Smith's form, but no one caused any trouble – they were always bored, lethargic, heads on the table, nodding off. He never bothered with the lads, anyway, just the girls. Me and that little goth girl at the front, we got chatting and she knew what he was.

She told me she could see the vampires too.

Mr Smith kept me behind after afternoon registration on the first day to 'check in' – see how I was getting on. He had this soft voice, always had a mint rattling round his mouth, too much aftershave. He was always on his own as well, it was like the other staff didn't like him either.

He asked me how I got my black eye. I could see he wanted to touch it.

I knew what I had to do.

I kept asking to stay back after registration, I told him about Mum; not too much, not enough to get social services out. I told him things were hard. I wore short skirts and black bras you could see through my shirt. I cried a few tears. He told me how women didn't understand him, how he couldn't relate to other adults. He told me I was special, that I wasn't like the others, he told me I was beautiful.

I felt beautiful.

After that, I went to see the head. It didn't take long.

It was all over town in weeks. I heard that Mr Smith got his windows put through, his car got egged.

When he topped himself, I realised I didn't care. That was how I knew. If he'd been a normal, real person, I would have cared. I would have had some remorse.

But you can't, you see. Not for them. You mustn't. Because that's how they get you – they make you feel sorry for them. That's why you've always got to be careful; you've always got to be on the lookout. Vampires don't come at you with fangs. They come at you with a smile.

I was only twelve. Then we moved to Ergarth, and another shitty classroom that smelled of sweat and floor cleaner and mud and damp, and all the things shitty schools smell of.

'Fresh start, fresh start' – that's all I ever heard from teachers. That's what they would say when I stood in front of a form group of bored-looking backwater kids who didn't give one fuck about me. The lads would look at my tits and the girls would curl their lips and suck their teeth and everyone would sit and work out the ways they could torture me or use me.

When I started at Ergarth High, I found out who the queen bee was straight away. There's always a boy one and a girl one. Sometimes one, sometimes more. I was good at identifying them soon.

—*I'm guessing you made a beeline for Elizabeth Barton?*

—You know; that's the funny thing because, yes, she was the one. But it wasn't her that I immediately was drawn to.

—*There was someone else?*

—Yes.

Gemma gives me the name and it's not one I was expecting. Love at first sight, perhaps? Gemma shrugs. She tells me she doesn't know what it was that drew her to George Meldby, the quiet one; the 'firebug'.

—I think I saw a lot of me in George; he'd had it hard too, growing up.

—*I don't really know George's story.*

—There you go. No one does. No one was bothered enough to try and get to know George. He was quiet and weird, and not like everyone else, so he wasn't worth getting to know. I think I saw in George the person I used to be.

I feel like I've learned quite a lot about George Meldby while making this series. I feel like I've got a grasp of his character and I'm interested in the side of him that Gemma was drawn to.

—So you got to know George – really know him?

—Yeah. He was quiet. Thoughtful. He only really spoke when he needed to and then it was barely a whisper. He was hard work; people couldn't be bothered to get to know someone like that. People couldn't be bothered to put the work in and draw him out of his shell. So he was labelled 'weird' and that was that. It's hard to live with a label all your life. It's hard to be attached to a story.

—What was George's story?

—I think one day he'll tell it. I hope he will. Sadly, right now, it doesn't matter.

George and I, we were friends first. He kept reptiles you know? Snakes and geckos and bearded dragons. He loved those things; his house was full of tanks, which he kept spotlessly clean. There was a load of his mum's dogs as well. I can see why people thought the Meldbys were odd. What people didn't know was that all these animals were abandoned: they were all pets that people bought to take photos with and then couldn't be arsed to look after. George took them all in. He just seemed to prefer these cold-blooded things to people.

Gemma sighs. We've reached the shade of an impressive Victorian mausoleum.

—That's what drew him to *her*, I suppose. That cold-blooded, inhuman-ness.

—Are we talking about...

—Elizabeth Barton? Yes. Of course. George had been in love with her since they were little kids.

—George Meldby was not the only one fixated on Elizabeth, to be fair.

—Oh, I know. Everyone in the town was obsessed with her. I was always playing second fiddle to Elizabeth when I was with George.

—Were you and George an item?

—We were, I guess. We didn't feel the need to broadcast it to everyone though. We didn't need to post pictures of ourselves kissing on Instagram. There was no need. It was between us.

I found out a lot more about Elizabeth Barton through George. I found out the things that didn't go with the whole 'Lizzie B' thing. Things that got conveniently edited out of her story.

—*George knew her since they were in primary school, right?*

—Yep. He was Elizabeth's only friend in primary school – until her parents found out and put a stop to it.

—*Why did they discourage their friendship?*

—Because they were as bad as she was. What makes a vampire?

—*Another vampire.*

—Exactly. George was too odd, too quiet, his family not rich or impressive enough to be friends with the great Elizabeth Barton. The Meldbys lived on the Prim, for fuck's sake. Harold and Mildred Barton wanted 'better' people to be friends with their little girl.

Harold Barton told me as much during our interview. He described the Meldbys as 'odd' but again, there was no real reason why George and Elizabeth shouldn't have been friends. I never challenged it either. Gemma looks at the elaborate Arcadian grave.

—It's like this thing. Six feet under; rich or poor, you're still just bones, but up here it's all about appearances. With the Bartons it was all about who you're seen with. That was drilled into Elizabeth when she was young. You know, George was her only real friend when they were little. No one else liked her.

—*George had his own issues didn't he? With fire?*

—Oh yes, he certainly did – stables, factories, schools … people.

—*There was an incident in primary school wasn't there? In the girls' toilets.*

—Yeah there was. But guess who actually tried to burn the school down? I don't need to say it do I? She did it because she wanted to be the one who put it out – be the hero, get all the adulation. And she was, what – nine years old? Poor George got roped into it and something went wrong. Of course, it wasn't Elizabeth Barton who got the blame, but weird little George Meldby. No one believed him when he tried to explain what actually happened. He only got into more trouble for blaming Elizabeth. That's where it all started. Once you get given a label like that, it's very hard to shake. Elizabeth understood that early on. George did too. That's why he's in prison.

—*Jason Barton told me something about some stables when I spoke to him.*

—I can tell you something about that too. Myrmirth stables was somewhere George and I used to like going, in the early days. Bit of a walk out in the fields, away from everyone, you know? Away from that tower. Bring a carrot and feed the horses. It was peaceful. It was nice.

—*Jason told me something not particularly pleasant about the stables.*

—It was the place where I told George he had to choose between Elizabeth and me; and he picked her.

—*So he tried to burn the stables down?*

—Hold your horses, eh?

Gemma sighs again and we begin walking. The path is shadier now and we reach a curve which leads down a wooded lane. This is where the woodland burials now take place.

—This is a long story. One that no one cared about then.

—*I'm listening.*

—OK, then. Everyone in Ergarth knew Elizabeth Barton. Everyone in Ergarth loved Elizabeth Barton. She was untouchable, so I made it my business to get close to her. I could never get there though. No one could. It was like she was ploughing this furrow all on her own, clambering over anyone so she could to get where she wanted to go. She went through the boys like a knife through butter. There was always drama afterwards. She'd cheat on them, and then make shit up about them, and because she was 'Lizzie B' everyone believed her. She had that power. She was the biggest fucking vampire I've ever seen.

—*Vampire? Figuratively … or….*

—Every fucking way.

Gemma's definition of a vampire makes sense. She doesn't mean in the traditional, undead-spirit sense, but something more modern.

Gemma tells me her definition of a vampire is someone who sucks the energy from others, who commands the attention of the room all the time. Gemma's vampires cannot feel love, they cannot feel empathy. Gemma tells me these sorts of vampires are on the constant hunt for attention and validation. A modern vampire is someone who is only out for themselves and leaves everyone exhausted in their wake.

—She took George away from me because she could. I knew he would choose her in the end.

—*Is that why Jason broke George's nose?*

—I mean, that was just the icing on the cake. Catching him trying to burn the stables was a good-enough reason for Jason. I've always wondered if she told George to do it? Burn the stables just because I liked the horses. Because it was something that was ours and not hers?

—*Why would she do that?*

—It was all about creating a persona. Elizabeth was the queen of that. 'Lizzie B' was going to be the next Zoella. Elizabeth helped create the 'firebug' – she got George excluded from Ergarth High not long after what happened at the stables. She set a fire in a sink in the art room. George Meldby got the blame. Again. He was gone. Simples.

—*That's awful. But why get him excluded?*

—I never understood that at the time. Either she was bored with him or what's more likely is that George Meldby had something on the Bartons that she didn't want coming out and ruining her 'Lizzie B' persona. Narcissists don't like it when the person they've created collides with reality. Who would believe George Meldby over the mighty Lizzie B?

—Did *George have something that Elizabeth didn't want anyone knowing? It had to be more than an incident at primary school?*

—It was more. Much more. I'll come to that.

—*You're painting a very different picture of Elizabeth Barton to the one everyone knows.*

—Elizabeth Barton was validated by drama and attention. Her sole purpose was to take from other people until she was at the top of the pile. If anyone got too close, she would chew them up and spit them out. Move on to the next. Somewhere inside George, he knew this, but he still kept trying to drink from that dry well. He was rebuffed by her, ignored by her over and over, unless she wanted something.

—*What kept him coming back?*

—Elizabeth Barton knew how to make people do things for her is what I'm saying, yeah? George took the blame for a lot of things in the name of Elizabeth.

—*Like burning down the Fellman's factory?*

—Yeah. Surprisingly enough, that had nothing to do with George.

—*Really?*

—Have you talked to Tommy Fellman about Elizabeth?

—*I haven't.*

—Missed a trick there, didn't you? That's what Jason meant when he said you were cold. You're looking in the wrong places. Tommy would have told you what she was really like.

—*I know that Tommy Fellman spread lies about Elizabeth online.*

—Lies! Tommy Fellman was one of the only people who dared tell the truth. He'd been to the Barton's house, he knew what they were all like. That whole family.

—*Did you know Tommy?*

—A bit. He was alright. He certainly didn't deserve what she put him through.

—*What did she do?*

—Oh mate, like, it got to the point where he had to record their conversations on his phone because he was so confused. She was either love-bombing him or ignoring him; their relationship seemed to be all about whether they looked good on her fucking Instagram.

Look at these.

Gemma pulls out a phone and shows me some screenshots from Tommy Fellman's Facebook page:

Tommy Fellman: How do you know if you're in a relationship with a narcissist?

1. You're not given any empathy ✔
2. She's arrogant and entitled as are her entire family ✔
3. Instagram likes are more important than real emotions ✔
4. She's totally weird about intimacy ✔
5. You're dropped immediately if someone else comes along ✔
6. You're dating Elizabeth Barton ✔ 😄

345 Likes 55 Comments

Gemma flicks to some of the comments. The majority are abusive toward Tommy, defending Elizabeth.

—He had to delete his account after that. She unleashed all her little fans on him. I think the comment about intimacy wasn't great though, to be fair. Everyone took it as sex, but I think he meant something else.

—*What did he mean, do you think?*

—If anyone got close to Elizabeth, she would find some reason to be horrible to them, or else use them to make herself more popular. If they said anything bad about her…

—*The flying monkeys would get them, right?*

—'Flying monkeys' – that's a good term for them. Look at someone like Amirah Choudhury. I'd say she was the closest to becoming Elizabeth's little pet, for a while. Poor girl couldn't believe her luck.

—*Snowball fight in Choudhury's.*

—Exactly. Amirah Choudhury is still running scared even though Elizabeth's dead.

George didn't burn down Fellman's. But Elizabeth had helped 'curate' his image, hadn't she? Of course, everyone believed it was him and he never denied it. But I knew it couldn't have been George. There was no way. He was with me that night.

—*Why didn't he say? Why didn't you?*

—That's jokes. No one would have believed him. Plus, he didn't dare.

—*Why on earth not?*

—Because if Elizabeth found out he was with me she would have destroyed both of us.

—*So who actually did it?*

—What did George Meldby want more than anything? Elizabeth Barton. What was his only way to reach her? *Who* was his 'in'? It had to be someone more like George. It was Jason. Jason burned down Fellman's. Everyone knew that. Jason Barton, the fucking 'mental hippy'. He did it because he knew he could make George take the blame and everyone would believe it.

—*George took the blame for Fellman's as a favour to Jason? Why?*

—To get closer to his sister, of course. For someone like George, you can't get what you want through the right means. There's systems and hierarchies and social constraints, aren't there? You have to pay a bloke to get in the back door. George didn't even have to say anything. He just had to keep his mouth shut and not defend himself when people said he'd burned Fellman's. And he did. For her.

—*And did it work?*

—George Meldby was with her right up until the end, wasn't he? His DNA was found all over her body. So Jason did keep up his end of the bargain. Suddenly little George Meldby was hanging out with Elizabeth Barton and her mates – helping her film her videos. If anyone asked, it was because of Elizabeth's wonderful fucking nature, taking in a little waif like George. He didn't care why she was doing it, so long as he got to be close to her. That's what vampires do; that's what they want – unquestioning adoration.

—*Jason Barton has had a hand in this story all along. He was the one who brought me here. To you. Did Jason break George's nose because of the stables or because he hurt you? What is the nature of your relationship?*

—Let me finish. Jason burned down Fellman's pasty factory, not because he wanted vengeance on Tommy Fellman. Jason was as much a victim of his sister as anyone else. He did it because he was trying to get at Flynn's Meats. He couldn't go burning down an abattoir though, could he? What about the animals? Plus the Flynns lived there didn't they?

—*So why Fellman's?*

—Where do you think most of the meat from Flynn's was

going? Jason had his own agenda, he was trying to bankrupt Flynn's Meats. Good thing too.

—*So this brings Martin Flynn into the equation.*

—Martin Flynn was always after Jason after that. He knew it was Jason burned Fellman's down, that Jason had it in for the Flynns. But he wouldn't do anything to Jason because he was also obsessed with Elizabeth. And she had him exactly where she wanted him.

—*How did she keep him there?*

—Sex. The same as George. Martin Flynn wasn't the brightest button and Elizabeth knew it. She had him always believing that one day she'd let him at her. Imagine doing that to someone for that long?

—*That's something else Jason told me. If it's true, it's a dreadful way to treat someone.*

Jason Barton had one more shot at Martin Flynn. In 2017 Justice for the Voiceless attempted to shut down Flynn's Meats once and for all. This time he did it from a distance, from right here in Bristol.

I wonder if his motivation was something other than animal welfare? I think about what Martin did to Jason's rescued bat, Jason's level of enmity for Martin Flynn and his family. Again, I can't help drawing comparisons with Elizabeth and her 'flying monkeys' – how, if she wanted someone destroyed, she didn't do it by halves.

Perhaps Jason was playing a longer game here, trying to make Martin Flynn finally snap. Or was Jason playing for insurance – burying Martin Flynn and his knowledge that Jason burned down Fellman's?

The similarity here between Jason and Elizabeth is striking; the degree of manipulation and control both display, making sure that their enemies are utterly wiped out. I wonder if Gemma's seen it too? It makes me wonder whether she's as autonomous in all this as she thinks.

—*You got to know Jason again when you moved down to Bristol? After the party when you were sixteen?*

—It was a few years later, yeah. We met here through a local animal rights group. He remembered me straight away. He remembered how Elizabeth had ruined me. I had to re-invent myself after what happened in Ergarth, become a completely new person. Be myself, finally. I'd lost myself, but Jason Barton found me. The real me. He let the real me come out; I didn't have to be something I wasn't anymore.

—*You were kindred spirits?*

—Yeah. Call it destiny. We'd both been through the ringer as well, when we lived in Ergarth. Elizabeth Barton ruined me up there, so when I first met Jason here I was scared. He knew exactly what his sister was though. She'd been abusing him since he was a little kid, but he knew that no one would believe him if he said anything. Just like George, just like Martin, just like me. The quiet ones, get reputations they can't shake.

I was still in touch with George, believe it or not. Despite what happened between us, we were still friends. I knew everything that was going on in Ergarth through him.

I ask Gemma to go back again in time, to that party she held. The one that went viral on Facebook. According to Amirah Choudhury, Gemma had deliberately not invited Elizabeth Barton.
Gemma nods.

—*This was how Elizabeth ruined your reputation, wasn't it?*

—Yeah. That was my plan that went all wrong. The thing was, Elizabeth had left school by this point; so I couldn't get to her that way. After I saw what she'd done to George, I realised Elizabeth was on another level. I saw how she behaved. I knew what she was and that party was just supposed to show people that, you know, there was more to life than Lizzie B – that she wasn't everything. I was just trying to bring her down a peg or two. And look what she did to me? You know she had no actual friends, right? She had no one who she actually liked, no one she could hang out with. For her, everything was about likes and subs and … God, that's fucking depressing isn't it?

—*I have to say I cannot find anyone who was genuinely close to Elizabeth Barton.*

—And you won't either. She had plenty of followers but no friends. It would be sad if she wasn't such a monster. That car of hers – that stupid red one with the fucking eyelashes and twee bumper stickers; there were some people in Ergarth who were terrified by the sight of it. There were girls who would start physically shaking if they saw it go by; they would start checking their phones, praying that they'd not said something bad; that they'd given Elizabeth's latest photo a like or a positive comment. It was terrifying. You know what we need to do with monsters; you've said it yourself on your podcast: shine a light on them. For this monster, though, the story doesn't quite fit.

— *To be honest, the majority of people I've spoken to have been positive about Elizabeth.*

— That was her power. I'm surprised at you for not seeing through it. Anyway, I saw her for what she was, even if you can't, yet. So I threw this party and I didn't invite her. Cos I knew that would hit her where it hurt.

Gemma explains that she had used her survival and social climbing to become quite popular at Ergarth High. Bear in mind, she tells me, she was only sixteen at the time. Elizabeth had left school by then and her YouTube videos were becoming incredibly popular. It was, Gemma thought, a good time to teach her a lesson.

—I was in a good place at school; top of the tree, year eleven, Elizabeth was gone. I thought I was ready. I thought I had enough about me; that this might undo her a bit. But it all went wrong. I was only young. I wasn't strong enough to tackle a creature like Elizabeth Barton yet. I also hadn't reckoned on Solomon Meer.

Solomon Meer has passed through Gemma's story so far without mention. As we begin our descent from the peak of Arnos Vale, I ask Gemma about him.

—People talk about Elizabeth weaponising George and Martin. That's not true, she just had those two at her beck and call. It was Solomon Meer she had her claws deep inside. He was like the other two, almost completely under her spell, under her control. He would have done anything for her. In fact he did do anything for her. Including locking me in a fucking toilet at my own fucking party. George was trying to get me out – so was Martin – but it was no use. That was humiliation. That was my lowest point.

Gemma's voice cracks and she begins to sob. We stop under a line of trees. The cemetery spreads out below us, still and silent. A few other people are moving quietly through the graves below, and a man sits on the seat of a council lawnmower, enjoying a cigarette, the sun on his face. I allow Gemma time to compose herself.

—Things were never the same after that party when Elizabeth invited all her followers, her 'flying monkeys', to destroy the house just cos she hadn't been invited. My name was mud and the landlord went batshit at Mum. We had to move. Again. This time it was across the country to here. Luckily we settled here. But I never forgot George, and I never forgot Elizabeth fucking Barton. I never forgot what she did to me.

These revelations, if they are true, are confusing – I'm struggling to get the story straight. George Meldby, Martin Flynn, Tommy Fellman, Jason Barton, Amirah Choudhury, Gemma Hines – they were all victims of Elizabeth Barton on her climb to the top. So far it is Jason and Gemma who have shown the most animosity to Elizabeth and I'm struggling to believe all of what they say is true. Gemma understands when I express this. Of course I don't believe it, Gemma says, because that's not the narrative. Popular, beautiful, powerful people, wannabe celebrities like Elizabeth Barton, aren't vindictive. But the stories she's told are the ones no one tells.

Suddenly I finally feel that I'm 'forcing the story'. I'm also starting to realise who might be its author.

I want to move on to the night Elizabeth died. Gemma, of course, was three hundred miles away by then. But, she tells me, through the Internet, no one is really that far away.

—Like I say, George and I were still in touch and his obsession with Elizabeth never went away. If anything, with me gone, it got even more intense.

—*Can I ask about Solomon Meer's involvement in all this? He seems a bit of an anomaly, yet it was he who is supposed to have orchestrated Elizabeth's death. Was that a story too?*

—It's all a story. Everything's a story. But stories have power – I found that out when I got in touch with Solomon Meer online.

—*You contacted Solomon Meer?*

—Maybe I'm more like Elizabeth than I think. Solomon Meer was a messed-up guy, he was vulnerable. Maybe I took advantage of that? Maybe it was for the best. In all stories, someone has to take the fall – for the greater good. That's just how life is. I learned that the hard way. George and Martin weren't supposed to fall too though. Blame Elizabeth for that.

The graves we pass are squeezed together, rows of wonky grey teeth in a green gumline. Birds twitter and hop on and off the path before us.

—I met Solomon Meer in Ergarth – everyone knew who he was. Back then though, I didn't have anything to do with him. Then I left Ergarth and pretty much forgot about him. But then he popped up again online.

—*Destiny again?*

—It was the Dead in Six Days thing – Solomon's famous video on YouTube. It was everywhere! I remembered how he used to talk about vampires all the time. He knew loads about them. Especially about the Beast from the East; the Ergarth Vampire. Yeah, he had his problems but I remember he had a good heart. I found him on Facebook and got in touch. Don't ask me why – I guess I was just intrigued to see what had become of him. He was still talking vampires, but there was something else he kept saying, he was right on the money with that.

—*What do you mean, he was right?*

—The Beast from the East. Solomon kept saying that the Ergarth Vampire had returned, and he had to get rid of it. At first I thought he'd just lost it, but then I realised he'd been right all along. There *was* a vampire in Ergarth; it just wasn't a vampire in the traditional sense.

—*Did Jason know you were in touch with Solomon Meer?*

—It was Jason who made the connection. He was the one who made me realise that a vampire *had* actually returned to Ergarth – in the form of Elizabeth Barton. The story goes that the farm lads in the legend never really killed the Ergarth Vampire. They never cut her head off. Elizabeth was its second coming.

—*And you believed that?*

—Not that there was an actual blood-sucking vampire. But it made sense in other ways. I think Solomon took it literally though.

—*Solomon believed in vampires.*

—Solomon was already running round Ergarth Dene dressed up as a vampire on Elizabeth's command, wasn't he? It took some work to make him realise that she had him under her control. As vampires do.

—*I wonder if you notice the irony of what you've just said, Gemma.*

I think about the vulnerable, pliable Solomon Meer and wonder just how much he was being manipulated from both sides. Gemma tells me that she indulged Solomon and watched as he concocted a plausible theory. Solomon had been researching the legend of the Ergarth Vampire and had come to the conclusion it was either a Siberian vampire – an 'Eretiki': a sorceress who became a vampire after death – or a Ch'ing Shih – originating in the lands between China and Siberia. The Ergarth Vampire was buried in Ergarth Dene and according to lore, if a person dies far from home and is not buried there, the Ch'ing Shih will return with red eyes, curved fingernails and pale skin. It feeds off the blood of men and has a voracious sexual appetite. Whichever one he finally settled on, Solomon Meer was convinced it was up to him to destroy it.

—Yes, I do see the irony. But you have to think to yourself, who was doing it for the right reasons? Me or her?

I think that somewhere here, the lines between reality and fantasy became blurred for Solomon Meer and perhaps Gemma realised this.

The Ergarth Vampire legend states the vampire, in whatever form it was, brought an eternal winter to the town. When the 2018 cold snap hit Ergarth, this only confirmed what Gemma was encouraging Solomon to believe: that Elizabeth Barton was the second coming of the Ergarth Vampire. As bizarre as it sounds, for Solomon Meer, it was the answer he'd been searching for all this time. It was the validation that he needed. His life suddenly had purpose. If I hadn't spoken to Jo and found out about Solomon's mental deterioration and his delusional behaviour, this would have been unbelievable.

—*It sounds to me, that the only person who was weaponised was Solomon Meer and not by Elizabeth.*

—I accept that yeah, it might have got out of control, if I'm honest, the vampire stuff. But did what I'd done really make a difference to what Solomon Meer thought? He was already obsessed with Elizabeth being a vampire. He was posting all over the forums about the second coming of the Beast from the East. He said he'd conducted some sort of ritual to stop her; burning flowers on her grave. He wasn't daft enough to name her – he knew what the consequences would be of talking shit about Elizabeth online. But then the cold snap came. I never thought he'd actually do it. I got worried and I texted George about it. I told him that Solomon Meer was after Elizabeth, he wanted to kill her. George and Martin appointed themselves Elizabeth's personal bodyguards, always keeping Solomon away from her. I know George threatened him if he went near Elizabeth again.

—*What did Solomon want to do with her?*

—I think it was a mess of fascination, adoration and hate. Those are the feelings most people had when they got close to Elizabeth Barton. Sol was more vulnerable that anyone else, though. And when someone was into her, she would encourage it, she would invite it. She loved the attention.

—*I'm still not sure why Elizabeth let Solomon Meer in, why she let him anywhere near her to be honest.*

—Solomon had got Internet-famous with his Dead in Six Days video, the one with all the dogs and the shopping trolley. That whole craze was going round Ergarth, and Elizabeth wanted a piece of that. It was that simple. He told me he was helping her make her videos and doing things for her social media; running round Ergarth dressed up as a vampire to scare people in the build up to her Dead in Six Days series.

—*I mention Jo's sighting of Solomon lying in the snow with vampire make-up on, taking photographs of himself.*

—Honestly, he would have done anything for her. It was pathetic really.

—*What was the Dead in Six Days challenge going to culminate in?*

—It was a meme or whatever, a craze. Elizabeth made up all her own challenges. That's what everyone did – made them up and pretend someone else had sent them. There was no 'vampire' – it was just a way to get popular online. Do a good video and you'll get likes and subscribers. Everyone knew that. Elizabeth was using it to supplement her channel, she had Solomon Meer helping her do these challenge videos, and they were getting edgier and edgier. At the end there was going to be some great big *thing* that they'd planned. God knows what it was. Solomon Meer was useful in more ways than one; if anything went wrong while they were making the videos, he would get the blame. She was smart, I'll give her that.

—*Elizabeth had hundreds, thousands of fans and followers, surely anyone else would have been a safer bet?*

—There was another reason she used him. He'd become the subject of Elizabeth's next 'project'.

—*This was going to be after Dead in Six Days, correct?*

—She was always one step ahead. Solomon Meer was more-or-less homeless. His mother wouldn't have him in the house because of his behaviour. I think she was scared of him. He was sleeping in the bookshop, Ergarth Dene, sometimes in Tankerville Tower. He was perfect for Elizabeth.

—*What does that mean?*

—Look.

Gemma pulls out a phone; it looks older, slightly scuffed; a crack in the screen. She unlocks it and scrolls through the photo gallery before stopping on a photograph. I reach out to look but Gemma holds it tight.

—Just look. There's plenty more like these.

The pictures start off rather blurry. They're dark and grainy. If I'm not mistaken, many have been taken inside Tankerville Tower. It's the lower level beneath the ruined staircase and there's a shape, coiled into a nest of muddy sleeping bags. It's a man, hair over his face. He looks like he's asleep. A few more, clearer now. This is Solomon Meer.

—Look at this.

Next is a short video clip. Meer is awake this time; he looks like he's in a bad way, shivering and filthy, his eyes rolling back into his head and his lips muttering. If this is staged, it looks horribly authentic.

—It gets worse.

A second video. Longer this time. Elizabeth Barton wanders into shot. She's dressed in immaculate woollen gloves and scarf, and is clutching a flask. She crouches in front of Solomon Meer, who takes the flask, looking at her with a puppy-dog expression. Suddenly there's a voice; a high, girlish hiss:
'Say thank you then, you prick.'
Elizabeth whips around and glares at whoever's holding the camera.

—Was that…
—George Meldby? Yes, I have them all on here.

There's more, a lot more. Elizabeth walking into shot with the flask from numerous different angles. Solomon Meer muttering to himself and thanking her in a reedy voice. There's another one: Solomon Meer sat beneath the echo bridge in Ergarth Dene, filthy, wrapped in a blanket. Elizabeth walks into shot and begins to talk to the camera. A gust of wind ruins the audio and Elizabeth tells George to cut. To come closer. Now I understand the videos Jason sent me earlier.

—These were all Elizabeth's?
—Of course. And there are outtakes too. Look at this.

Gemma shows me a clip of the video I watched on the bus. This time, it's a longer shot, and there's sound. Elizabeth enters the alleyway, her face a mask of benevolent concern. I realise now that whoever was shooting it was crouched on the floor, behind the bins in the alleyway. It's slightly lighter in this one, and as Elizabeth gets close, she proffers a steaming cup of something, her perfectly painted lips now smiling. She is genuinely beautiful.

A grimy hand reaches up to take the cup. Then there's a cough from somewhere. Elizabeth's face switches instantly into a snarl and she looks around. A hulking figure is visible in the periphery. Elizabeth stands up.

'Fuck's sake, Martin!' Elizabeth says, her eyes rolling. 'Go and get yourself a fucking sandwich or something.'

Martin Flynn grunts and moves out of shot. Elizabeth stands up straight and takes a drink from the cup, sighing dramatically. She looks back into the camera. Gone is any sort of beauty from earlier. The difference is striking.

'Maybe you'll actually get to have a little drink this time,' she says, her voice thick with poison. 'Can you do something with your hand? Make it look a bit more…'

The camera moves down and out of focus; there's an unpleasant scraping noise.

'Is that any good?'

'Not bad. Can you make it bleed a bit more?'

'Sure.'

More scraping. The camera moves up again and we see Elizabeth nodding. She turns to the camera.

'Turn it off, then.'

'Sorry.'

I don't recognise the other voice. Gemma smiles and shakes her head.

—One more?

This time Elizabeth is being filmed from the side. She's walking down the alleyway again, no Martin Flynn in sight. I realise I'm holding my breath as Elizabeth bends down. There, in a nest of old blankets and newspapers is Solomon Meer. He reaches up for the steaming cup and Elizabeth holds it just out of reach. The knuckles of one of his hands is red raw, a little blood trickling down between his fingers. Elizabeth's face has slipped again as she turns to the camera.

'Cut? Yes?'

'Yes. Sorry.'

'Wake up, George, for fuck's sake.'

Elizabeth takes a swig of the hot drink and storms out of shot.

Gemma shakes her head, slowly, and scrolls through the phone to a picture of a logo. Red on black. Some words and the unmistakable, austere block that is Tankerville Tower.

— When all this shit went out on Elizabeth's channel, she was going to be untouchable. Believe me, she had press releases all planned out; a strategy to go global.

—*What on earth was going on here?*

—This was the famous 'Elizabeth Barton Tower Foundation'. She'd paid someone to make her a fucking logo for it with the fucking Vampire Tower front and centre. This was her ticket to superstardom. She was going to go beyond Ergarth – she wanted the country, the world. Like vampires do, right? Her narcissism knew no bounds.

—*What about George?*

—Stupid boy. As soon as this went big, she would have dropped him like yesterday's rubbish. I wish he'd known that too.

—*And Solomon Meer?*

—Another pawn. Her initial idea was that she was going to befriend him – get him the help for his mental health that he needed. She was going to be his saviour.

—*How do you have these pictures, these videos? How do you know all this, if you were down here in Bristol the whole time? This is getting rather tangled.*

—It's a tangled story. George was filming all this stuff for her, using his phone. Then he was sending it to me. Why? To show off I think. He still thought that he was going to be part of Lizzie B's rise to superstardom. Idiot.

—They all kept it a secret. George threatened to burn Tankerville Tower with Solomon in it if he spoke up. When we spoke to Solomon ... well ... we just wanted to show him that he was being taken for a ride. He was just a puppet. An accessory like all the homeless people she took photos of in town to make herself look good.

Finally I understand what Jason had over George. All his life, George Meldby had been hanging on Elizabeth's coat-tails and this was his chance, his ticket to ascend with her into sainthood. All his past misdemeanours cleansed. All he had to do was take the rap for Fellman's. Gemma nods her head when I put this to her.

—Yeah. It wasn't as if George was going to tell anyone. Nor Martin, nor Solomon.

—*This makes sense. If it had got out, people would have had a hard time believing any of those three.*

—Yeah and anyone else might have given away her secrets, about the challenge, about how she got Martin Flynn to steal a lamb from the abattoir for her stupid videos. How the Ergarth Vampire was Solomon Meer running round in make-up whenever she asked him to. Solomon Meer was utterly in her control and she loved it. That's the heart of it: she loved the attention, the adoration.

But that was her weak spot. And that's how we got to her.

—*What happened on the night Elizabeth died, Gemma? Who locked Lizzie in the tower?*

—That's the question, isn't it? The big one. What do you want to know?

—*What we all know for a fact is that Elizabeth got a text from Solomon Meer, asking her to meet him in Tankerville Tower that night. I just don't understand why.*

—It was freezing cold that night. It was the worst one up there. Minus ten by the sea. Elizabeth had changed her plans. Getting help for Solomon Meer was far too much effort for her. She was now hoping Solomon Meer would die in the tower. That would have made her video all the more moving wouldn't it? She had done her best to help him. She had all the videos she needed. She'd have made a montage of it for her channel; all to the sound of a Coldplay tune in the background. Everything was in place. The Elizabeth Barton Tower Foundation was going to help the most vulnerable in society without Elizabeth actually having to do much work. She would have taken all the adulation for it too. Makes you sick doesn't it?

But something went wrong that night.

—*Clearly.*

—Look at her last YouTube video; she posted it not long after that text from Solomon was sent. Why do you suppose that was?

—*I'm not sure.*

—That video is all messed up cos of the weather. If you listen carefully, she's asking people to come and help. She's asking her followers to come to the tower too!

—*Why?*

—It wouldn't have looked good would it? If she got there and he was dead. She needed backup, unquestioning backup. She needed people to film this. She needed to be the hero, not a suspect. And I think she was scared too. If he could text her, he could text someone else, he could call the authorities and tell them she'd got him sleeping outside in a fucking blizzard.

—*Wait. Elizabeth made Solomon sleep in Tankerville Tower?*

—Solomon was sleeping in the bookshop, sometimes in the Dene. He wasn't stupid enough to sleep in the tower; but he was stupid enough to do what Elizabeth told him to.

—*Her reputation would have been in ruins if anyone had found out she'd told him to sleep there – no 'Elizabeth Barton Tower Foundation'.*

—Exactly.

—*But no one came. Save George and Martin. Why not?*

—Everything she had was online. She'd got these thousands of followers and subscribers, and she genuinely thought they were all going to come and meet her at the Vampire Tower at night, in the freezing cold. I think she didn't realise that all that online stuff is bullshit. People liked to sit in their bedrooms and watch her open boxes, for fuck's sake. They liked to live vicariously through her.

No one actually wanted to be her friend or actually spend time with her unless they were going to get something out of it. Not really.

—*What about the snowball fight?*

—It didn't take much effort did it? Going down the street and throwing snowballs in a corner shop. Trekking out to Tankerville Tower in a blizzard, though, to watch Elizabeth meet a 'vampire' when you could be at home in the warm, watching it? No contest really. That's how shallow her followers were.

—*You think those lines between reality and fantasy blurred for Elizabeth too that night?*

—Yeah. I do. George Meldby and Martin Flynn were the only ones who actually cared enough about her to brave the weather. Everyone thinks Martin Flynn brought that knife to kill Elizabeth and cut off her head. What if he'd brought it to defend her instead?

—*Defend her from who?*

—What if Elizabeth didn't want to be alone with Solomon Meer? What if he'd already tried to do something to her?

—*This could explain Solomon in the Bartons' house.*

—It also explains why she didn't grass him up for it either. She needed him dead in Tankerville Tower. Why else did she make him go there that night? In that weather? He was either going to be dressed up as a vampire for her Dead in Six Days video or else he was freezing and she was going to 'find' him there, dead. I don't think any of us will ever know. I think she was going to go there for the challenge and be 'shocked' to find Solomon Meer dead or at least passed out. Her numbers for the Dead in Six Days videos were *huge*. The whole world would have been able to watch her being the hero, as per. This was her ticket to superstardom. That's what I think, anyway. And George and Martin followed her there, just in case something went wrong.

—*But what actually happened?*

—I know that George and Martin were late; very late. The weather made it really difficult to reach the tower. By the time they got there, Elizabeth was already dead. Those two broke in to the tower to try and rescue her; they tried to resuscitate her, but it was no use.

—*What about the video on Solomon Meer's phone? 'What have we done?'*

—Look at it. Look at it hard. George and Martin are just stood there. The wind's screaming all over the place. It's Solomon's voice, he's whispering. The other two didn't even know they were being filmed.

—*How do you know all this? You were here. Three hundred miles away.*

—Because George called me that night. He was panicking and didn't know what to do. His and Martin's DNA was all over Elizabeth's body. '

—*What happened?*

—They panicked, they ran away.

—*Why didn't they call the police?*

—Why do you think? Who was going to believe they had nothing to do with it? They'd realised Martin had dropped his knife when they were trying to save Elizabeth. So they had to go back. Just think what would have happened if it was found with their fingerprints on it. But when they got back to the Vampire Tower, Solomon Meer had stripped Elizabeth's body and cut off her head. He was stood there with that knife from Flynn's Meats. George and Martin ran again, hoping that the evidence would be enough to convict Solomon alone. It didn't work out that way, unfortunately.

—*You said that Solomon removed Elizabeth's clothes. Wasn't it assumed she'd undressed herself?*

—Yes, it was. But she was clothed when George and Martin tried to resuscitate her. When they came back for the knife, she was naked.

—*Gemma. Why on earth is none of this public? Why haven't you told anyone about this?*

—Who's going to believe me? The girl who was famous online for being a little slag who had a party that a thousand people turned up to? A girl who was dumped by the little weirdo firebug George Meldby? The evidence was too strong. Who was going to believe me or any of those three? I told George to throw his phone over the cliff, get rid of all the video evidence. That way he'd get a lighter sentence.

— *You're getting yourself off the hook here.*

—I didn't do anything wrong did I? I didn't touch her. I didn't believe she was a vampire. I didn't tell anyone to do anything. I didn't cut off her head. Am I sorry she's dead? Not really. Maybe she was a vampire. Of sorts. Maybe we did the right thing?

This is the second time Gemma has slipped into a plural. Who does she mean by 'we'?

—Why didn't the other two just blame Solomon Meer, rather than stay silent?
—What would have been the point? George and Martin knew fine well that no one would believe them. No one ever had, no one ever would. The forensic evidence was all over Tankerville Tower. Maybe the three of them made some sort of agreement with each other that night? I don't know. I wasn't there. All I've got is what George told me, before he sent me all these pictures and videos then got rid of his phone. It might be true. It might be all lies. I guess we just wanted you to know that there were other ways of seeing the story of Elizabeth Barton. She wasn't the only victim.

I'm utterly shocked. I also notice that plural again. I'm astounded that Gemma can be so blasé about what happened to all four of them that night in 2018. Surely she cared enough about George Meldby to protest his innocence, to be his voice when he couldn't. I put this to Gemma and she shrugs again.

—George had a choice – me or her. And he trotted back to Elizabeth Barton like a little puppy dog. Why should I reward that? Why should I have helped him after he gave no shits about me?
—Because neither George Meldby nor Martin Flynn really deserved what happened to them.
—Didn't they? Are you sure? Martin Flynn, a thug who liked to beat people up, who helped run an abattoir with his family, slaughtering innocents every day, a place investigated for animal cruelty?

I remember who it was who called me here to meet Gemma. Now

I realise who 'we' were. Gemma's protestations that she didn't do anything wrong might actually have substance.

—Tell me about Jason, Gemma. What was his part in all this?

—Jason's a survivor. Like me. Sometimes you have to be tough to survive. Jason was abused by his sister all his life. But he knew her, he knew what would work.

—What are you telling me, Gemma?

— What I can tell you is that Jason managed to escape that family. He made it out intact. Just. We met here, in Bristol, long after we escaped Ergarth. I know all about what it was like for the Barton children. Their parents showered them with gifts, they had TVs and PlayStation and things, but when either of them had a problem, Mum and Dad were nowhere to be seen. All they gave a shit about was how that family looked from the outside.

I'm surprised Jason has turned out so stable. We've both got our darkness, and we share it. We're there for each other when it becomes overwhelming. Is Jason sad about what happened to his sister? I don't know really, not for sure. Sometimes it's not nice to say what you really think. Sometimes that's not acceptable, is it? But when he suggested the world would be a better place without her, I was inclined to agree.

I see now what role Gemma played in the manipulation of Solomon Meer to kill Elizabeth. It smacks of the sort of thing that the Elizabeth Barton Gemma hated might do – taking advantage of a mentally vulnerable person. Yet I have no way of proving her story. I open my mouth to speak and there's a crunch of tyres from the entrance to the graveyard. We turn to look and Gemma begins to pick up the pace. A car sits at the entrance, unmoving. I can see a figure at the wheel. They wave and Gemma waves back. I realise that this is my last chance.

—I guess my question is why?

—Why what?

—You two got away with it. All of it. This was the perfect crime. Almost. Why not leave it at that?

—Meaning what?

—*Meaning I think you and Jason are more like Elizabeth than you think. You all couldn't bear doing something in secret, doing things for yourselves. 'Who locked Lizzie in the tower?' – that was what drew the eyes of the world back to Ergarth. You two wanted to show off how you killed Elizabeth Barton and landed three young men in prison. It was all about validation. Attention. It feels to me like if what you say is true, you two are just as bad. Maybe worse.*

—And you were the perfect vessel for us. Unfortunately though, right now, it's your word against ours. Don't think we don't have plans to disappear. Again.

—*What if you stayed? Handed yourselves in?*

—I could give this to you.

She waves the phone under my nose and pulls it back.

—I won't though because that would spoil everyone's story. The story of perfect Elizabeth Barton and her crazy brother. It would ruin the story of firebug George Meldby and evil Solomon Meer. It would wreck the legend of poor Mr and Mrs Barton who cared so much for their children. You see, if there's one thing I've learned in life, it's that sometimes you have to be a little bit of the thing you hate. Jason knows it too. He learned from the best. You have to be a little bit of a vampire to get on, to get where you want to go.

—*One thing. Please. Before you walk away.*

Gemma looks at me, then back to the car, then back to me again.

—*I spoke to Jason. Why didn't he tell me any of this?*

Gemma shrugs.

—Sometimes, you have to let people tell their own stories. Their own way. You needed this story as much as we did. You needed to escape your own story, deflect the spotlight, push it onto some people who deserved it for once, perhaps?

—I finally forced the story?

Gemma Hines smiles. I watch her walk away, get into the car and close the door.

I recognise the driver. Jason gives me a quick smile before he reverses out of the cemetery gates and away.

I could have snatched that phone but what then? What exactly would have happened next? I could have taken my evidence to the police. They could have sifted through the phone and found that George Meldby called her on the night that Elizabeth Barton died.

And what then? Would that be enough to convict Gemma? Maybe alongside this interview?

Gemma Hines told me that vampires have to move with the times. She's right. I could have taken that phone and maybe we would have had tangible evidence that Gemma Hines is to blame for the death of Elizabeth Barton? I don't know. I'm no legal expert.

Gemma didn't give me the phone, and I didn't snatch it. Is that me playing some part in this whole story too? I believed, when I started this series, that coming to Ergarth was my own choice. But was it really? Instead, did the message on the Bartons' wall draw me here like a lure in the dark, on the end of some terrible, deep-sea predator?

I am inclined to think so.

You see, I don't believe Gemma Hines is responsible for the death of Elizabeth Barton. I think that she was actually a proxy. Because vampires are smart. Vampires move with the times. I think back to something Gemma said earlier: what makes a vampire? Another vampire. This has stuck with me and got me thinking.

On that phone that Gemma waved at me before she disappeared, there'll surely be enough to at least bring her to court; along with her interview with me. What there won't be on that phone is any evidence that Jason Barton was behind a plan to help kill his sister and leave their parents with the pain he's carried all his life. I don't believe Jason was there that night. He's too clever for that. I think he conducted proceedings from afar.

And there's a detail that looks to me like his fingerprint. It can only have been Solomon who stripped Elizabeth naked, before beheading her. There's nothing I've read that says a vampire needs to be naked to die; so why would Solomon do it? I believe Jason, via Gemma, persuaded him to, as an extra piece of revenge against the sister who forced him to remove his clothes and stand out in the snow all those years ago.

I'm forcing a story here: what makes a vampire? Another vampire. Jason knew Gemma from school; he liked her. He watched while she did what she had to do to make herself popular; he watched her climb the rungs of the social ladder and when she had nearly reached the top, he watched her fall. Spectacularly. He also saw who it was who pushed her. Did Jason Barton see someone who was willing to change fundamentally who they were, just so they would fit in? Did he see someone with motive to harm his sister? And when he met Gemma again, several years later, did he then seize on this unexpected opportunity. To put it plainly, did he manipulate Gemma Hines and Solomon Meer to rid the world of his sister? Did he create his own 'flying monkeys'; those creatures from an old story? If that's what happened, he knew how best to do it; he's learned from a master how to manipulate and curate a life.

Why do I think this? Well, it's been Jason who's been in charge of this series, hasn't it? Of course, it's still me, unmasked, meeting people face to face; but Jason's the one who brought me here, pushed and pulled me towards this ending. Like Gemma says – vampires move with the times. Jason Barton's learned a new way to tell stories.

Was this how it all unfolded? I don't know. I'm no expert; I just tell stories too.

And stories are powerful things, they can make a person and they can break a person. We tell each other them to guide us, to warn us, to learn things about ourselves and to learn things about the world around us.

Whatever really happened to Elizabeth Barton on the night of the third of March 2018, I fear, will remain just a story. For some it will be about a beautiful and popular young girl who was killed by three unhinged thugs. For some it will be about a narcissistic and shallow young woman getting her comeuppance for what and who she was.

Or a little boy who stood outside a house naked on a freezing morning, dreaming up revenge.

For some it will be about a vampire.

And maybe the truth is all of those, maybe a bit of some, a bit of another, because that's how stories are; a mix of truths and lies and conjecture.

And all we have now are stories. Stories vying for attention, for truth. Grinding up against each other like glaciers. Lies or not, they all stand, festooned with rumour and mystery, like towers on the edge of a cliff. Like cold in the fingers that will not shift; like a winged, black shape that creates a blot on the horizon; like a glitch on a video, or a crack on the screen of a phone.

I believe that one day, whoever locked Lizzie in the tower won't be able to contain themselves. Whoever locked Lizzie in the tower, really, will want the world to know their story on their own terms.

For my part, I have given you six.

And I have been Scott King.

https://www.reddit.com/r/realvampires/

posted by u/AVHellsing 1 week ago
New Lizzie B Video WTF??
Um ... guys ... this just got uploaded from that Lizzie B channel and idk what to think ... is she back from the dead??? Haha
Link:
http://bit.ly/Lizb6

Livindedgrrl 1 Point ·2 days ago
Who's Lizzie B????????????

TheBl00dizthelyf 1 Point ·2 days ago
Dude. That's not her.

AVHellsing 1 Point ·2 days ago
Whoosh!

Lizzie B

33 subscribers

Hey guys, story-time with Lizzie B! Yes guys it's lil' ol' me, back from the dead; not so pretty now: a bit masculine maybe, with a bit of stubble – but unfortunately some desperate make-up brand hasn't used me for free advertising for aaaages. Sowwee!

As you can see, I'm by the fire, look at me, lying here with my dressing gown a little bit open, just to keep the incels going. Ooh! Don't shoot up a school, lovelies!

I've got this lovely throw on and my bunny slippers. Here's a cup of cocoa. Look at all the stuff *I have, look at all my* things *that companies sent me because they're as fucking vapid and empty as me! Look at what I have and what you* don't *have!*

Yeah all this make-up might be tested on animals, all these clothes might be made by kids in sweatshops, but who the fuck cares*, right guys? Who cares, cos you're all looking at me, and you all either want me or want to be me – and that's all we need, right?*

Anyway, lovelies! I just came back from the dead for a little while to tell you guys a story! Yeah, being dead makes you look a little bit like a man in a wig, but, hey, I'm fucking great, so it doesn't matter.

I just want to let you guys know about what happened to me, cos I know there's this sudden interest in me again – which I'm totally loving by the way – after that podcast went out.

But I'm the fucking storyteller here guys, OK? Let's get that straight.

Six Stories. *Yeah, cool. I'm fucking dead and I'm the story. You only need one. Mine.*

Um, so yeah, as you can tell, I've got my head fixed back on specially to let you lovely people know that everything in Six Stories *was good, but not quite right. I just need the final word, okaaaay?*

Soooo, let's just imagine that, like, when I was alive, I was a nasty, abusive, piece of shit, yeah? Maybe I was really good at hiding it, yeah? Maybe there was only one person who knew how to kill a vampire?

And maybe he didn't get the credit he deserved....

Oops, slip of the tongue there, lovelies...

Maybe I had a little brother. Maybe I made his entire life a fucking misery ever since he was a fucking baby. Maybe he found out I used to drop him, squeeze his throat, punch him and pinch him, then tell our parents that I'd saved him. Silly little brother, always walking into doors. Good old Lizzie B to the rescue. Maybe that silly little brother spent his childhood terrified of me, and when he got older and decided to speak up, no fucker ever believed what happened to him.

What happened to him? You're all asking that, I know. Well what if I made him stand, naked in the garden when it was fucking freezing, just for the fun of it? Imagine that? What if I made him squeeze boiling-hot tea bags with his little fingers; what if I made him terrified in his own house; what if I made it so his mam and his dad wouldn't have believed him even if he'd dared speak out? What if I utterly destroyed his childhood just for my own pleasure? Just because I could?

No, you say, not perfect Lizzie B. She wouldn't do something like that, right guys? She wouldn't destroy someone like that – break them into bits when they were a kid and make them just as broken as an adult? No ... not lovely ol' me. I'm not that type of gal!

Maybe that silly little brother did once try to speak up for himself but was told he was a liar. What a silly little fool he was, thinking anyone would believe him, even his own parents. Maybe that silly little brother decided then that he'd get his revenge. Maybe he decided he'd take something away from the two people who were supposed to look after him. Maybe he'd take away the thing they loved most of all.

And maybe it was easy – cos, look at me: I'm the perfect victim, aren't I? I'm young and pretty and female. I'm the perfect story – dead as well as alive! So getting rid of me was easy. Everyone bought the story. And they were soooo sad I'd gone.

Ooh! Jump-cut. I'm back again and look at this delightful hat – so cute, huh? Maybe some company will send me another one for free cos I'm just totes adorbz?

Hey guys ... do you know how to kill a vampire?

'Cut off its head so it can't come back?'

That's the one! Well done!

Vampires are slippery though; vampires can shift shape, they can pretend to be wonderful, beautiful people and really, on the inside they're all wizened and dead. You have to be smarter than a vampire in order to kill it. Maybe that silly little brother was – shock horror – smarter than me!

You see, the thing about silly little brothers is that they do a lot of observing, a lot of learning. Silly little brothers watch their evil big sisters and they learn things. They learn how to get what they want, when they want, starting with mammy and daddy. They learn how to *manipulate and control, they learn how to keep people on the end of a fucking string, dangling like a little worm. As silly little brothers grow up, they learn how to be not-so-silly adults. Soon enough, silly little brothers are big, smart grown-ups who know exactly how to find and exploit a weakness in someone else.*

It becomes second sucking *nature to them.*

Silly little brothers learn from their masters – or mistresses – how to become the best manipulators. And that's when silly little brothers get their revenge.

And all thanks to lovely Lizzie B! Yaaaaay!

Oops, sorry guys. I said it was story-time and we haven't even started yet! You see, I want to talk about vampires. You know the thing with vampires? You've got to invite them in first. I know someone who did that. Tonight's story is about three naughty little boys who fell in love with a vampire. They let her in, they let her get her nasty little fingers into their brains.

Two of them were scum: they hurt things, they burned things, they broke people's hearts. Those two needed punishing and the best way to punish them? Take that vampire away. But how does one get rid of a vampire when one lives so far away?

Eyes and ears everywhere, that's how – whispers and spies. Opportunities. And the perfect opportunity dropped right into someone's lap. My silly little brother's, of all people! Imagine that! He found the perfect proxy. She lives somewhere else now, somewhere far away; but she still had eyes and ears in the vampire's lair, and she knew the naughty little boys. After that it was easy.

But sometimes you have to return home to make sure your plan is going to work. Sometimes someone just needs that last little push, to convince them about what to do. Sometimes you have to burn flowers on a vampire's grave to stop it coming back and … oh noes guys! It didn't fucking work! The vampire's back! Kill it!

Five people punished.

A beautiful story.

The end.

You see guys, you have to make the story your own. Because sometimes, lovelies, no one listens to you; sometimes it feels like no one has ever listened to you; so sometimes you have to force the story … right? Anyways, lovelies, make sure you hit that like and smash that subscribe. Why? Because I fucking need it, because likes mean love and I'll do fucking anything to be loved. I'll trample over you, I'll humiliate you and I'll throw my fucking face into the ether in the vain hope that someone will like it. I've got nothing else. I've got a black void where a heart should be; a grasping, sucking, empty place that just needs to be filled by anything and anyone.

In death like I did in life.

Cos I guess that's all really what anyone wants. Someone to love and who loves them back.

That's what we all want, isn't it, guys?

Isn't it?

Comments have been disabled for this video

Acknowledgements

I'm grateful to a huge amount of people for their help bringing *Beast* to publication:

To my publisher, Karen Sullivan for her unrelenting and unwavering faith in both me and my work from the very start. My agent, Sandra Sawicka for her enthusiasm, support and constant encouragement, *dziękuję bardzo!* The king of editors, West Camel, for the belief and assistance – all and any errors are entirely my fault! Luke Speed at Curtis Brown, for helping me fulfil a dream. Sophie Goodfellow at FMcM for the hard work with publicity. Cole Sullivan at Orenda for the magnificent social-media visuals; and the inimitable Mark Swan, the dark sorcerer of all book covers. To Helen, James and the rest of the staff at Forum Books in Corbridge, for making every visit, whether it be a book launch or a wintery afternoon browse, memorable.

To Anne Cater and the book bloggers: every single one of you who takes the time to read and then write a review – you are the ones I strive to impress. Your dedication means the world, and I am forever in your debt.

To Ben Bryn and Jimmy Bunker, my middle-aged *Fortnite* squad – you guys help keep me sane. Richard Dawson and Sally Pilkington – aye, your music's canny but your company is exquisite. Thank you also to every member of team family!

Cheers Katie Stone, for saving me from looking like a divvy when I asked for your advice on children's lit.

Massive thanks to every other writer who's appeared on a panel with me or made me feel welcome at book events; also, to the booksellers, volunteers and wonderful attendees – you are hugely appreciated.

Thanks every single person who attended an event, a signing or even just came over and said hello. I'm terrible at remembering names but I never forget a face. OK, so sometimes I forget a face too, but that's my fault not yours!

I know you don't want me to put you last, but this is how it's done, OK? Sarah Farmer, Farm-a-tron, Farmazoid, Farmz, Dr Tiggy. Where the hell would I be without you by my side, playing Pokemon Go? Your support and love is everything. I adore you.

Finally, my little lad Harry, who's not so little anymore; it's such a pleasure to see you grow into the coolest, funniest little fella I've ever known. I love you so much, and all of this is always for you.

And what about you, dear reader? Here we are again. I'm so glad you've stuck with me. Hopefully we'll meet again soon.

—*Matt Wesolowski*